Wait for Me

J.M. McKenzie

ISBN: 9798591049423

DEDICATION

To my fellow survivors of the Monroe Zombie Apocalypse, and my nemesis, The Abomination (aka Stevie J. Douglas).

J.M.MCKENZIE

ACKNOWLEDGEMENTS

The author would like to acknowledge the support of her fellow writers and members of JAMS Publishing: AJ Jones, of Get It Write UK, who did the proofreading and editing; Michael Andrews, who did the formatting for publication; and S.J. Gibbs for her unwavering support and encouragement.

The book was written on the advice of those fellow writers, after they gave the author feedback on her first attempt at another novel, *The Ice Factory*. *The Ice Factory* is an ambitious project on a serious topic, and they suggested that she "cut her teeth" on something a little lighter.

At the time, the author had recently taken part in a reality TV show on BBC3, *I Survived a Zombie Apocalypse*, and had developed a small following on social media. She has always had an interest in all things related to apocalyptic scenarios and zombie-related ones in particular, so it seemed like a good place to start.

The "journey" theme of the book was inspired by a novel that J.M. had read and enjoyed, called *The End of the World Running Club* by Adrian J. Walker. Some of the locations in this book were familiar to J.M. and she wanted to weave the idea into her own story by taking an ordinary woman on an extraordinary journey, through the author's own local environment.

Last but not least, she would like to acknowledge the patience and encouragement of her partner, Mike, and all of her family and friends.

J.M.MCKENZIE

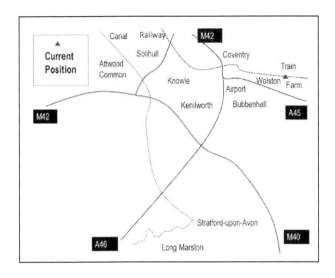

Chapter 1

Day 1 - Wolston near Coventry

Wide-eyed and gasping for breath, Lisa braced her back against the wall to counter the rocking of the train. Her trembling legs threatened to buckle underneath her. Her chest was tight, and her throat ached as she gulped in air. Black spots floated across her vision, and she felt fuzzy and light-headed. She scrabbled in her pocket for her inhaler, almost dropping it from her shaking fingers before she shook it and inhaled a couple of rapid puffs.

Along with the roar and rattle of the train, the sound of her blood pulsing in her head was deafening. Her mind was in overdrive, fuelled by the adrenaline surging through her body, and she struggled to process what was happening. Aware that she was in survival mode and functioning at the most basic level, her analytical self battled to regain control. She knew that, if she could not pull herself together in the next few minutes, she was almost certainly going to die, and not from an asthma attack.

The Ventolin kicked in. She closed her eyes and tried to steady her breathing. Forcing herself to inhale deeply through her nose then out through her mouth to the count of four, she felt her airways gradually begin to relax. Her heart slowed and her head began to clear, but it took a full minute before she could open her eyes.

She was in an absurdly bright and shiny, windowless train toilet. The smell of industrial-strength disinfectant barely concealed the odour of stale urine. There was movement outside the large concave door: shuffling and bumping, moaning and scratching. Further away, there was screaming. Her eyes registered a big red button with a white padlock on it and she reached out and banged it with her fist.

Shit! The dull clunk of the lock activating was followed by an increase in noise from outside.

The realisation that the door had been unlocked shook her. She had to calm down, think clearly. She couldn't afford to make stupid mistakes.

2

She looked around the small cubicle. There were a multitude of buttons and signs on the walls. The lid of the toilet read:

> *Please don't flush Nappies,*
> *sanitary towels, paper towels, gum,*
> *old phones, unpaid bills, junk mail,*
> *your ex's sweater,*
> *hopes, dreams or goldfish*
> *down this toilet.*

She read it a couple of times trying to decide if it made sense or not, deliberately testing her focus and mental clarity. Despite herself, she acknowledged the bizarre attempt at humour.

She wasn't alone. On the floor, head down, knees hugged against her chest, a girl was whimpering and muttering. She looked about twenty, in tight jeans, impressive trainers and a leather jacket. Her long black hair was braided and piled loosely on top of her head. Her nails were ridiculously long and intricately painted. Lisa couldn't see her face.

Standing by the sink, was a tall, thin, elderly man in a light grey suit and charcoal overcoat. Both lenses of his wire-framed glasses were broken, and the bridge of his nose was cut. Blood trickled slowly down his face and neck, staining the collar of his crisp white shirt.

Behind him, in the mirror, a woman was staring at her. She barely recognised her own reflection. Her freckles were stark against her ashen skin, and her wide, blue eyes were framed by a mop of unruly, auburn hair. She'd not straightened it that morning, and it was escaping from the loose scrunchy she had used to try and control it.

The man was staring at the opposite wall with intense fascination. Lisa followed his gaze.

The whole wall was one huge photographic image of a recently-harvested cornfield in soothing hues of yellow and gold. Tyre tracks in the corn stretched into the distance. Lisa's eye was immediately drawn to the orange emergency panel positioned neatly between the tyre tracks. On the panel, was a speaker and another red button, this time with an alarm bell on it.

She lunged for the button, but before she reached it, all three of them were thrown violently forward as the train screeched to a halt. They landed in a tangled heap at the bottom of the cornfield. Outside, a series of heavy thuds indicated that whoever was on the other side of the door had suffered the same fate. There was a brief silence before the shuffling and moaning resumed. The distant screaming had stopped.

Lisa gingerly got to her feet and helped the man, whose cut was bleeding profusely now, to stand up. She pulled some paper towels from the dispenser and pressed them against the bridge of his nose. Taking his hand, she coaxed him to apply pressure to the wound.

"Here, press. Like this."

"Are you okay?" she asked the girl.

"I think so," the girl answered. "What the hell is going on?"

She stood up, unfurling surprisingly long limbs to reveal a tall, athletic physique.

"I think it's an … attack, or something," Lisa replied, shaking her head in disbelief.

"What d'you mean, an attack? What kind of attack?"

"I don't know … I just think …"

"Oh, my god! Oh, my freakin' god! We're so gonna die." There was rising panic in the girl's voice. She moved towards the door. "We've gotta get out of here! We've gotta get away."

"No! Stop!" Lisa gripped the girl's shoulder. "Wait! They're right outside the door."

"Who's right outside the door? Who are they?"

"Some of the other … passengers …"

"But who are they? What's wrong with them? Why are they …? Man!"

The girl put her palms flat against the door. Her head dropped.

"Has anyone got a phone on them?" Lisa asked. "I left my bag in there."

The girl shook her head. "Me too."

They both turned to the man. He fumbled in his coat pocket and pulled out an ancient Nokia. His hand shook as he held it out to Lisa.

"What is *that*?" the girl hissed.

"Thank you." Lisa shot her a glance. She took the phone, tapped some numbers into the tiny keypad then stopped and stared at the screen. "No service."

"MAN!" The girl kicked the door, triggering a frenzy of banging and crashing outside. The door rattled and shook under the impact.

5

"Stop it! Calm down!" Lisa grabbed her shoulders. "They can't get in, or they would've by now. Someone stopped the train. Someone else will call for help. We just need to wait in here." She took the girls face in her hands. "Be quiet and wait. Ok?"

She tried to smile, but her mouth struggled to remember how to do it and the result felt more like a grimace, but it seemed to work. Nodding, the girl sat down with her back against the door and crossed her long legs. Lisa sat down beside her and took her hand.

"I'm Lisa! What's your name?" She coughed. Her mouth was dry. Her tongue felt thick and sticky.

"Anita."

"Look, Anita. We're going to be ok. Someone will come," she whispered.

After the first hour, they knew that help was not coming. Silent and still, crouched on the floor, they strained to hear what was going on outside, exchanging occasional brief, whispered reassurances and anxious looks when the activity outside increased. At first, they were expecting, then hoping for, the sounds of sirens, vehicles and voices that would signal their rescue. The man, Brian, sat mostly with his eyes closed. His nose had stopped bleeding, but he was deathly pale and sweaty. He hadn't said a word the whole time, except to croakily reply when Lisa had asked him his name. Anita was more composed now, and, like Lisa, was listening keenly to every sound from outside, trying to understand what was happening

6

and what their options might be.

Again and again, Lisa went over everything that had happened since she'd awoken in her seat, to someone shaking her violently and the sounds of a disturbance. For a moment, she had no idea where she was, before her thumping headache reminded her that she was on a train on the way home from London, nursing a serious hangover and the effects of a very late night. Anita, in the window seat beside her, was standing and staring in horror towards the other end of the carriage. There was screaming and shouting, and other unrecognisable wet and guttural noises. She remembered thinking that a wild animal had got onto the train, and that she must be dreaming, maybe even hallucinating. It had been a really heavy night. Then Anita shook her again, even harder.

"Wake up! Move. Move. Move!" Her tone was quiet but urgent.

On her other side, Brian was standing in the walkway between the seats. The three of them were in the back row of the carriage, next to the entrance. Initially, Brian had looked as though he was moving towards the disturbance, but then he'd turned and begun fumbling with the button that opened the carriage door. Lisa saw the look of sheer terror on his face, and she stood up, instantly wide awake.

"What's wrong? What's happening?" she said.

As soon as Lisa rose, Anita moved like lightning, leaping behind her across the seats into the aisle. She hurtled into Brian, who'd managed to open the door, pushing him out of the carriage where he fell, face first, to the floor. Still not sure what she was running from, Lisa followed them. As she exited the carriage, she turned and looked back.

She was stunned by the scene in front of her. Her eyes took in the visual information, but her brain refused to accept it. On the floor, at the far end of the carriage, a screaming woman was lying in a pool of blood. A man was kneeling over her, tearing at the soft flesh of her belly with his teeth. He was drenched in blood. Some of it was the woman's, but most of it was bubbling from a wound on his own neck, where a huge flap of flesh had been torn away to reveal bone and cartilage underneath.

All around the couple, other attacks were taking place. Blood and gore spurted, sprayed and splattered. The air was filled with a metallic stench and the sounds of ripping flesh and crunching bone. Again, she thought she must still be asleep, and was just having a terrible nightmare.

People were screaming and shouting, pushing and shoving, clambering over seats, stepping on the dead, the dying and the living, in their frenzy to get away. Closest to her, a lifeless young man in a green hoodie was sprawled on his back. He had to be dead. He couldn't possibly have survived his terrible injuries, but, as she watched, he twitched, opened his eyes and struggled to his feet. His skin was grey-green and his eyes opaque and completely devoid of consciousness. He fixed her in a milky gaze and his features distorted into an expression she could only describe as rage, before he staggered towards

8

her. She turned and ran.

Nothing she had seen could be rationally explained. She had no point of reference. She was a problem solver by nature and intention. Facts were her friends. They were the only thing that could be trusted and believed in an increasingly complex and challenging world. Every day, she separated fact from fiction, analysed and drew conclusions to develop foolproof plans and strategies. But here, today, some of the facts were so implausible that even they couldn't be believed. She had seen people attack and kill each other with their bare hands and teeth, and that was horrifying. But there would be a reason for that. It would eventually be explained somehow. What could never be explained, because it was scientifically impossible and totally and utterly inexplicable, was that she had seen a dead boy get up and walk.

She retched as a surge of bile rose in her throat. Her chest tightened again, and she took another couple of puffs from her inhaler.

Anita squeezed her hand. "Are you ok?"

"Asthma. I'll be fine in a minute."

The rasp of the inhaler and the sound of their voices prompted more banging and moaning from outside. Brian's eyes snapped open and he flapped his hand towards them in a downwards movement.

"Keep it down," he mouthed.

"Piss off." Anita mouthed back. She looked anxiously at Lisa.

"It's just ... they were killing each other. Biting and

9

tearing." Lisa whispered.

"I know, I saw." Anita's reply was barely audible.

"And … and … "

"… the dead were coming back." Anita finished her sentence for her.

"But … it can't be … it doesn't …"

"I know … shh … " Anita placed a finger over her lips as the moaning outside grew louder.

The two women huddled closer together.

Brian closed his eyes again.

Lisa's brain continued to process. Piecing together information, examining it from all angles. The activity outside reduced when they were quiet, but quickly resumed when one of them spoke or changed position to relieve stiff limbs. It was odd that their pursuers hadn't followed them into the toilet. The door had been unlocked long enough for them to have got in. The illuminated OPEN button would have been in plain sight. The boy and a couple of others had been close behind, as they had scrambled inside. Anita had frantically banged the CLOSE button again and again, as if it would make the door close faster. Lisa had watched, knowing it would make no difference. The few seconds it had taken for the curved door to slide shut had felt like the longest of her life.

But she had something to work with. It was small, but it was potentially important. She recalled the boy's milky gaze. Whatever had happened to them, had affected their mental ability. They hadn't been able to work a simple door mechanism. It was a start, something to bank for later, but now the only thing she did know for certain, was that they were in serious trouble, and it didn't look like help was coming anytime soon. If they were going to survive, they would have to think very carefully about every single decision they made, and every action they took. And already, it felt as though she was going to have to take the lead on that. Anita seemed a bit impulsive, reckless even, and Brian ... well, Brian ... didn't seem to be coping very well, and that was putting it politely.

She ran back through the rest of the day, looking for signs that might help explain what was happening. Anything she might have missed. Her day had begun in the Park Plaza Hotel, near Victoria Station, where she'd been at a two-day business meeting. The meeting rooms were all in the lower basement level, where there were no windows and no phone signal. They'd been in there all day, effectively cut-off from the outside world, apart from occasional visits from hotel staff with meals and refreshments. And, they were all pretty groggy from the night before, so it was possible ... But it didn't make sense. Some people had logged on to check their emails, so they would have seen any *Breaking News*. Besides, the hotel staff would have had said if anything untoward was going on. However she looked at it, everything had been completely normal.

Lisa was one of the first to leave. She couldn't wait to get out of there. She hated these events. Forced fun and compulsory socialising with people who weren't her friends, under the guise of so-called teambuilding. It was all so fake. Wide grins, banter and backslapping concealing a cesspit of backstabbing, petty jealousies and Machiavellian office politics.

For her, it was particularly hard. She was a natural introvert. Apart from Neil, and a handful of close friends, she found it difficult to spend long periods of time with other people. There was only so much pointless chat she could tolerate before she ran out of things to say. What made it worse was that she could tell that people felt awkward around her. She knew that they tended to avoid getting stuck in a one-to-one situation with her, reluctant to put themselves on the wrong side of one of her uncomfortable silences. That knowledge sucked her deeper into a spiral of self-conscious paralysis.

Alcohol helped a bit, hence why she always ended up overdoing things in that respect. It helped her relax and made it easier to think of things to say. It got her through events like the past couple of days, even if she did pay for it the next morning. But it was simple, she'd always much rather be on her own in front of her computer or snuggled up with Neil on the sofa at home.

So, she'd rushed off the minute the meeting was over. She'd used the Express Checkout Service, grabbed her bags and headed straight to the station, a two-minute walk away. She'd picked up cash for her taxi at the other end, and jumped on the Victoria Line, eager to catch an earlier train than the 17.25

she'd reserved a seat on. At Euston, she'd still had time to pick up her sure-fire hangover cure combination, of a bottle of coconut water and a packet of Percy Pigs from Marks & Spencer.

At the station, everything had seemed perfectly normal, apart from the fact that it seemed unusually busy. She'd briefly registered a couple of policemen in their high visibility jackets, talking on their radios as they walked swiftly through the crowds, but had assumed they were simply heading to some minor incident.

She caught the 16.43 to Edinburgh, via Birmingham, her destination. As she was boarding, a station announcement had reassured the public that the increased police presence in the station was due to a routine operation and there was no cause for alarm. She hadn't given it another thought.

Because she didn't have a seat reservation on the earlier train, she'd headed to the front, furthest away from the gate, hoping it would be quieter. She found an unreserved pair of seats right by the door to the carriage, and had taken the aisle seat as usual, hoping to deter anyone from sitting next to her. She always told herself it was to give her a spare seat for her bag and the privacy to get some work done, but more importantly it avoided having to engage in conversation with any over-friendly fellow travellers.

The train was busy and soon filled up. Irritatingly, Anita, had taken the window seat, forcing Lisa to move her bag with a tight smile. "Of course. No problem."

The train was hot, and exhaustion soon overwhelmed her. She drank her coconut water and attacked the Percy Pigs.

Who was she kidding? The way she felt, she was never going to get any work done. She closed her eyes, and by the time the train pulled out of the station, was deeply asleep. The next thing she knew was Anita shaking her awake.

Anita was talking to her again now. The girl nudged her.

"I said, was anyone expecting you home by now? Will anyone realise that you're missing?"

"No, my partner's working away. He's not due home himself till tomorrow. You?"

Anita sighed. "No. I'm going back to Uni. Loughborough. My parents wouldn't expect me to call till late tonight."

They both looked across at Brian, who simply shook his head.

Lisa wondered what Neil was doing. A freelance cameraman, he was away on a job in Lincolnshire. Filming was due to finish today, but he wasn't planning to head back until the following afternoon, when they'd dismantled the rigging and loaded the vans. He wouldn't call until after seven at the earliest, when she was due home, but he would probably leave it until he got back to his hotel, around nine or ten. It could be hours before he realised she wasn't there.

God, she wished he was here. She never thought

she'd hear herself say it, but he'd know what to do. He always assumed command in a crisis. It was irritating, verging on patronising, but right now she would have welcomed it with open arms. As much as she teased him about being an "alpha male" and reminded him that she had managed fine on her own for years before he was around, she had to admit she secretly always felt safe when he was with her.

Even though she'd lived alone for almost a decade before she met him, now, when he was away, the house seemed empty and scary when she turned off the lights and got into their big empty bed. She liked to keep the TV on for company as she fell asleep.

More than the comfort of his presence though, she missed her nightly ritual of cuddling up to his broad, smooth back and kissing the tattoo of a sun between his shoulders. He would reach for her hand, pulling it across his body and holding it to his chest as they fell asleep. He always said, as long as he had the sun on his back, he was happy, so she'd bought him the tattoo for his 30th, while they were on holiday in Miami.

When she left yesterday morning, he'd been perched on the edge of the bed watching BBC Breakfast in his bath towel. She'd given him an absent-minded peck, before rushing off to catch her train. She wished she'd said a proper goodbye. She felt sick. What if they never saw each other again. What if she died here, today and that had been their last moment together?

She replayed the scene. This time, she turned his

15

head away from the TV, looked him in the eyes and told him how much she loved him. He took her face in his hands and kissed her back. Told her that he loved her more.

She felt so far away from him. So alone. She saw him in the sunshine, winding cables and packing away cameras, laughing and joking with the crew, completely oblivious to the fact that she was cowering in a train toilet with a bunch of deranged killers waiting outside to rip her throat out. Her lip trembled and a single tear rolled slowly down her cheek.

Before she could sink deeper into a well of self-pity, the power went out. They were plunged into darkness and the door mechanism let out a long, slow hiss.

She felt Anita tense beside her. "The door. It's unlocked!"

Brian groaned.

But it was completely silent outside. Neither the hiss, nor the groan had triggered a response. She waited for a moment, then tapped lightly on the door and felt a tiny seed of hope begin to swell within her when there was no response.

She knocked again; this time louder.

Again, complete silence.

"I think they've gone," she spoke into the darkness.

"How d'you know?" Anita's voice startled her as it came just inches away from her face.

"Listen."

16

They both held their breath and listened, then Anita did a bit of theatrical coughing and crashing around. It provoked nothing. Not a sound.

"I think you're right. Sweet!" Anita said as she got to her feet. "How do we open it?

"Just wait. Wait. Let's think for a minute."

"What about? They've gone and I'm outta here." The girl rattled at the door.

"We don't know for sure. Let's just try and open it a bit and see."

"I agree." Brian's voice was stronger.

Working together in the darkness, they managed to jiggle and slide the door open a crack, letting in a slim shaft of early evening sunlight and a waft of cool fresh air. When no crazed passengers appeared, ready to tear them apart, they opened it a little more. They continued like this, sliding it open, inch by inch, until the gap was wide enough for Lisa to stick her head out. She immediately pulled it back, with a sharp intake of breath.

"What?" Anita barked.

Although she'd been half expecting it, the horror of the scene took her breath away. Blood, body fluids and fragments of flesh and bone were splattered over the walls and floor. The smell of death hit her like a wave. Putrid and metallic.

But there was a light breeze coming from her right. It was cool and refreshing above the stench of the train and the stale air of the windowless toilet. She pushed her head out once more, a bit further this time, alert and ready to react to any sound or sudden movement.

Anita gripped her arm, trying to see around her. "What can you see?"

"Shh. Give me a minute." Lisa looked further round the edge of the door towards the source of the breeze.

All the train doors were wide open. A glimpse of blue sky, white clouds and green grass was tantalizingly close. To her right, the glass door to the carriage they had been in was closed. Blood and gore obscured her view inside. She turned to her left. The door to the next carriage was also closed and smeared with bloody matter. The space between the carriages was empty. Whoever had been outside was gone.

"It's ok. Let's open it a bit more so we can get out. Slowly. Quietly." Lisa whispered.

They eased the door open wide enough for her to step outside. Standing there, between the two carriages, she was overwhelmed by a feeling of exposure. She was torn between the urge to lurch for the open door and run, or to fling herself back into the safety of the toilet and curl into a ball. She forced herself to stand still. To wait. To listen. To breathe. She put her finger to her lips as Anita emerged from the toilet to stand beside her. The girl's eyes widened in terror as she looked around. Brian remained inside. Lisa thought she could hear him praying under his breath.

They began to explore, tiptoeing between bloody puddles, making sure not to touch anything, or look at it too closely. Anita went to the open door. Lisa focused on the carriage that contained their bags and, more importantly, their phones. They had to call for help. She had to call Neil.

Finding a spot of clear glass, she squinted inside. Stifling a scream, she fell backwards. Instinctively reaching out to steady herself, her hand landed on a slippery, clotted mess. She lost her balance and sat down heavily. Something squelched beneath her.

She almost screamed but stopped herself by biting her lip. Retching in disgust, she scrambled to her feet and wiped her hand on her dress. She frantically signalled a silent warning to Anita, by pointing furiously at the carriage and shaking her head. Anita crept over and they squatted low, peering inside.

It was full of shuffling, twitching creatures that had been their fellow passengers. They shambled around, jostling each other in the narrow walkway between the seats. The door was blocked by a barricade of luggage that had fallen from the storage shelves. Their heads drooped on their shoulders and they seemed to be in a sort of stupor.

There was none of the loud moaning and ferocious growling from earlier, just an occasional low groan or snuffle. Their bodies were in various states of terrible destruction. Bloodied and torn. Gaping wounds and tattered flesh. Their skin was the same grey-green colour as the boy's. They all had the same cloudy, unfocused eyes.

Lisa and Anita looked at each other. No words were needed to communicate their fear, revulsion and confusion. Anita indicated towards the other carriage and Lisa nodded. Moving slowly, they

19

crossed to the other closed door and looked inside. The scene was the same. A throng of wretched, ruined souls, ambling about amidst the detritus of a frenzied, violent attack.

They went to the open door and stood for a moment, breathing in the fresh air. They were in the countryside. The train was high on an embankment, and they could see for a good distance. Across a recently harvested field (so similar to the one on the toilet wall that Lisa thought again that she might be dreaming) was another field and, beyond that, a cluster of farm buildings.

The view from the open door on the other side was similar - endless rolling fields dotted with occasional clusters of trees and small groups of buildings.

"That farm looks closest." Anita pointed to the first farm. "It's only a couple of miles away. Let's go." She prepared to jump down from the train.

Lisa grabbed her sleeve. "Hang on! What are you doing? What about Brian and the … others?"

"What others?"

"The ones that were outside."

"Gone. So?"

"But they could be out there."

"Can you *see* them? Even if they are, we can outrun them. Easy."

"*We* might be able to, but what about him?" Lisa nodded back towards the toilet.

"What about him?"

"We can't just *leave* him."

"Why not? He'll slow us down."

20

"Anita. Come on. Please."

The girl rolled her eyes. "Ok, but he's got to come with us. We can't stay here."

Brian looked at them expectantly, as they slipped back into the toilet. Lisa described what they had seen and told him that that they were going to leave. Head for the farm. Where they could get help.

"Is it safe?" Brian asked.

"I don't know." Lisa was honest.

"Then why not stay here until help arrives?" Brian whined.

Anita's impatience was building. "It's not coming. That's the point. We don't have a choice. We need to go. *Now*."

"Brian." Lisa tried to reassure him. "If anyone was coming, they would be here by now. Don't you think?"

"Well ... " he glanced towards the door.

"It's going to be dark soon," Lisa continued. She checked her watch. "It's almost seven already. I'm sure you don't want to be here in the dark. I know *I* don't. The farm is only a couple of miles away. We can be there in half an hour."

"Less if we run," Anita added.

"I'm just not sure ... " Brian shook his head.

"Look, I know you're scared. I'm scared. We're all scared. But it's the right thing to do. The safest thing to do." Lisa pleaded with him. "This train is full of ... of ... them. We have to get away."

Brian sighed deeply. "Ok, ok. You're determined to go, and I can't stay here on my own. What choice do

I have?"

"Good man!" Anita took his arm and guided him toward the door.

"Let's do this!" Anita jumped down from the train. She looked from side to side. "It's fine. Come down."

Lisa dropped down beside her and squatted as she looked around. Apart from a few bloodstains on the ground and some bloody footprints leading down the embankment, Anita was right. It was fine. It was more than fine. It was a massive relief to be off the train. Conscious of the relatively insubstantial glass doors that contained the occupants of the carriages behind them, and the likelihood that every other carriage on the train contained a similar threat, again, she fought the impulse to sprint down the embankment and across the fields as fast as she could. Instead, she waited patiently as Brian stiffly eased himself down beside them. He was trembling.

Anita was not as patient. She was striding away from the train. "Let's go."

Lisa looked at the expanse of open space between them and the farm. "Before we go ..." she started.

"Oh, for God's sake." Anita rolled her eyes again.

"It's going to be a long walk and, once we leave the cover of the train, we'll be very ... exposed," Lisa said.

"Come on. Let's get out of here. We're wasting time."

"No really, we're so close to the driver's cab. Why don't we check it for anything ... useful? For ... protection." Lisa couldn't bring herself to say the word *weapon*, but that was what she was thinking. That conjured up some implications and mental images that she wasn't quite ready to embrace.

Anita looked at the farm, then along the carriage towards the front of the train. It was close.

"Yeah, yeah. Good call. Maybe I'd feel better with something solid in my hand. There might even be a phone or something in there."

Brian pressed the palms of his hands together with his forefingers touching his lips in a praying gesture.

"It's ok. We won't be long." Lisa rubbed his arm.

"You can keep watch," Anita winked.

Lisa led the way as the women moved silently along the side of the train. Brian cowered close to the open doorway, glancing anxiously from side to side.

"Hurry up, please," he called after them.

About two-thirds of the way along the carriage was another open door. It was smaller than the main doors and led into a large storage compartment. Apart from a couple of bikes stacked in a corner, the space appeared empty. The door on the opposite side was open too.

Anita was up and inside before Lisa had time to think. When she joined her, the girl was standing staring at the door to the driver's cab. It was slightly ajar. The back of a blue seat and part of the control console was just visible.

Anita moved towards the door then hesitated. She pointed towards a plastic water bottle resting in a holder. Lisa looked at the bottle and gave Anita a quizzical look. Anita gestured more emphatically towards the bottle. Lisa looked at it again and was about to speak, when she saw it. A single bloody smear on the white label of the bottle.

Nothing was out of place in the storage area. The bikes were stacked neatly against the wall. A door that led back into the passenger carriage was firmly closed. There were no signs of a struggle and no other bloodstains. It could be nothing. Anita pointed back outside and made a circling motion with her finger.

They stood at the front of the train and looked up towards the dark sloping window of the cab. It was impossible to see anything clearly inside except shadows and outlines, but there was no sign of movement.

"Come on," Anita said. "It's empty."

"I wonder where the driver is?"

"Long gone, if he's got any sense."

"What about the blood?"

"It's one smear. It could be anything."

"Oh god. I don't know ..." Lisa could feel her chest tightening again. She turned and looked out across the fields, taking a few deep, calming breaths. "Give me a minute."

In the far distance, she could see the grey outlines of some high-rise buildings. Given the time the train had stopped, and the fact that they had not reached the city yet, she reckoned that they must be somewhere between Rugby and Coventry.

It was eerily quiet. No cars or tractors. No planes

in the sky. No signs of everyday life at all. And the emergency services had never arrived. A small, cold, ball of unease formed in her stomach. She felt for her inhaler in her pocket but tried to calm herself without it. It was nearly empty, and her spare was in her bag back in the carriage.

"Trust me. It'll be alright. There's no-one in there." Anita put a hand on her shoulder.

"It's not that. It's ... "

A sudden crunch of gravel underfoot caused them both to spin around. Lisa froze and Anita instinctively coiled into a defensive posture.

Another crunch. Lisa raised her palm to Anita who was now poised as if to strike.

And another.

Lisa held her breath then let out a sigh of relief as Brian appeared from around the side of the train. Anita launched at him and her hands were at his throat before Lisa could stop her.

"What the hell are you doing, creeping up on us like that!" the girl yelled.

"Anita! Stop it!" Lisa pulled her away.

Brian massaged his neck. "What have you been doing? I thought something had happened."

Anita snarled at him. "It nearly did, but to you, not us. You idiot!"

"We're just making sure the cab is empty," Lisa explained.

"Are you sure this is a good idea?" Brian sighed. "Don't you think we should just get moving? It'll be dark soon."

"Yes, we are!" Anita snapped. "And we know it's

getting dark soon. But, it's a long walk to that farm and Lisa's right. What happens if we meet some of *them* on the way? Anyway, it's empty. The driver's gone. We're going in now."

"Oh, whatever you want. Just hurry up, *please*." Brian anxiously scanned the fields around them.

The women looked up at the cab once more, before making their way back onto the train.

As soon as Lisa stepped into the cab, they saw each other. He was stooped motionless in the corner, but his head snapped up and he let out a scream of rage as he lurched towards her. Anita was in the doorway blocking her exit and all three of them tumbled out of the cab as he barracked into them, teeth bared, hissing and snarling.

The fall winded her badly. She was on her back, his body pinning her to the ground, his face close to hers, a mask of rage and snapping teeth. His hands clawed at her body. She managed to free one arm and tried to push him away, but he was too strong. She couldn't breathe, her empty lungs crushed under his weight. His face moved closer to hers. His mouth opened wide. His breath was fetid. She tried to scream but nothing came out. She closed her eyes.

There was a loud thud - the crack of something solid hitting bone - and he rolled off her. Air flooded into her lungs, and as she exhaled, she released the scream that had been trapped in her chest. She felt herself being dragged along the floor and then tumbling from the train onto the gravel below.

26

Dazed and panting, she crawled onto her hands and knees and looked up. Anita was standing in the doorway facing into the train. Her arms were braced against the frame. Behind her, the driver was moving towards her. Not fast, but slowly and steadily, one step at a time. Arms outstretched. Growling.

Anita lifted her legs and coiled them to her chest. She timed it perfectly. When he was just close enough for maximum impact, she shrieked and released both legs in a single explosive kick. It caught him in the centre of his chest, propelling him backwards and out of sight. Anita followed him.

Lisa pulled herself up so she could see into the train. Anita was standing at the other open door looking down. She took a single step back as the driver appeared in the doorway, still growling. The train was high. Only his head and shoulders were visible. He was wearing a Virgin Trains name badge. His name was Craig. Craig made no attempt to climb back into the train. He strained and stretched to reach Anita. He snarled and screeched. He grimaced and leered. He clawed and scratched. But he seemed totally incapable of climbing back inside.

Anita dropped to her knees and vomited.

Lisa looked down at herself. Her denim jacket had protected her. She was filthy and smeared with blood, but the fabric of both her dress and jacket was intact. She was shocked and winded, but she wasn't injured. She sank to the ground shaking uncontrollably.

27

The light was fading by the time they recovered and searched the cab. As Craig continued to scrabble in the doorway outside, Anita salvaged a crowbar and a large heavy spanner from a toolbox under the console, and Lisa found a screwdriver in a wall cabinet. Anita gave Lisa the hammer and handed the screwdriver to Brian with a sneer. He looked at it curiously, then, as she went to snatch it back, tucked it into his pocket.

They half slid; half stumbled down the embankment. It was steep and thick with shrubbery. Once they were all at the bottom, they started walking briskly towards the farm.

It was getting dark. They couldn't waste another second. They had to get there.

The women broke into a light jog.

Brian hurried behind them.

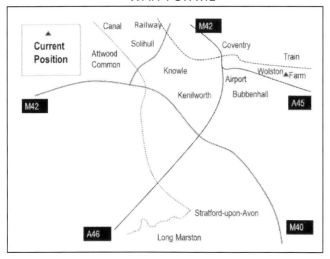

Chapter 2

Day 1 - Wolston near Coventry

They reached the farm as dusk gave way to darkness. It had been a tense walk. They didn't talk much, each lost in their own thoughts about what had happened and what they would find out when they reached their destination. It had taken about half an hour. They could have been quicker, but for a huffing and puffing Brian stumbling along behind them and stopping from time to time, bent over with his hands on his knees to catch his breath.

Lisa was grateful that the dress code for her meeting had been business casual. She was wearing a loose-fitting short dress, a denim jacket, and comfortable flat pumps. She would have struggled if she'd been in her usual business attire of a tight-fitting suit and heels.

The tension had eased a little, the further they got from the train. It felt good to be moving purposefully towards the farm, and there was even a growing sense of relief that their ordeal would soon be over. Out in the fresh air, surrounded by normal sights and sounds, what had happened over the last few hours began to feel like a bad dream. Lisa even noticed that it was a lovely late autumn evening. It was warm and the setting sun cast a red glow across the horizon.

Her thoughts drifted back to Neil. He should be back at his hotel by now. She pictured herself standing in the cosy farmhouse kitchen, calling him on the phone. Breaking down. Telling him what had happened. Heard him comforting her, telling her it was going to be alright; he was coming to get her.

But, all feelings of relief and hope that had begun to surface gradually dissipated as they got closer to the farm. Nobody vocalised it but they all felt it. Even though it was now almost completely dark, there were no lights coming from any of the buildings. They could make out a large barn on the left, and a sprawling farmhouse on the right. The buildings were connected by some outbuildings and open stables, all of which faced into a large, cobbled courtyard, bordered by a low wall. They headed for an open gate in the centre of the wall.

Unconsciously, they'd slowed down, and walked towards the gate with some trepidation. As they approached, a dog began to bark, which was strangely reassuring and alarming at the same time. The large dog suddenly bounded out from behind a building, barking loudly, warning them to stay away. It stopped in the open gateway growling menacingly. In the dark they couldn't see it clearly but could sense that it was bristling with aggression. They stopped.

"Man, I hate dogs," Anita grumbled.

"Me too," Lisa agreed. "What do we do now?"

Brian stepped forward.

"What are you doing?" Lisa grabbed his arm. "Be careful."

Brian turned to her. "Don't worry".

The women watched in amazement as Brian confidently stepped forward and, when he was about four or five metres from the dog, dropped onto one knee and held his hand out.

"Here, boy. Come here, boy. There's a good boy."

Astonishingly, the dog stopped growling and padded over to Brian who ruffled its fur and rewarded it with a series of rubs, pats and kind words. It began panting and whimpering.

"He's just upset and frightened," Brian said.

"What of?" Lisa and Anita spoke in unison.

They walked warily towards the farmhouse accompanied by the dog. It stayed close to Brian, growling quietly as they neared the building. The two-storey house was in darkness, but the front door was ajar. To the right of the door was another small building: a lean-to that was attached to the main house but with its own separate door, also ajar.

They approached the farmhouse. The dog's growling intensified. They huddled together, pausing after every step, gripping their makeshift weapons tightly, raised and ready to strike. Even Brian had his screwdriver clenched in his hand.

There were noises coming from the lean-to: wet guttural noises that were now horribly familiar. They looked at each other. Anita signalled to back off.

The dog rushed forward to the door and started barking again. There was movement from inside. They froze. The door burst open and a figure staggered into the courtyard.

Lisa recognised him immediately. His image was burned into her mind. It was the undead boy in the green hoodie from the train.

Later, when she tried to work out exactly what happened next, it was a blur. There was no time to think, only act. The boy lunged for Brian. The man struck out with his screwdriver, but the boy caught the sleeve of his coat and pulled his arm towards his mouth. Brian screamed in pain and shock as the boy sank his teeth into the side of his hand.

Almost at the same time, the dog leapt up, snarling, and knocked the boy to the ground. Brian reeled backwards clutching his hand. Then, Lisa and Anita were on the boy, striking and stabbing at him, as the dog tore at his arm. The boy was incredibly strong, seeming to barely notice the frenzy of blows that were reigning down on him. He snarled and struggled, grabbing and biting at them for what seemed like an eternity. A deep penetrating blow to the head from Anita, finally stopped him and his body went limp.

Lisa rolled off him and crawled a few feet away before she began to vomit. Shaking and crying, on her hands and knees, she heaved and retched again and again, bringing up nothing but acrid, foul-tasting bile. Her eyes streamed and snot drooled from her nose and mouth. She wiped it away with her sleeve.

Anita seemed to have taken this one more in her stride. She stood over the boy staring down at him, crowbar poised in case he should stir again. The dog went over to Brian, who was kneeling and examining his hand. It licked his face.

"Are you ok, Brian?" Anita asked.

"Yes, all things considered," Brian replied.

"Only a flesh wound, as they say," he almost joked.

Lisa glanced up at him, surprised by how jaunty he sounded. She was about to reply when the dog started growling again, low and threatening, looking towards the lean-to. They all looked in the same direction.

Standing in the doorway was what used to be a man. There was practically nothing about him that was recognisable as a human being. He was in his socks, which were still remarkably intact, but every inch of the rest of his face and body was ravaged and torn.

He had been tall and heavyset. He was wearing outdoor work clothes. They were ripped and torn, as was the flesh beneath. His legs and arms were mauled down to the bone in places. Ribbons of torn skin, muscle and tendons trailed on the floor behind him. The contents of his abdomen had tumbled out of a yawning wound and dangled between his legs. His face had gone, except for one eye hanging down his cheek.

It was amazing that he could stand, there was so little left of him that was solid, but he dragged himself towards them, arms outstretched, mouth open, not moaning like the others had been, but gurgling and rasping.

Anita strode over to him and, confidently swerving to avoid his grasp, plunged the sharp end of the crowbar into his forehead. He crumpled to the floor.

"Sorry, Matey." She pulled the bar out using her foot as a lever and wiped it clean on what was left of his shirt.

"I think we've worked out how to kill them."

She was learning fast, Lisa thought. Too fast for comfort, maybe.

The dog padded over and began sniffing and pawing at the body.

"Must be his owner," Brian observed. "He's a Springer … Springer Spaniel. Great farm dogs," he added.

"Random," Anita muttered. "Do you think there are any more?" she asked.

"Dogs?" asked Brian.

"Of them, you idiot! In there?" She gestured to the lean-to. "Or in the house?"

"He seems more settled." Brian ruffled the dog's fur. "I think he would sense it."

Lisa got wearily to her feet. She felt drained. She'd had more than enough for one day.

"There's only one way to find out, and we need to get help. We're completely out of our depths with this." She walked towards the door.

Anita pushed past her to look in the window. "Wait."

It was now so dark they could barely see anything inside, but there was no obvious movement.

Lisa rapped on the window. Nothing. But then the dog took matters into his own hands. He left his dead master and slipped in through the door. They heard him greedily slurping water inside.

"God, I need a drink too," Lisa followed him in.

She fumbled around the door frame, feeling in the dark for a light switch. Her fingers found it and flicked it down. The room filled reassuringly with light. They were in a large room with windows on two sides and patio doors on another. It was empty.

"Shut the curtains!" Anita hissed. "It's too bright!"

Working quickly, Lisa pulled the heavy curtains over the windows on the left, as Brian did the same on the right. Anita closed the blinds on the patio doors.

It was a huge space, surprisingly modern, open plan with a low beamed ceiling. On the left was a raised kitchen area with solid beechwood units and expensive granite worktops. Warmth radiated from the AGA on the far wall, along with the comforting aroma of something tasty cooking inside. In the middle of the room was a long dining table and chairs. Two places were set at one end, complete with an open bottle of red wine and two glasses.

The other half of the room was a cosy sitting area

with three substantial sofas arranged around a low coffee table scattered with books and magazines. There was an unlit wood burner nestling inside a rustic red-brick fireplace and a flat screen TV in the corner.

Scanning the space quickly, Lisa headed to another closed door in the far corner of the kitchen area, hesitating with her hand on the doorknob, glancing questioningly at the other two.

"We need to be sure it's safe," Anita nodded.

Lisa slowly opened the door, revealing a small hallway with a wooden staircase directly opposite and another door on the left. All was quiet apart from the dog still happily slurping from his water bowl. Once again, listening carefully for any sounds from within, she slowly opened the second door.

The next room was cool and dark but the light from the kitchen was enough for her to see that it appeared to serve as a combination of a pantry and a laundry room. White goods ran along one wall and the other was lined, floor to ceiling with well-stocked shelves. Another door at the far end looked as though it led back outside to the side of the house. Satisfied, she closed the door and joined Anita at the bottom of the stairs.

Anita led the way as they crept upstairs, weapons poised once again. They paused when the staircase turned halfway up onto a small landing. The silence was oppressive. They continued up to a wide square hallway with five doors leading off. The light from downstairs was still just enough to see by. Four doors were open slightly and one was closed. They stood for moment in the gloom, watching the doors and waiting, ready to react.

Lisa's stomach cramped and she felt bile rise in her throat again. She was shaking again too, but this time it was as much with exhaustion as fear. Her mouth was dry. Her head was aching. She was so tired. She honestly didn't think she had the strength for another terrifying encounter. It was too much. But she had no choice. She had to do this, had to keep going for just a bit longer.

Anita, on the other hand, seemed calm and alert. She moved quickly, kicking the four partly open doors wide open, one at a time, karate style, each time with a loud bang that resonated through the house.

"It's fine. There's no-one here. Don't worry. We'd know by now if there were." She was matter of fact.

Without any sign of fear, she opened the final closed door, then kicked it hard and fast like the others. It slammed wide on its hinges, bouncing back before it settled, revealing the interior of the room.

Immediately, her whole body tensed, and she stepped back raising the crowbar high, as if to strike. Lisa braced herself. A woman screamed, but she instantly recognised it as a healthy human scream.

She grabbed Anita's arm.

"No!"

Standing in the middle of the room, eyes wide with fear and arms raised defensively in front of her, was a small dark-blonde woman. She looked around fifty, but could have been older, trim and fit, in black and pink lycra running gear and trainers. She was crying and cowering.

"Please don't hurt me. Please."

"It's alright," Lisa reassured her. "Sorry, we thought you might be one of them."

Anita switched on the light and crossed the room to close the curtains. The woman sank down onto the bed, sobbing.

"What's happening? Who are you? Where's John?" she asked between sobs.

"We're from the train, out back." Anita waved in the direction of the train.

"We need help. Have you got a phone?" Lisa asked.

"They came from the train. I saw them. I tried to warn him. Where is he? Is he alright?"

She stood up again and looked at their faces. "Where's my husband?"

"I'm really sorry," Lisa said. "If he was outside, I think he's dead."

She looked at them in silence for an instant, as if struck, then collapsed onto the bed. Her hands covered her mouth and she issued a long high-pitched wail of despair, followed by more wretched sobbing and choking. She was inconsolable, but her unchallenging acceptance of her husband's fate suggested to Lisa that they had just confirmed what she'd already suspected.

They watched her, both struggling with their own emotions. Her pain was hard to watch.

Lisa wondered how *she* would react if someone

told her Neil had died ... what he would do if she did? It was cheesy, she knew, but they were everything to each other, and had been since the day they'd met. She couldn't imagine her life without him. If he died, she supposed she would just curl up in a ball and wait to die too. He was her lover and her best friend, and all the more precious because she found it hard to make friends ... hard to form any close relationships, in fact.

She was aware that she was an introvert. Always too busy analysing and working out what was going on, to just enjoy the moment. Always wondering if people really liked her ... whether she was doing and saying the right things and worrying that she was going to mess it up. She could count on one hand the number of people she'd truly ever been able to call her friend, and, even then, they had come and gone at different stages of her life. She *knew* lots of people, but for her, a friend was someone you could trust and be yourself with, free from fear of judgement or criticism. Someone like Neil who loved her unconditionally for who she was.

The woman on the bed was still weeping. Suddenly, the enormity and horror of what had happened over the past few hours hit Lisa hard. She started crying too. She dropped to her knees and buried her face in her hands. They had *killed* this woman's husband. How could they tell her that? The boy in the green hoodie was someone's son, and Craig was probably someone's father.

Her mind was rebelling. She was seriously

39

conflicted. Her instincts had told her what they needed to do to survive, but her head was telling her that they had crossed a line. A line to a place they could never return from. They had *killed* people. Nothing could ever be the same.

She spoke to the woman. "I'm so sorry, I'm so, so sorry."

"This is so messed up." Anita turned and left the room.

"Look! Listen to me for a minute. Something awful is happening," Lisa appealed to the woman. "We don't know what, but it's really, really bad. We need to get help. Have you got a phone?"

The woman pointed to a mobile on the bedside cabinet.

Lisa picked it up and dialled 999.

No service.

"Mobiles don't seem to be working. Have you got a landline?"

"Downstairs," the woman nodded.

"Come with me. Show me."

Lisa took her by the shoulders and gently stood her up. With one arm around her waist, she helped her from the room. Barely able to see through her tears, the woman allowed herself to be guided down the stairs.

In the sitting room, Brian had turned on the TV and was standing in front of it, his injured hand wrapped in a table napkin. He barely glanced in their direction when they entered the room, concentrating on the screen and fiddling with a remote control. Anita was watching him impatiently.

"Turn it up! Give it to me!" She snatched the remote control from him and turned up the volume.

The woman pointed out the telephone, on a small low table by the kitchen window, before falling to her knees as the dog ran over to her.

"Oh Matthew," she wept, burying her face in its fur. It licked the salty tears from her hands and face.

"Matthew!" snorted Anita. "What sort of name is that for a dog?"

Lisa frowned at her and shook her head.

Picking up the phone handset, Lisa realised that, without her mobile, her recollection of any numbers, including Neil's, was extremely limited. She never memorised them, just rang them straight from her contacts. As it happened, it was irrelevant, as every number she tried just rang out. She tried 999 first but no-one answered.

After a few tries, she was pretty sure she had Neil's mobile right but, despite calling it several times, she kept getting the "number unavailable" message. She was also confident about their landline number. Even though she knew he wouldn't be there, she dialled it anyway. It rang for a while before it went through to their answerphone.

"Neil, it's me. I'm in trouble. I'm so scared. I don't really know where I am. I don't know what's happening. I'm so scared, Neil. I don't know what to do. I need you. I really need you."

She called over to the woman, "What number is this? What's your number?"

"024 2356 2134," the woman replied nasally,

blowing her nose loudly on a crisp white cotton hankie. She had stopped crying and was sitting on the edge of the raised kitchen floor, also now watching the TV. Matthew was nuzzling in her lap.

"If you get this message, ring me here on 024 2356 2134 as soon as you can. I love you." Her voice cracked. "I love you so much. I'll try you again later."

"I can't get through to anyone," she said as she put the phone down.

"I'm not surprised," said Brian. "Come over here, listen to this. We're in the middle of a national disaster."

But, Lisa's first priority was to quench her raging thirst. Opening and closing cupboards until she found a glass, she filled it from the tap and gulped it down. She closed her eyes. The water was ice cold. It soothed away the raw dryness in her throat and she felt her entire body sigh with relief. She took a deep breath, before refilling and drinking again. She drank three glasses. Water dribbled down her chin; it had never tasted so good.

She took a couple of glasses over to Brian and Anita as she joined them in front of the TV.

"Here. Drink."

The BBC News Channel was playing. All four of them watched in silence, unable to believe what they were seeing. Anita's mouth was open. Her jaw slack with disbelief. Brian's lips were pressed tightly together. He was shaking his head.

Repeated amateur footage of scenes of carnage, like the ones they had witnessed on the train, were being broadcast, with warnings to viewers about the disturbing nature of the content. They were occurring in towns and cities all over the country. The video clips were interspersed by wide-eyed, dishevelled journalists and various, hastily assembled experts, speculating about what may, or may not, be happening.

In a few short hours, it appeared that the entire country had descended into chaos. Terms like "coordinated bio-terror attack", "chemical warfare", "outbreaks of cannibalism", and "reanimation of the dead" were being used freely. The rolling newsfeed at the bottom of the screen provided regular updates of areas that were affected, and the steps that were being taken to try and regain control of the situation. An emergency meeting of COBRA had been called and was in session. The army was being mobilised to support the emergency services who were unable to cope with the unprecedented demand.

The "attack" had been large scale, sudden and completely unexpected. No-one had claimed responsibility. Most outbreaks appeared to have started on trains and buses that left several major cities, including London, Manchester, Glasgow and Cardiff, between four and five that afternoon. Some, like theirs, had failed to reach their destinations, but many had arrived in towns and cities, spilling their infected occupants out into busy stations and city centres.

The speed and scale of the event meant that the government and the authorities had been initially slow to react, and things had rapidly spiralled out of control. The public were advised to stay in their homes, make sure all doors and windows were shut and locked, keep the TV or radio on and await further advice.

Standing in front of the TV, it was hard to accept what they were seeing and hearing. Complete disbelief and fear were mixed with a strange feeling of relief that there was an explanation for the nightmare they had found themselves caught up in, and that they were lucky to have survived. Really lucky, if the TV footage was anything to go by. Lisa was certain in her belief that the authorities were working to get everything back under control. If they could stay safe overnight, she was sure things would be getting back to normal tomorrow, or if not tomorrow, at least in a few days' time.

The others all tried phoning their families with little success. Anita tried her parents and brothers but didn't get through, but Brian managed to speak to one of his two sons at work. He was trapped in his office in London with some colleagues, but the building was secure, and they were prepared to wait it out until it was safe to leave. After what Lisa observed to be a very matter of fact and emotionless conversation in the circumstances, he wished his son good luck and hung up.

Brian's view was that they should also follow government advice and wait at the farm until morning, or until the advice changed. The women agreed.

They systematically checked the whole house, making sure all the doors and windows were locked and all the blinds and curtains closed. They switched off all the lights except for a table lamp in the sitting area, and gathered on the sofas in front of the TV with the volume down low - loud enough for them to hear what was being said, but quiet enough to hear any sounds from outside.

They sat and watched the flickering screen for hours. Early on, Lisa thought she heard moaning and scraping sounds outside, but they eventually stopped. Matthew had growled on and off at first, but as time passed, he also settled down.

Around 11pm, Anita announced that she was hungry and the farmer's wife, whose name was Lynda, produced a slightly dried out, but otherwise tasty, lasagne out of the depths of the AGA. Although, she didn't think she was hungry, Lisa took a small plateful and surprised herself by finishing it and going back for more. Lynda picked at hers and Brian didn't touch his, but between them Lisa and Anita finished the lot. It was delicious and, although she hadn't consciously realised that she needed food, Lisa's mood and energy levels lifted perceptibly soon after she'd eaten. Even her headache began to ease.

"Aren't you hungry, Brian?" She gestured towards his untouched plate. "You should eat."

Brian was red-eyed and slightly flushed and sweaty, as though he had a fever.

"Are you ok?" she asked. "You don't look well."

"I think I'm just tired," he replied. "I might have a lie down."

"Did you clean your hand before you bandaged

it?"

"I don't suppose I did. I got distracted by the news."

"Here, let me have a look at it."

She took him over to the sink and unwrapped the makeshift bandage. Deep teeth-marks formed a half moon shape around the entire edge of his hand. Already, it was evident it was infected. The wound oozed watery fluid and pus, and his whole hand was red and swollen. Dark red lines threaded up his wrist and forearm. It was spreading already.

Lynda brought over a first aid box. Frustrated with herself that they had left it so long before cleaning it, Lisa put on some plastic gloves and washed the wound under the tap. Brian winced and turned his head away. Lynda then rinsed it with TCP, causing Brian to flinch even more. Lisa applied some Savlon and bandaged it up again.

She felt his forehead. "You have a fever. It's a nasty infection. When we get out of here in the morning, you'll need to see a doctor."

They spent the next few hours in the sitting area, drawing some small comfort from being together. They kept the TV on, but no new information came through. The same video clips were replayed, the same endless uninformative discussions and analysis continued. In between patrolling the house and making rounds of hot drinks, they talked about their lives, why they'd been on the train, and where they'd been going.

Anita went first. She was a first year Sports Science student at Loughborough University, and had been making her way up there from her home in Epsom. She was an athlete - a sprinter - and had chosen Loughborough because it meant she could get the training and support she needed for her athletics career and continue her education at the same time. This was going to be her first experience of living away from home. Her parents had already been up to Loughborough with her the weekend before, to settle her into her accommodation. She'd been having a final few days at home before her first term began. She had older twin brothers, one of whom had just graduated and was back home trying to find a job. The other was a chef on a luxury yacht, currently somewhere off the coast of Croatia, as far as she knew.

Although she was young and relatively inexperienced, during the short time they'd spent together, Lisa was already impressed by her bravery and resilience. Yes, she was a bit impatient and impulsive, but she could tell that she had a depth of character and inner strength that were going to help her recover from what had happened to them, and what they'd had to do.

It was harder to get Brian to talk. As well as feeling increasingly unwell, he was struggling generally with the whole situation and just seemed reluctant to talk about himself … or anything else for that matter. They did learn that he was from London and was a director of a national animal rescue charity. He'd been travelling all the way to Edinburgh for a conference. He was divorced and lived alone but did have two grown up sons who also lived in London.

Lynda described, in between bouts of weeping, how she'd been preparing dinner in time for John to get in. While it was cooking, she'd gone for a run and then went upstairs to change. She'd seen the train on the embankment from the bedroom window before she'd gone out, and was surprised to see that it was still there when she got back. She'd been out for over half an hour. Trains occasionally stopped in the same place during busy periods, waiting for clearance to continue into Coventry, but they were never there for more than five or ten minutes at a time. She watched it for a while, wondering what was going on. She assumed it had broken down. She was about to jump in the shower, when she saw a small group stumbling across the field towards the farm. Something in the way they moved wasn't right.

She continued to watch and, as they got closer, could see that they all seemed to be injured. Their clothes were heavily bloodstained, some of them were limping and dragging limbs, and others were holding their heads in unusual positions. She looked back at the train. There didn't appear to have been an accident. They were moving surprisingly fast. For a reason she didn't fully understand, she was suddenly deeply afraid.

Just as they disappeared out of sight behind the building, she heard Matthew barking, signalling John's return. She hurried downstairs.

She described how she'd opened the front door

and seen John's back in the doorway of the boot room. He was bent over taking off his boots and completely unaware of the hideously disfigured boy in a green hoodie behind him, dragging his blood-soaked body towards her husband.

"John!"

"I'm coming, just taking my boots off," he called.

"John! Behind you! Look ..."

John turned his head. Too late. The boy lurched towards him, knocking him into the room and onto the floor.

"John!" she'd cried again, backing off in shock as the boy fell on her husband, snarling and moaning like an animal.

At that point Lynda couldn't go on, but they knew the rest and didn't push her.

Lisa explained that she was on her way back from a meeting in London, heading to Birmingham to catch another train to her local station. They had established that they were, as Lisa had suspected, between Rugby and Coventry. The farm was close to a village called Wolston, near Coventry, and she lived only twenty or thirty miles away, near Solihull. She lived there with Neil, her husband of fifteen years. She worked as a business analyst for a large engineering company that supplied the motor trade.

"Have you got children?" Anita asked.

"No. No children," she replied.

"Oh, why not?

"No reason really. I don't know. We just never got

around to it, I suppose."

It was the truth. She honestly wasn't sure why they hadn't had kids. Initially, she'd been trying to get her career established before she started a family. Then there were other things they wanted to do before they settled down. Places to visit, things to see and experiences to have. The years had just slipped away. At forty-four, she was well aware that her biological clock had probably stopped ticking. Sometimes, little pangs of regret floated to the surface but most of the time she was happy just the way they were, and so was Neil. Or at least that's what he told her. All they really needed was each other.

It had always been like that with them. Other than Neil, the only other people she was close to were her family, consisting of her parents and two sisters, and Sylvia, a woman who lived across the road. She had known Sylvia for a while. They had both joined a local pop choir at the same time and, discovering that they lived close to each other, they had started walking to rehearsals together.

For Lisa, they only became *friends* a year later when they spent four hours on a coach together, travelling to and from a performance in London. They had talked all the way there and back, and Lisa had really liked the older woman for her openness and generosity of spirit. Since then, she had grown to love her and now, saw her as a true friend. Nothing shocked or surprised Sylvia, she never judged or criticised and she had become one of the few people Lisa could talk to openly and enjoy spending time with.

It had been the same with lovers. First and foremost, they had to be someone she could call a friend, by her own definition, overthinking or not. If she only had a few real friends, the list of lovers was even shorter. She'd met Neil in 2001 when she was working for Jaguar in Coventry, her first job after graduating. He'd come to film a documentary about the decline of the British car industry in the Midlands. For a couple of days, she'd watched him working with the rest of the film crew from behind her computer screen, drawn in first by his unguarded smile, but later by a baser appreciation of his broad, powerful shoulders, his lightly tanned forearms and obvious, even inside his jeans, muscular thighs and buttocks. When, on the third day, he asked if she fancied a drink after work, she was terrified. She tried to say no, but he had already got her sussed and had arranged where and when they were going to meet before she could think of a good excuse.

From that day on, she had adored him. He made her feel loved, safe and secure, and normal. He balanced her out, checked her when her mind was taking her too far in unhelpful directions. She trusted him completely, and he had never let her down.

At some point around 3am, the programmes stopped and were replaced by an Emergency Broadcast Screen. Every thirty seconds, a woman's voice, slightly robotic but with a soothing authoritative tone, repeated the same message. Her voice reminded Lisa of Moira Stewart's.

"This is not a test. Repeat! This is not a test. A state of emergency has been declared in the entire United Kingdom. If you can, stay in your home or find a place of safety. Repeat! Stay in your home or find a place of safety. Ensure that all doors and windows are secure. Await further advice."

After that, Lisa and Anita took turns to stay awake and doze on one of the sofas for an hour at a time. Anita slept deeply and Lisa had to shake her hard to wake her. Lisa, on the other hand, found it impossible to sleep when it was her turn. Flashbacks of the horror of the previous day would jolt her awake every time she drifted off. Brian lay on another sofa covered with a blanket. He was getting sicker by the hour, shivering and moaning in his sleep. Lynda was subdued and tearful sitting at the dining table, still in her running gear.

Around 4am, they heard helicopters thumping overhead and heavy vehicles rolling by on the road that ran past the farm. But they stayed inside, afraid to go out or even to look through the curtains until it was light. The Emergency Broadcast continued. No further advice came. The phone never rang. It was as if they were the only people in the world.

Knowing that they were so close to the city, it seemed crazy that help was potentially so near yet felt so far away. Lisa tried phoning 999 again once or twice with no success. She tried Neil's mobile and the home phone again, but the outcome was the same. Where was he? Was he ok?

She remembered the last time in her life she'd felt a bit like this. It was not long after she and Neil had moved in together, a few months after they'd met, when, in the aftermath of September the 11th, there had been a few hours where it appeared that the whole world might descend into chaos. She'd been in a meeting in a hotel near Gatwick Airport. A man had slipped quietly into the back of the room. He waited for a gap in proceedings, then took the floor to explain what had happened. Everyone had left the meeting room to watch the TV coverage in the hotel bar for a while. There were rumours of other impending attacks in London and around the world. Everyone was anxious to get home to their families, so they'd agreed to abandon the meeting and go home.

She hadn't been able to get in touch with Neil. She wasn't even sure where he was working. She remembered the loneliness and anxiety she'd felt, being so far away from him and her family in a time of such shock, fear and uncertainty.

That night, they'd held each other tightly and whispered a promise to each other. If anything like that ever happened again, their first priority would be to make their way home to each other. Whoever got there first would wait for the other. Whatever happened next, they would deal with together. They could deal with anything as long as they were together. She wondered if he remembered their promise.

She wondered if he would go home and wait for her.

Around 5am, she called their landline again and left another message.

"It's me again, Darling. I'm ok. Sorry about before. I'm in a farm near a village called Wolston, near Coventry. I'm not far away. I'm safe at the moment. I'm with a few other people. I was on one of the trains. It was awful, but I'm ok. I don't know how, but I am ok. I'm going to stay here until the morning, then try to get home. If you get there before me, wait for me. I love you. Remember! Wait for me! I'm coming home."

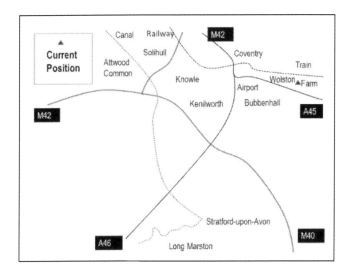

Chapter 3

Day 2 - Wolston near Coventry

It was around seven when it got light and Anita opened the kitchen curtains. The yard was empty apart from the bodies, a gruesome reminder of the previous evening's activities. Ironically, it was another lovely day. Matthew seemed relaxed and they were as confident as they could be that anyone, or anything, who'd been outside last night was gone. Sitting at the dining table with steaming mugs of freshly brewed coffee, the women discussed their options.

Brian was still very unwell, worse, in fact. His

whole arm was red and swollen and he had developed a cough. Despite their protests, he painfully eased himself off the sofa to join them at the table.

"I'm not dead yet," he joked.

Lynda glanced at the bodies in the yard.

Lisa winced.

Anita sucked her teeth.

No-one laughed.

"Coffee?" Lynda offered.

"Couldn't face it, I'm afraid," Brian said.

"You better drink some water. You'll get dehydrated." Anita filled a glass and thrust it at him.

Brian took a half-hearted sip and spluttered, stifling a cough. Anita scoffed and turned her attention back to the discussion.

No further advice had been issued through the Emergency Broadcast System. The message on the screen was the same as it had been all night. They'd not heard a helicopter, nor a vehicle go by for several hours. They weren't even sure whether the advice to stay indoors still applied.

Lisa started.

"I'm so close to home. I'm only half an hour away … by car." She glanced at Lynda.

"I just want to get back to Neil. The A45 is just down the road. That'll take me to the M42 and then it's pretty much a straight run most of the way."

Anita spoke next.

"Honestly, I can't just sit here doing nothing any longer. It's driving me mad. I need to get out. Move on. Do something. Maybe, I could come with you for now, Lisa, and then try to get back home later, when things settle down?"

"Yeah. Of course. I'd feel better if you came with me. I'm not going to pretend I'm not a bit nervous. And, I promise we'll do whatever we can to get you home too ... as soon as we can."

They all acknowledged that Brian needed a doctor. If he stayed at the farm with his infection untreated for much longer, he was in danger of becoming seriously ill.

And so, they agreed that they would leave.

Lisa looked at Lynda, who'd been very quiet throughout.

The older woman spoke quietly, but there was determination in her tone.

"I'm going to stay here. With Matthew and ... John ... until it's all over. Besides, I haven't heard from the kids. I need to be here if they call or try to come home."

Lisa nodded. "I get that. But, as long as you're sure you'll be ok here ... alone?"

"I'm sure. I want to stay. You can take John's old X-Trail, though. I don't need it ... now."

Lynda's eyes filled with tears, and she got up from the table.

Lisa stood up and put an arm around her shoulder. "Thank you. Thank you so much. I promise we'll bring it back ... after."

"The only thing is," Lynda almost whispered. "John still has the keys."

She choked on a sob and left the room.

"We're gonna have to move both bodies." Anita was pacing up and down and chewing her thumbnail.

Lisa looked at her.

Anita continued. "We can't leave her here alone with a couple of mangled corpses outside her front door."

Lisa reluctantly agreed. "I suppose ... who knows how long this will go on before anyone comes to move them? What if her kids come back and see their Dad ... well, you know?"

Anita started rummaging in the cupboard under the sink. "Let's do this and get the hell out of here!"

Armed with rubber gloves from the kitchen cupboard, the two women stepped outside, closing the door behind them.

Lisa sighed. It was a beautiful morning: fresh and clear, beneath a blue and cloudless sky. Birds were singing, oblivious to the *National Emergency*. If there hadn't been a couple of mutilated bodies lying in the yard, you would never have known that anything was wrong.

But it was wrong ... very wrong! A plume of black smoke billowed into the sky from the direction of the city. Flies were buzzing around the bodies. Close up, in the light of day, the scene was horrific. The smell of death, sweet and putrid. Lisa's heart was thumping, her chest tightening. She took a couple of puffs from her inhaler.

Anita knelt by John's side and started groping

58

around in his tattered, soiled clothes. She retched as she wriggled her fingers inside his trouser pockets. Lisa took a deep breath and crouched down to help her. There was nothing there. He was wearing the remains of a checked flannel shirt but no jacket.

"They're not here," Lisa said. "They must be inside."

She stood up, spitting as bitter saliva pooled in her mouth.

They went into the boot room.

The floor was covered with blood and torn flesh, and it was hard not to slip in the sticky mess. A heavy waterproof jacket was lying on the floor, along with John's discarded boots. Lisa went through the pockets of the jacket.

"Got them!" She jangled the keys triumphantly.

She turned to Anita, who was examining something in the corner of the room, beside some shelving.

"What is it?" Lisa asked.

"Look at this," Anita said, stepping aside to reveal a large shotgun leaning against the wall. Lisa looked at the gun. She was horrified. Not by the weapon, but by the realisation that her heart had leapt when she saw it … leapt with excitement because this was going to make any killing they had to do so much easier. What was happening to her?

"Come on. We can use this," Anita picked it up. It looked heavy. She held it awkwardly by the barrel.

"Do you know how to work it?" Lisa asked.

"It can't be that hard. Point and fire. I used one in

Tomb Raider once. I don't know how to load it though."

"Tomb Raider?"

"The game. You know?"

"This isn't a game, Anita."

Anita rolled her eyes and huffed.

Lisa went back out to the bodies.

Anita leant the gun against the wall by the front door of the house and Lisa put the car keys on the window sill.

They looked at the bodies.

"Let's get this over with," Anita said.

Since the start, this was by far the worst thing they'd had to do. All the other awful things they'd seen and done since the previous afternoon had happened when they were in shock, fuelled by fear and adrenaline. Their memories were a blur of hazy images and sensations. Now, every gory and disgusting detail was on full display in the bright morning sunshine. Lisa was about five-four, and just under nine stone. She tried to keep fit but her desk job made this a challenge at times and her strength was limited.

Anita was tall, around five-ten, and lean and muscular, but it took a lot of effort from both of them to drag John's heavy carcass into the boot room. He was a dead weight and the parts of him that were loose snagged on the cobblestones, leaving gory blobs behind in the dark, red-brown smear that trailed behind him. The boy was a bit easier, lighter and somehow more compact.

With both corpses inside the boot room, they closed the door, taking care to check that it was secure. The smell was going to get bad as the day warmed up.

Back inside, they prepared for the trip. Lisa was convinced it would only take half an hour or so, but Brian and Lynda didn't think it would be as straightforward as she hoped. Lynda insisted they took some bottled water and a bag of cereal bars from her abundantly stocked pantry ... just in case. She gave them a couple of boxes of shells for the shotgun and showed them how to put the safety on and off, and how to load and fire it.

They all tried the phone again before they left.
No-one got through to anyone, not even Brian this time.

It was about eight-thirty by the time they finally left the farm in the old Nissan. Lisa drove. Anita sat next to her, with the shotgun between her legs, and Brian lay across the back seat under a blanket.
He was not doing well. They'd had to help him into the car. Lisa was concerned about how quickly he'd become so ill. The boy had clearly infected him with something, which was hardly surprising. But what was it? Was it related to the virus or just a normal bacterial infection? Maybe they'd find help for him first, rather than taking him all the way? Maybe they could find a hospital to drop him off at on the way?
Following Lynda's instructions, they set off down

61

the short farm track that led to the road and turned left towards the A45. Almost immediately, they passed a small crossroads with a signpost for the village of Wolston pointing to their right. The roads were quiet: no other traffic or pedestrians. It was like a Sunday morning, but it was Friday. It should have been busy with people making their way to work or taking the kids to school. It was eerie and disconcerting. They tuned the radio in to Radio 4 and kept it on but, like the TV and all the other stations they'd tried, the same Emergency Broadcast message was on repeat.

They moved quickly down the winding country road, with fields and hedgerows flashing by. Lisa was confident she would be home in no time if they continued like this.

Just when she thought they must be close to the main road, they reached a bend where a couple of cars were blocking the way ahead. Beyond the cars, just visible over some bushes, was the top of a tall, narrow, pointed structure. Lisa instantly recognised it as the obelisk in the centre of the roundabout on the A45, where it crossed the old Roman road, the Fosse Way. She had her bearings. She knew where she was, and she knew her way home easily from here.

She slowed to a stop about a hundred metres from the cars. They had hit each other head on and were both badly damaged. Broken glass and metal littered the road. The impact had spun them both sideways and they were effectively blocking the road to all other vehicles.

All four doors of the car closest to them were open. It was a dark grey saloon of some kind. She didn't really do cars. As long as they looked good, and reliably got her from A to B, she was happy.

Neil loved cars. Maybe it was something to do with the fact that he drove a van most of the time. For his birthday a few weeks ago, she had bought him a Driving Experience in Thruxton. He'd been ecstatic. They were due to go next weekend. She hoped this would be all be over by then. He'd be so disappointed if it was cancelled.

Further away was a smaller red car. It was more badly damaged. The front had completely crumpled. There was someone in the driver's seat. They were moving.

Lisa gasped. She recognised the unnatural, jerky movements straight away. An ice-cold ball of fear formed in the pit of her stomach. Her hand instinctively went for her inhaler.

"Oh, shit!" She looked at Anita. Her inhaler rattled as she shook it, but didn't take a puff. She took a few long slow breaths instead.

Anita was staring at the red car. She had seen it too.

"Just get a bit closer so we can see," the girl suggested. "Go slowly. We're ok in here and we can just drive away if anything happens."

"Except that we're facing the wrong way and I'm not great at reversing," Lisa muttered as she put the car in gear and began to roll it slowly towards the accident.

They stopped again, a few feet away from the

vehicles, and sat there for a minute with the engine still running. The grey car was empty, all four doors were wide open, and both front airbags had been activated.

In the red car, an infected, undead woman was trapped in the driver's seat by her seatbelt. She looked young, maybe late twenties, in jeans and a blue, heavily blood-stained jumper. She was straining to get out of her seat, leaning forward and rocking from side to side within the confines of the belt. Lisa was transfixed. It was morbidly fascinating watching her from the safety of the car. She clearly couldn't work out how to release her seatbelt. She got more and more agitated the closer they got, and her moaning changed to a low growl. She glared at them menacingly, baring her teeth and snapping her jaws.

"What do we do, Nita?" Lisa asked.

"Can we get around?"

"I don't think so, not in the car. But the A45 is just over there."

"We can't *walk*. And besides, I wouldn't feel safe out of the car." Anita shook her head. "And what about him?" she gestured towards the back seat.

"You're right," Lisa said. "We'll just have to go back the way we've come and find another way."

She managed to do a laborious, gear-grating, five-or-six-point turn that got them facing back in the direction they'd just come from.

Anita put a hand on her arm. "Wait!"

Lisa looked at her. She was staring down into the red car.

"What?" Lisa leaned forward to see what she was looking at. There was a car seat in the back. She could just see the top of a small blond head and two tiny, kicking feet in striped socks.

"Oh, God!" Lisa stared at the road ahead. The engine idled. It would be so easy just to drive away.

"Oh, God!" She said again, as she laid her forehead on the steering wheel and closed her eyes.

Anita banged her fist on the dashboard. "Man!"

Before Lisa could protest, the girl had opened her door and got out.

She lifted the gun and pointed it out in front of her, its butt resting in the crook of her shoulder. Her finger hovered over the trigger. She actually looked as though she knew what she was doing, computer games or otherwise.

"Keep the engine running. Be ready to move."

Marvelling at her bravery, Lisa watched in the rear-view mirror as Anita moved behind the X-Trail, pointing the gun from side to side and behind her like some sort of commando. She shocked herself when she had to suppress the urge to giggle a little. It was all so ridiculous. Instead, she concentrated on checking the trees on either side of the road for any movement, jumping every time a branch twitched or a leaf fluttered.

After less than a minute, a breathless Anita climbed back into her seat. She fastened her seat belt with trembling fingers.

"Just drive."

Lisa didn't ask. She didn't need to. They headed back in the direction of the farm.

They could clearly see the farmhouse ahead on the right when they reached the small crossroads again. Lisa slowed to a stop. On their left was the village of Wolston and a small sign identified the road on the right as Coal Pit Lane.

"Let's go left. Through the village," Lisa said. "It's the right direction and I reckon we can get back onto the A45 further up."

"You know where you're going," Anita responded. "Do what you think."

"Brian?" Lisa asked, craning her head to look at the man lying on the back seat. She realised he'd not made a sound since they'd stopped at the accident. "Shit. He's worse!"

Anita undid her seatbelt and knelt on her seat, leaning into the back to gently shake Brian by the shoulder.

"Mate, how are you doing back there?"

There was no response. His eyes were closed, and his breathing was laboured and painful.

"Jesus. We've got to get him to a doctor. I think we need to do it now, before we do anything else. He looks really bad. He's burning hot. Unconscious."

"Oh, God! There must be a surgery in the village, or at least someone who can help."

She turned left towards Wolston.

They'd only travelled a few hundred yards when they reached a T-junction. The left turn led straight into the village. The right doubled back at a tight angle.

As soon as she turned, Lisa saw them.

A crowd of people were wandering about in the road in front of a small row of shops. Their unsteady gait, blood-stained clothes and pallor left no doubt that they were infected. There were so many. She counted at least thirty. They milled around as if performing some strange and ghastly dance. Lisa's mind kicked into analytical mode. A million questions formed in her head. What had happened here? Why were they there? Why so many? What were they doing?

As the women watched, partly in horror and partly in morbid fascination, a tall man in a business suit who was closest to them suddenly stopped moving and stood stock still, his head cocked as if he was listening. He slowly turned his awful head towards them and fixed them for an instant in his gaze. He wailed loudly and, arms outstretched, began to haul his broken body up the road towards them. As his wailing intensified, the others joined in the chorus and started moving with him. The noise built quickly to a deafening pitch. Anita put her hands over her ears. Lisa was paralysed by a mixture of terror and perverse interest.

The crowd of hideous undead, all in various states of mutilation, was moving steadily towards them. Some were horribly wounded like John had been, but others bore little or no signs of obvious injury. They all had the same grey skin and empty eyes. There were men, women and children - people in business and work clothes, some still in their night wear. One woman was naked, and another man was wearing just his boxer shorts. The businessman reached the car and started banging on the bonnet with outstretched hands. His clawing fingers leaving long, dirty streaks of gore.

"Lisa, move it!"

Anita's cry shook Lisa out of her daze.

Panicking, she struggled to get the X-Trail into reverse, the gears screaming in complaint as she jammed the stick into various positions before it found home. The man was now groping his way round to the passenger side. Lisa slammed her foot on the accelerator and the car shot backwards. If her reversing in normal circumstances was bad, now it was truly terrible. She zig-zagged crazily back up the road, hitting the verge a few times and scraping the side of the car against the hedgerow. At one point, the tyres on the passenger side slipped into a shallow ditch and the car tilted dramatically to the side.

"Jesus!" Anita shouted, gripping the dashboard.

Eventually, they hit the main road and, tyres screeching, Lisa swung the car round to face the other side of the crossroads. Getting back into first gear far more easily than she had reverse, they sped off down the winding lane. She drove fast for a full two or three minutes, looking behind them in the rear-view mirror more than she was looking forwards, until she slowed to a halt. Lisa took a couple of puffs of her inhaler and, for the second time that morning, rested her head on the steering wheel with her eyes closed.

"Jesus! You weren't kidding when you said you

couldn't reverse!" Anita started to laugh.

Lisa turned her head to look at the girl. She was laughing hard. For a moment, she considered the possibility that she might be hysterical. Then, despite herself, she felt her lips curl into a smile, and she chuckled into the steering wheel. As Anita laughed even louder, slapping her hand repeatedly on her thigh, Lisa gave in. She sat up and began to laugh too. The pair of them laughed until it hurt … until snot dripped from their noses, tears poured down their cheeks and they were choking and gasping for breath.

Each time they began to calm down, they would look at each other and start again. Lisa knew it was weird and inappropriate, but that somehow made it even funnier and harder to stop. She knew it probably was hysteria, but it felt good. It felt like a huge build-up of tension and emotion was finally being released.

When they eventually recovered, they sat quietly for a while, wiping their eyes and noses on their sleeves.

"Jesus! What was that?" Anita muttered.

"We'd better get going." Lisa broke the silence, straightening herself into a more comfortable position and checking her face in the mirror. "Shall we keep going down this lane and try to get back onto the A45 further up?"

"Might as well," Anita replied. "We can't go back the way we've come. I think Brian was right. This is bad, and I don't think this journey is going to be as easy as we thought. D'you think we should even head back to the farm and wait there for a bit?"

"Maybe, but that still means going back the way we've come. Besides, what about Brian? We need to get help for him. Let's just press on and see what it's like. If we get into trouble again, then that's still an option."

"Ok. Your call."

They carried on down Coal Pit Lane for a few miles. It was a narrow, tree-lined, winding road with few buildings or turn-offs other than the occasional cottage or driveway. They saw no signs of life, infected or otherwise. They toyed briefly with the idea of stopping at one of the houses to see if they could get help but were too afraid to stop for fear of what they might find. Eventually, they reached another T-junction on a sharp bend. Lisa paused, to decide which direction to take. She was about to take the right turn, which would take them back to the A45, when a car sped round from their left. It careered past so quickly that they couldn't see the occupants and presumed that they hadn't seen them either.

Lisa followed the car, not saying anything, but feeling slightly more positive, now that they had seen their first vehicle, apparently being driven by other healthy, living people. What was more, it was heading in the same direction as they were.

Sure enough, a few minutes later they reached the large dual carriageway. It was solid with traffic and they came to a stop at the back of a queue of cars waiting to join it. Lisa felt weird. Confused. One minute they'd been driving around like the only people in a crazy new world full of walking dead people, and now they were sitting in a traffic jam.

"Thank God," she murmured.

"Thank you, Jesus. People!" Anita concurred.

The London-bound carriageway was nose-to-tail with cars heading south, away from the city. Most cars seemed to be waiting to get into that stream of traffic. Anita got out, and approached the car in front, the one that had just passed them at the junction. A man in his fifties was in the driver's seat with a woman of a similar age beside him. They both ignored her and continued to look straight ahead.

Anita tapped on the glass. "Excuse me, can you help us?"

Their backs stiffened and they continued to stare straight ahead. The woman fiddled with her glasses and the driver eased the car a few inches forward. She tapped again.

"What's wrong with you? We need help. Please!"

The woman opened her window a few centimetres. She was trembling. "We all need help sweetheart. You'd better get back in your car."

She held Anita's gaze for a moment and added pointedly, "It's not safe out here."

She closed the window and her husband moved the car forward again, as another one somewhere down the line had slipped into the flow.

Anita stood and looked at the car in astonishment. She started to walk after it, then stopped when she saw a clearly infected man staggering around at the head of the queue. He was moving between the cars, clawing at doors and windows, moaning and

71

growling. The cars began to rev their engines, edging and pushing to get away and out onto the main road. Someone sounded their horn, and someone else shouted. The man became more agitated, banging on the back-passenger windscreen of one of the cars. Children screamed. Anita hastily retreated back into the X-Trail, slamming the door and fastening her seatbelt.

"What did they say?" Lisa asked.

"Nothing. They're scared. Just as scared as us."

"I think we should keep moving."

"Definitely." Anita nodded toward the infected man. "We should get outta here before some of his mates turn up."

"Look, most traffic's going south. We actually need to go north, back towards Coventry. There seems to be hardly any traffic going that way. Let's give it a try?"

"Whatever you think. Just go." Anita shuffled in her seat, frowning, clearly anxious to get moving.

They left the queue and took a turn off to the left. Another couple of turns and they were over the bridge that crossed the carriageway and down the slip road onto the north-bound side. No-one else was heading to the city. It was uncanny. One side of the road was choked with slow-moving traffic, and the other was completely empty.

A few people gestured at them to turn around. Lisa felt a tiny seed of doubt take root. Were they heading straight into something that everyone else was fleeing from?

She *had* to get home. She had to get back to Neil.

Nothing was going to stop her. Until now, she'd worked hard to think clearly and logically, to give them the best chance of survival. But was she still doing that? Or had she started allowing her judgement to be clouded by her irrational desire to get home? Was she making a mistake?

She looked at Anita who was still frowning and chewing on her thumbnail again, as she watched the endless stream of cars on their right inching their way away from the city. She didn't want to reveal her unease in case the girl suggested turning back.

If Anita was thinking it was a bad idea, she didn't say a word.

"This is better." Lisa tried to make her voice sound cheerful and upbeat. "Better than sitting in that procession waiting for God only knows what." She forced her lips into a smile.

"Yeah." Anita sounded unconvinced.

Lisa picked up speed, taking advantage of the empty road. It should be ok until they got to the other side of the city, and then it would probably be jammed again heading down the M42. It might take longer than she'd thought, but at least they would be moving in the right direction. If they kept moving and didn't meet another crowd of infected, they were relatively safe in the car. They had a full tank of petrol. They'd be fine.

But what about Brian?

Brian! She'd almost forgotten about him. The prospect of a longer-than-expected journey might not be so good for him.

"How's Brian doing, Nita?"

Anita twisted in her seat to look at him. "He's not as flushed." She reached back to touch his hand. "Jesus, he's freezing now."

Lisa glanced over her shoulder. Brian was now deathly pale with a grey tone to his skin. His fingers and lips had a blue tinge to them. His breathing was shallow, and his eyes were partly open, even though he was still deeply unconscious.

"He looks bad, Nita. He might be dying."

"Jesus, what can we do?"

"Nothing … except try to get him help as soon as we can."

She pressed down on the accelerator a bit harder. The engine revved and they picked up speed.

They carried on for several miles until they reached the obelisk roundabout they'd seen when they'd had to turn back earlier. The two cars were still blocking the road back to Wolston and the farm. The roundabout was gridlocked. Most traffic was still heading in the opposite direction, but some was slowly peeling off towards Princethorpe and Southam.

It took them a good ten minutes to create a gap to squeeze through, the other drivers gripping their steering wheels and avoiding eye contact as they anxiously pushed onwards to their destinations. Tired, nervous passengers eyed them with fear and suspicion. Wide-eyed, fearful children and family pets stared from back windows surrounded by piles of clothes, bedding and hastily packed bags.

Once they got over the roundabout, they made

good progress for another few miles. Still, the route into the city was disconcertingly clear. When they crossed the brow of a hill, they got their first proper view of the City of Coventry on the horizon. Plumes of black smoke rose into the sky and the whole city seemed to be enveloped in a dusky haze. A couple of dark helicopters circled over the east side of the skyline. The queue of traffic on the other side stretched as far as they could see.

They pressed on, negotiating a second roundabout near Ryton more easily than the first, even though the oncoming traffic was now almost stationary. Less traffic was turning off here, and the exit for Leamington was almost completely clear. Lisa briefly considered taking it herself, but the thought was in and out of her head before she could decide.

The mental effort of working through the implications of a new, longer route was too much for her overloaded system. She was on autopilot for the M42. She was aware on a deeper level that she needed to dig deep and do what she did best. Her usually rational and logical thinking was clogged by fear, desperation and a lack of reliable information.

Just after the roundabout, the edge of the little village of Ryton spilled across the road with a few houses and shops on both sides. On their right, the stream of traffic had now completely stopped. A few infected wove between the vehicles, and a few more ambled about on the roadside. They had to swerve to avoid some on their side of the road, reaching out with claw-like hands, their faces distorted with ferocious rage as the car passed by, out of their reach.

The closer they got to Coventry and the major island Lisa knew as Tollbar End, the worse it got. The numbers of infected were increasing dramatically and now they were all around them. Some cars on the other side were surrounded by small groups, banging and scratching at their windows. A few people had left their cars and were running for safety into fields and gardens, pursued by slow-moving but determined groups of diseased.

A metal crash barrier running down between the carriageways prevented most of the infected crossing over onto their side. Although it was only just over knee height, they were walking into it and pushing against it, but seemed unable to climb over. On their left, a tall metal fence lined the road, marking out the edge of a business park. More infected roamed around in the car parks and service roads of the complex.

Rows of distorted faces pressed against the fence, grasping through the bars with torn and bloodied hands. Lisa's fear and mental paralysis gave way to sheer terror and despair with the gradual realisation that they had driven straight into the middle of a nightmare. After all they'd been through, they were in as much, if not more, danger now as they had ever been.

Anita had her head down and was repeating the same words over and over. "We're going to die … We're going to die … We're going to die … We're going to die …"

"We're not, Nita! We're going to do this! Look!"

Straight ahead a cluster of dirty green vehicles and piles of sandbags blocked the road. Armed men, dressed in the same shade of dirty green, were standing or crouching around the blockade. One was furiously waving them. As they approached, two others stood up and pointed their guns directly at them. The first came to Lisa's window, signalling at her to lower it. She obliged.

"Just where do you ladies think you're going?"

"We're trying to get to Solihull. To the motorway."

"No way, Ladies, you need to go back. Now!"

"Please ..." Lisa started.

"Turn around and get out of here, now!"

In the background, was a burst of what Lisa thought sounded like gunfire, although she'd only ever heard it before on TV.

"We have a really sick man in the back. Please can you help us?"

The soldier peered into the back of the car. "I'm sorry," he said, his tone softening a little. "I can't let you through. We're evacuating the city and we can't let anyone back in."

The gunfire intensified behind him. He glanced over his shoulder.

"You need to get into the countryside like everyone else ..." He pointed at the traffic queue.

"Where there are less people and less infected. Designated Emergency Centres are being set up. Keep tuned into the Radio and TV. You should head to one of them. Look, Darling. It's out of control in there. It's overrun. You wouldn't last five minutes.

77

You'll *have* to go back the way you've come. I'm sorry." He turned and walked away.

The two soldiers with their guns pointed at them remained in position.

"Jesus!" Anita was out of the car before Lisa could react. She started to follow the soldier. The other two raised their weapons higher and pointed them at her.

"Get back in the car!" one of them shouted. "Get back in the car … right now!"

Anita hesitated.

"Anita, get back in! Don't be stupid!" Lisa called to her.

One of the soldiers took a step towards her, and Anita stepped back. He indicated towards the car with his weapon. Unbelievably to Lisa, she gave him the finger before reluctantly getting back in.

"Jesus!" she muttered, slamming herself back into her seat, bristling with rage.

"We've got to go back, Nita. They're not going to let us through."

Lisa manoeuvred the car to face back up the empty carriageway they'd just come down. A few other cars had made their way through a gap in the crash barrier and were now heading south on the northbound side. They followed them.

They had barely travelled a few hundred metres when a low gurgling moan emanated from the back of the car.

Anita glanced behind her and screamed so loudly Lisa nearly lost control.

"Stop! Stop the car! Get out! Run, Lisa!"

Lisa hit the brakes and the car lurched into a stall. Anita grabbed the shotgun and was out of the car in an instant, sprinting across the road towards the Holiday Inn on their right.

Shaking and fumbling with the release button for what seemed like an eternity, Lisa struggled out of her seat belt. She didn't look behind her, but she could hear and sense the movement in the back seat. Just as she got her door open, her head was yanked back as Brian grabbed her hair. Screaming and struggling to get free, only the headrest protecting her from his snarling and snapping teeth, she managed to kick the door open. Still screaming, she threw herself out, sprawling onto the tarmac. Hair ripped from her scalp. Scrambling to her feet, she slammed the door shut against his angry grey-green face. It pressed against the glass, features distorted with hate, eyes glassy and bloodshot, open snarling mouth drooling with frothy blood-stained sputum.

She ran for her life.

She followed Anita past the hotel entrance. The lobby was teeming with infected, pushing and shoving against the glass doors. Dodging cars and a couple of infected, she ran through the car park to where Anita was waiting by a low, wire fence.

Clambering over the fence and barging through a hedge, they burst into a field and ran. They ran until they couldn't run any more … ran until they fell to the ground gasping for breath in the cover of a cluster of trees.

They didn't speak for a while. Anita was on her

hands and knees, head down, panting. Lisa lay flat on her back beside her. She was struggling to breathe. She forced herself to stand up, leant against a tree, and closed her eyes. Her mouth was dry. Her head reeling. She shook her inhaler. It sounded empty but she took a puff anyway.

Stunned by how things had gone so wrong, so quickly, she tried to think.

Her head was a jumble of confusion and questions.

They'd lost the car. There were infected everywhere. It was *way* worse than they'd thought. She was still miles from home. She had absolutely no idea where they were. It was a complete mess. They were worse off than ever.

She was furious with herself. She'd been stupid ... stupid *and* irresponsible, dragging Anita along with her in her desperation to get home at all costs ... Stupid for ignoring her internal voice when it told her to turn back ... Stupid for ignoring all the public warnings and advice. What had she been thinking?

She hadn't. That was the problem.

She had to do better. Had to work harder. To think clearer. Had to work out what to do.

She opened her eyes and looked around.

They were near the edge of a river. On the other side were several large industrial-looking buildings. A few radio masts sprung up here and there among them.

Of course! She knew where they were.

From where they'd been when they abandoned the car, she was pretty sure that she was looking at Coventry Airport. That meant that the river was the

Avon and she knew it flowed from Coventry to Warwick and beyond, into the Warwickshire countryside. She knew Solihull was to the north of Warwick and, while she didn't know the Coventry area particularly well away from the main traffic routes, she was familiar with some of the small villages between Warwick and Solihull. Once she hit somewhere she knew, she could work out the rest.

So what if they'd lost the car? They'd only travelled a couple of miles since they'd left the farm anyway, and it was now almost eleven. They'd probably be better off on foot. Twenty miles or so was a walkable distance. Possible to do in a day, but definitely in no more than two. And, they could keep away from main roads … keep away from populated areas like the soldier had said. It all made sense. She took a deep breath. She was ok. It was going to be ok.

Ahead of them, the river meandered along a stretch of open land until it disappeared into a wooded area.

Anita broke the silence.

"Jesus. Brian! … What the …"

Lisa just nodded.

"What do you think is …?" Anita stopped, shaking her head.

"I honestly don't know. But for now, I think we should get moving. We can think about it later … Talk about it when we get somewhere safe."

"Where are we going?" Anita looked up at her. Her face was streaked with sweat and mud. She looked exhausted. Young. Scared. Vulnerable.

"Don't worry, I know the way."

"But, how are we going to get there?"

"We're going to walk."

"Walk? But, how far is it?"

"Walkable. Come on."

Lisa took her hand and pulled her to her feet. She held her grip for a moment and looked her in the eyes.

"It's going to be ok. We're going to be ok."

Anita didn't answer. She tucked the shotgun under her elbow with its barrel pointing to the ground and checked the safety was on, like Lynda had shown her.

They started to walk.

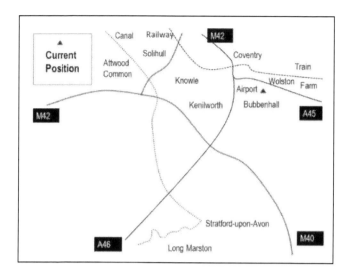

Chapter 4

Day 2 - Coventry

They made slow progress. The ground was rough and uneven. They had to weave their way around trees, bushes and boulders. At times, they were forced to backtrack when the route became impassable. At one point, the river took them close to the fenced boundary of the airport, and they could see crowds of infected in and around the buildings. Eventually, they left airport buildings behind, and moved further into open farmland.

Despite the sunshine, it was still muddy in places

from some heavy rain a few days ago. Lisa's shoes were caked with dirt, and her tights were shredded by constantly snagging them on twigs and branches. Anita's jeans gave her more protection, and her trainers were far more suitable for the task than Lisa's pumps.

Anita's movement was hampered by the gun, which was heavy and awkward to carry. But she wouldn't give it up. She kept the barrel pointed to the ground, frequently checking the safety lock and taking care to keep her fingers away from the trigger.

They were both filthy. Lisa tried to remember the last time she'd had a shower and brushed her teeth. She thought it had been on Thursday morning in the hotel. It felt longer. Her hair was tangled and starting to matt in places. She licked her teeth. They felt coated and disgusting, and she was parched again. She visualised the bottles of water in the back of the X-Trail, scattered loose in the boot, wet with condensation. Why hadn't she taken them into the car? Put one in her pocket? She imagined picking one up and twisting its cap, the snap as the plastic seal broke and the soothing sensation as the cold liquid trickled down her throat.

It was well after one when the square bell tower of a church appeared above the treeline. They were close to exhaustion. So, with no better plan, they headed towards it, assuming that was likely to be as safe as anywhere.

But they hit a problem. They passed through a thin row of shrubbery and emerged onto a wide, recently mown lawn. At the far end of the lawn was a large, sprawling bungalow. It was modern, with multiple glass doors and windows opening onto a wide patio area that stretched around the property. Three cars were parked on a nearby driveway.

Lisa instantly felt exposed and vulnerable. There was nothing between them and the house. She imagined multiple pairs of eyes watching them from within. Hungry infected about to burst out and come for them across the grass. Without speaking, they both picked up speed and hurried across the lawn into the cover of a thickly wooded area.

They picked their way through trees and bushes until they hit another barrier.

A tall red-brick wall.

Behind the wall was a conifer hedge and, to their left, they could see the upper floors of a large house. The red-brick wall was dotted at regular intervals with security cameras. It was a large secure property and it lay directly between them and the church. There was no way through or over, so they would have to go round.

They followed the wall away from the building until it turned and ran along the bottom of the property. The woods ahead were dense. The trees blocked out the light. They couldn't see beyond. They were both instinctively afraid to enter its ominous depths.

They loitered at the edge of the treeline and deliberated anxiously.

"The church should be just through there." Lisa pointed straight ahead through the trees. "It can't be far."

"Jesus! It's dark, though!" Anita whispered. "What if there are some of *them* in there?"

Lisa looked at her. "We can't go back."

"We could go round?"

"We've got the river on one side and the house on the other. God knows where we'll end up."

"What does it matter? We don't really know where we're going, anyway."

"We do." Lisa was indignant. "We're heading for the church. We agreed that it was probably a … safe place."

Before Lisa could stop her, Anita had snatched up a large stick and started banging it against a tree. The sound reverberated through the forest.

"Shh!" Lisa hissed at her. "What are you doing?"

Anita stopped banging and looked into the darkness.

She put a hand up to hush Lisa. "Wait."

They both jumped as the silence was broken by a small bird that fluttered from a nearby bush, soaring into sky and away to safety. Nothing else moved.

Anita tittered. "Come on. Let's go."

They crept between the trees, Anita in front with the shot gun pointed out in front of her. This time she had unlocked the safety and kept her finger loosely on the trigger. The wood was cool and still. At first every small sound startled them. Every rustling leaf, snapping twig or creaking branch caused them to swing towards the noise and freeze. But, as they got used to the natural sounds of the environment, they moved more quickly towards the light shining through the trees from the other side.

After what felt like a lifetime but was probably only five or ten minutes, they emerged into a small walled garden. Straight ahead on their left was a pretty little church surrounded by a small graveyard dotted with old, lichen-covered gravestones leaning at various lop-sided angles.

They moved quickly towards the building. A neat, modern extension had been added to the side of the main church. The extension had one small, high window and a single, solid dark wood door. Lisa tried the handle. Unsurprisingly, it was locked. They headed to the main entrance on the other side of the building. The original entry had been re-fitted with polished, new, light-wood double doors and the old brickwork on either side was decorated with modern, shiny black wrought ironwork. They were locked too.

"So much for churches being places of safety!" Lisa muttered.

The front of the building was more exposed than the back and in plain sight of a nearby house. Uncomfortable about the possibility of being seen, they returned to the back and the small extension. Anita rattled the door by its handle. It didn't budge. She turned her attention to the small window.

Standing on her tiptoes, she could just reach the sill.

"Give me a lift up, Lisa."

Lisa cupped her hands for Anita to hoist herself up. She was heavy. Lisa's whole body shook under her

J.M.MCKENZIE

weight.

Anita pushed at the window. "It's locked! But I could smash it?"

"We can't break into a church, Nita!" Lisa whispered.

"Jesus, Lisa! What other options have we got? I'm sure they'll understand in the circumstances! It's not as if we're going to steal anything."

"Ok! But just be quick. I can't do this much longer. I'm going to drop you!"

Anita pulled her sleeve down over her fist and impressively punched a hole in the window.

She opened the window from the inside.

"Give me another push."

Lisa summoned every last ounce of strength she possessed to push the girl a few inches higher. Anita wriggled through the space. There was a thud and a crash followed by swearing. But a few seconds later, the heavy door swung open and a grinning Anita gestured her inside.

Lisa closed and bolted the door behind them.

The room was surprisingly large. It was dim, the only light coming in through the small window. A single, closed door led into the main building. The room was evidently the vestry. It had the appearance of an office come dressing room. There was a desk and chair, and the walls were lined with bulging bookshelves. A wardrobe stood in the corner next to a small sink with a mirror above it.

Lisa made straight for the sink, turning on the tap and sticking her head under it. She slurped water from the cupped palm of her hand. When she'd had her fill, she stood back allowing Anita to do the same.

"Should we check out the rest of the building?" Lisa asked.

"Probably," Anita mumbled between swallows.

When Anita had finished drinking, they cautiously opened the vestry door and stepped into the silent church.

Lisa had expected the space to be gloomy and scary, but there was something soothing and tranquil about the interior of the old building. It was cool. The light that filtered through the stained-glass windows was soft and welcoming. She wasn't religious but felt safe and protected for the first time since it had begun.

The windows were so high they couldn't see out, but that also meant they couldn't be seen. They knew the doors were locked. As Anita wandered around checking corners, nooks and crannies, Lisa sank onto one of the cushioned pews with a deep sigh.

She was shattered. She hadn't slept the night before and the stress and trauma of the morning was taking its toll. Her head was aching again, and her throat and eyes felt dry from lack of sleep.

"Do you think it would be safe to rest here for a bit, Nita? I feel like shit. I need to sleep."

"Yeah, me too." Anita stretched and yawned. "I'm done."

They decided the small vestry was the safest place to rest. They dragged some cushions from the pews into the room and, combined with some thick tablecloths salvaged from the wardrobe, made a surprisingly comfy bed on the floor. They pushed the desk against the door that led into the church for added peace of mind.

Some letters fluttered from the desk as they were moving it. Lisa read the address at the top of one of the pages as she picked them up.

"We're in St Giles' Church, Bubbenhall," she told Anita.

"Jesus, where's that?"

"We haven't really come very far. It's just another small village near Coventry."

"Let's hope it's not like Wolston then," Anita whinged.

Before they settled down, they washed at the sink and drank more water.

"I look as bad as I feel. Worse in fact." Lisa complained as she dried her face on the hand towel, examining herself in the mirror. She was a mess. Her hair was out of control. Wild auburn curls framed her pale, drawn face. Dark circles surrounded her bloodshot eyes. Her hands were red and scratched, the nails thick with dirt. Her clothes were splattered with grime and gore.

With their shoes on and the gun close at hand, they lay down, side by side, covering themselves with a tablecloth for comfort, rather than for warmth. Although she was exhausted, Lisa couldn't get off to sleep. She lay on her back and stared at the ceiling, the events of the past couple of days and a fog of unanswered questions swirling in her mind.

Should they have stayed at the farm? Should they have headed away from the city like everyone else? Would she *ever* get home? Was Neil alright? Had he made it? Was he waiting for her?

Anita was already snoring softly. Lisa turned over onto her side and tried to slow her mind … tried to make it go blank … to stop the stream of questions. But then memories of the past few days began to come in. The awful face of the boy in the green hoodie coming at her on the train, the tiny kicking feet in the red car, the mob of infected in Wolston moving menacingly towards them. They became mixed up with daydreams. Neil's smiling face looking at her from the passenger seat of the X-Trail. Neil in a green hoodie, opening the front door of their home, grinning at her as he took her hand and pulled her inside.

She must have drifted off. It was completely dark when they were both awoken by a banging at the outside door. Lisa was up and awake instantly, groping for the shotgun in the dark and stumbling and tripping over the nest of cushions. She could make out Anita's silhouette as the girl slowly sat up, rubbing her eyes, confused.

"Shh! Someone's outside," Lisa whispered.

A wavering light shone into the room from the small window and a man's voice called out softly. "Are you in there?"

Lisa went over to the window. She paused before replying as assertively as she could.

"Yes, who are you?"

91

"I live nearby. I want to help."

"Why? How did you know we were here?"

"Just let me in, quickly! Please! It's not safe out here. Then I'll explain."

Lisa looked questioningly at Anita who shrugged.

"Please!" The man sounded frightened.

Anita got up and unbolted the door. She pushed it partly open and stood back as a tall, bulky, male form, pushed past her into the room. He closed the door and turned to face them. In the dark, all Lisa could see of his features was a crescent of perfect white teeth.

"Well, hello, Ladies. I'm Richard. Gosh, I'm not ashamed to say I was a tad nervous out there. It's bloody creepy."

"Hello." Anita sounded suspicious.

Lisa remembered she was holding the gun and raised it, so it was pointing towards his abdomen.

He took a step back. "I'm sorry. Let me explain. Look, we saw you this afternoon, at the back of our house, on the CCTV. We knew you had to come out onto the lane through the churchyard. It's the only way you could have gone. But you never appeared. We guessed you might be in here. Well, my wife did. We just wanted to make sure you were ok. To help if we could. Two women … on their own … out there." He gestured towards the closed door.

Still fuddled by sleep, Lisa and Anita just looked at him with something akin to wonder.

He continued. "By the time it got dark we were really worried. Charlie - that's my wife - insisted that I come out to look for you. I saw the vestry window was broken and … well, here I am."

Lisa lowered the gun. "Gosh, I don't know what to say. Thank you. I …we …" She didn't know where to start.

"Look!" Richard said. "It's only a short walk to our gates. Let's just get out of here and into the house. We can have a proper talk then."

Lisa looked at Anita.

The girl shrugged again. "Why not?"

Half relieved and half bemused, they left the safety of the vestry and followed Richard, guided by the swaying torchlight. He was right. It was incredibly creepy picking their way between the gravestones in the dark. The main gates to the church opened onto a small lane. Richard headed straight for an illuminated intercom on the wall ahead. He pushed the button and it crackled.

An echoing voice spoke from somewhere inside. "Is that you Richard? Did you find them?"

"Yes, it's me, and, yes, I did. You were right, as always."

"Oh! Thank God."

The intercom went off and there was a low grinding and creaking as the heavy, cast iron, double gates began to part. As soon as they could squeeze through the gap, they slipped inside onto a gravel driveway. Richard waited until the gates had fully opened and closed again, and then he strode up the drive towards the house. The women followed him.

The drive swept up to a large two-storey house. Even in the dark, its ivy clad façade was impressive. A curved flight of stairs rose up to a set of double doors. One of the doors opened and a blonde, heavily made-up woman in her late forties tottered out in a pair of dangerously high heels, glancing anxiously from side to side.

She hurried them all inside and closed and locked the door, resetting an alarm via a panel on the wall. It beeped four times, followed by a long tone lasting a few seconds. Richard indicated to Lisa to leave the shot gun by the door as the woman ushered them down a corridor and into a vast sitting room with a spotless, cream-coloured carpet, huge, dark brown, soft leather sofas and heavy, dark curtains.

Lisa looked down at her muddy shoes and slipped them off before she entered the room, although her stockinged feet were not much cleaner. Anita strode in without a second thought and sank into one of the sofas, looking around the room with unconcealed admiration.

The room and its occupants, Richard and Charlie, oozed wealth. Now they could see Richard properly, he was tanned and well-groomed, with close-cropped silver hair. The furnishings were opulent, yet tasteful. The artwork looked valuable. Another door led into an equally large room with a bar, a pool table, and a huge, flat-screen TV.

Charlie insisted on making them coffee and sandwiches, which arrived on a large platter, beautifully garnished with salad and different coloured vegetable crisps. The coffee smelt delicious. They were starving and devoured the sandwiches as Charlie and Richard looked on patiently, waiting to hear their story.

The foursome spent the next hour recounting their experiences of the past 24 hours and sharing what they had learned.

Lisa and Anita went first, leaving out some of the more gruesome details as, although Richard listened with interest and admiration, Charlie went pale and became very distressed when they described what they had seen on the train.

The couple had been at home most of the previous day. Richard had been working from home and was tucked away in his office. He owned a medical equipment company. Charlie had been out in the morning to have her hair and nails done and had been pottering around the house in the afternoon, taking delivery of the shopping and preparing dinner. It was around six when Richard had joined her in the kitchen for a glass of wine and had put on the TV to catch the early evening news. That was the first they knew about what was happening.

Since then, they had followed government advice and stayed put. They had activated their alarm system and constantly monitored the TV, radio and social media for information and further advice. Charlie had kept watch on their immediate outside world via their CCTV system but had seen nothing untoward at all until she saw the two women earlier that afternoon.

Richard was able to give them a bit more information. The UK, along with the majority of other countries in Western Europe, had been attacked simultaneously using some kind of lethal biological weapon. It was believed that deliberately infected individuals - essentially biological suicide bombers - had been positioned on trains, planes and buses making their way between major towns and cities throughout the affected countries during Thursday afternoon.

After they had succumbed to the infection, they had reanimated as crazed, cannibalistic, killing machines. The infection had then spread quickly. People who died in the first attack also reanimated and killed or infected others within the confined spaces.

By the time the vehicles arrived at their destinations, most, if not all, of their occupants were infected. Once the infected passengers spilled out into busy stations, city centres and airports, the infection began to rage through the affected towns, and beyond, at an exponential rate.

Anyone who was bitten or scratched became infected and, if their injuries were minor, they appeared to survive for only 12 to 24 hours. Many infected people with minor injuries had made their way home and unwittingly spread the contagion even further.

As Lisa and Anita already knew, from the outset, the official government advice was to stay indoors, at home, or in a secure location. The same message had been posted on the Emergency Broadcast Screen for the last 18 hours.

However, many cities had had to be evacuated due to the rapid spread of the infection in densely populated areas. In some places looting and rioting had added to the chaos. Increasingly on social media, people were being advised to get away from populated areas and await further advice. The chatter was that the situation was out of control. There were suggestions that the army was in the process of identifying and securing safe zones, but this had not been officially confirmed or denied, and no details had yet been released. So far, the power and internet were still working, but most telephone networks were down.

Lisa and Anita were able to add to the picture from their own personal experience. What had happened to Brian confirmed what Richard had said about the infection being spread by bites or scratches and eventually killing everyone it touched.

Their encounter with the army had made it abundantly clear that it was every man, or woman, for themselves for the moment. Their current focus was evacuation and containment. They had said to watch out for news about the creation of safe zones, but rescue for survivors was evidently further down their list of priorities.

The women also had first-hand experience of the reanimated and were able to share their observations that the infected were slow and clumsy, and that they were unable to navigate around barriers directly in their path. They seemed to react to noise. They had also learned that only a penetrating head wound would disable an infected completely.

Richard had a variety of electronic devices in his

office. Lisa and Anita spent another hour sitting at his desk, scrolling through their Facebook, Instagram and Twitter feeds, and logging in to their email accounts trying to fill in the gaps and track down the whereabouts of their friends and family.

During the first few hours of the attack on Thursday, there had been a lot of activity. There was too much to take in and most of it was repetitive: people posting images and video footage of their own terrifying experiences, sharing their fear and concern, speculating about what was happening, and trying to find or contact loved ones. Into the night, and throughout the following morning. the chatter had gradually slowed down and now was almost silent.

That silence frightened Lisa more than anything she had seen or heard. Where was everyone? What were they doing? She tried to reassure herself that they were probably using all their energy to focus on actually surviving, rather than documenting it. But a small insistent voice in the back of her head kept telling her that it might be due to something more sinister. People might be silent because they were unable to post. The chatter might have stopped because most of the population had been infected.

Anita had received an email from her brother on the boat in Croatia. They had attempted to moor up in a small town just north of Dubrovnik but had been forced to head back out to sea for their own safety. They were part of a small flotilla that was moored just off the coast, considering heading south to North Africa, which was so far unaffected. He'd sent a flurry of emails since Thursday evening and was frantic with worry about her and the rest of the family. She emailed him back telling him that she was safe and that she was with good people, and not to worry.

She had heard nothing from her parents, nor her other brother. Nothing had been posted by any of them, and no emails had come from them since she'd left home at lunchtime on Thursday. She feared the worst and became tearful and subdued.

Lisa tried to reassure her. "You don't know what's happened, Nita. They might just be trapped at work or have been evacuated or something."

But Lisa's experience was similar, and she was struggling to stay positive herself. There was nothing from her parents who lived in Leeds, one of the worst affected cities according to Richard, and nothing from her sister Judith, who lived with her family in Sussex. However, an email had come through from her other sister, Gina, letting her know that she was safely ensconced in her isolated, but solid, old barn conversion in the Yorkshire Dales, with her two children, her husband and her mother-in-law.

They had seen no direct evidence of any infection in their area yet. They had no phone signal in normal times, but Gina had sent several emails to Lisa over the past 24 hours, pleading with her to get in contact just to let them know that she was safe. It felt good to be able to email her back to say that she was ok and making her way home to Neil.

Disappointingly and disturbingly though, there

was nothing from Neil himself. Nothing on Facebook nor Twitter, and no emails - just total silence. She sent him an email anyway.

Hi Darling, it's me again. I'm still safe. No longer at the farm but in a house in Bubbenhall. Been an awful day, but some great people have helped us. I'm still coming home. It's not going to be easy, but I'm getting closer. We're going to stay here tonight and set out again in the morning. If you get there first, just wait for me. Please just wait there, and I'll come. I promise. If I get there before you, I'll wait for you. Like we promised. I love you so much. Please be ok, my darling. Lisa Xxx

Eventually, when they had exhausted all avenues of enquiry, they joined Richard and Charlie in the lounge again, where Richard opened a bottle of expensive red wine and Charlie served an elegant selection of sophisticated nibbles.

To Lisa, it seemed as though their lives were almost untouched by the crisis. They had been in regular contact with their own family throughout and knew that they were all safe in different secure locations around the country.

They seemed to be simply waiting for it all to be over so that they could resume their normal lives. They were good, kind people, though, so who was she to judge? Maybe it was just their way of coping? Lisa was beginning to suspect that there was a strong possibility it might never be over, or at least not for a very long time.

The property was enormous and seemed to be completely secure. The high wall with the conifer hedge that had blocked their path earlier completely surrounded the house and spacious gardens, which included a large outdoor heated swimming pool. The whole place was effectively concealed from the rest of the world. The electric gates at the end of the small lane were so innocuous you would never imagine that a property of this magnitude nestled behind them on the edge of the River Avon, in the sleepy little village of Bubbenhall.

The lounge was warm, and the lights had been dimmed. This, combined with the wine and their emotional and physical exhaustion, quickly made both women very sleepy. The conversation dried up, everyone lost in their own drowsy thoughts. Anita failed miserably in her attempt to stifle a couple of large yawns.

It was around one when Charlie showed them to a twin guest room on the first floor, complete with, soft, white, fluffy towels, brand new toothbrushes and toothpaste, and miniature bottles of Molton Brown toiletries. They had been offered separate rooms but had chosen to share. Lisa had seen the look of anxiety that flickered across Anita's face at the prospect of being separated, and the relief that took its place when Lisa said she'd be more than happy for them to sleep together.

They both took long hot showers and brushed their teeth. They'd borrowed a couple of Richard's T-shirts to sleep in.

It felt unbelievably good to be clean and fresh

again. Charlie took their dirty clothes and offered to wash and dry them overnight. When she slipped underneath the light fluffy duvet, luxuriating in the cool softness of the expensive sheets, Lisa felt like a little girl scrubbed and clean after her evening bath.

In many ways being in this house with Richard and Charlie felt more like a dream than the wild and frightening nightmare that was going on outside. She wondered briefly if they should think about staying here for a few days. It felt so safe and comfortable, and totally protected from the outside world. At the same time, she knew in her heart that this was not an option for her. She wouldn't be able to stay here knowing that Neil was either at home waiting for her, or out there somewhere trying to get home. Her overwhelming desire was still to get back to him.

That might not be true for Anita, though. Anita might want to stay for a bit.

Anita was snoring softly. Lisa envied her ability to drop off so quickly. She turned onto her side, drawing her knees up to her chest, and snuggled deeper under the duvet. They could talk about it in the morning, when they'd both had a good night's sleep, and they could work out exactly what to do next.

She closed her eyes.

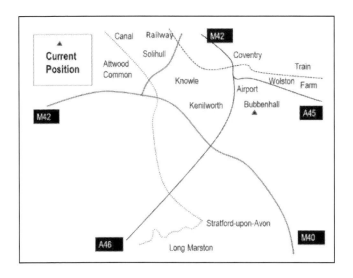

Chapter 5

Day 3 - Bubbenhall

Lisa woke the next morning to the smell of bacon cooking and fresh coffee brewing. Dishes clattered from somewhere downstairs. Morning birds chirruped outside. Sun streamed in through the net curtains; they hadn't even bothered to close the heavy drapes the night before.

She yawned and stretched. She felt fresh and rested. The thoughts from the previous night about staying for a few days threatened to return, but she pushed them away. She had one plan and one plan only, and that was to get home to Neil.

She reluctantly pushed the fluffy duvet back and swung her legs round to sit on the edge of the bed. Her toes sank into the deep pile of the carpet. Anita still slept soundly in the other bed. Padding across to look out of the window, she viewed the property properly in the daylight for the first time.

It was another fine day. Clear blue skies were dotted with occasional cotton wool clouds. Beneath the window was a large patio area and, beyond that, extensive lawns and neatly manicured gardens. The high conifer hedge concealed everything beyond except the very top of the bell tower of the church next door.

There was a knock at the door. An immaculately dressed and fully made-up Charlie greeted her with a neat pile of their washed and freshly ironed clothes.

"I hope you don't mind, but your tights were in such a state I threw them away," she said. "I've popped a pair of leggings in there that you can borrow if you want," she beamed at Lisa.

"You two are so kind," Lisa thanked her. "You have been amazing. We honestly can't thank you enough."

"Oh, I'm sure you'd do the same, if the tables were turned," Charlie replied.

"No, seriously, you've been wonderful." Lisa gratefully took the pile of clothes.

"Breakfast is nearly ready," Charlie called over her shoulder as she left the room.

Lisa showered for the second time in twelve hours, not sure how long it would be before she got the opportunity to do so again. When she was dressed, she went downstairs to the kitchen and perched next to Richard on a high stool at a long, shiny breakfast bar, while Charlie served her fresh coffee and a bacon sandwich. She told Richard about her plan to try and get home.

Shortly, they were joined by a rumpled looking Anita. Yawning and rubbing her eyes, she climbed onto a stool.

"Morning, Darling." Charlie handed her a mug of coffee. "No need to ask if you slept well. How are you feeling?"

"Yeah. Good, thanks." Anita took a big gulp of coffee. "I could have slept forever."

Charlie placed a bacon sandwich in front of her.

"Lisa is still determined to try and get home, Anita," Richard said. "What are you going to do? You're more than welcome to stay here as long as you want, until this whole thing blows over."

"You do what feels right for you, Nita." Lisa put a hand on Anita's arm. "Honestly, I completely get it if you want to stay here for a while. There's a part of me that wants to, too, but I just can't. I'm so close to home that I have to try and get back. Neil should be there by now. He'll be frantic. I couldn't live with myself if I didn't try."

Anita put her hand on Lisa's, shaking her head. "I'm coming with you. We started this together and I want to … you know … finish it with you. We've done ok so far. We're a good team. What I'm saying is … no offence Richard and Charlie … you guys are amazing … but I'd really like to see it through with you, Lisa, to the end ... whatever that is. Besides there's no way I could just sit here knowing you were out there on your own. That's just crazy!"

"Nita ..." Lisa started.

"No! It's not up for discussion. I'm coming with you. I can't wait to see this bloody Neil, anyway. He must be something really special the way you carry on about him all the time."

Lisa squeezed her arm. "Thanks. I can't wait for him to meet you, too."

She spoke to Richard and Charlie. "If it's ok with you guys, we should get going as soon as we can. God knows what it's going to be like out there, or how long it will take us."

"Well," Richard replied. "You've got to do what you've got to do. I understand that. But, please, be careful. I'd offer to drive you, but I can't leave Charlie here on her own, and I'm not taking her out there ... the ways things are."

"Honestly, guys, you've helped us so much already. Don't even think about it. Please. We wouldn't want you to do that. We'll be fine," Lisa reassured him.

Charlie looked at Richard and he nodded. "Look, we'd like you to borrow a car," she said. "You won't stand a chance on foot."

"Sound!" Anita mumbled through a mouthful of bacon.

"If you're sure! That would be amazing!" Again, like Lynda, Lisa couldn't believe their generosity. She found herself wondering if she and Neil would have done the same. She hoped they would.

Within the hour they were ready to set off. The "car" was a practically new Land Rover Discovery. Richard insisted that they take some blankets, pillows and warm jackets in case they got stuck again. He loaded them into the back seat of the car. He also gave them a map and a torch. Charlie produced a picnic of cheese and pickle sandwiches packed neatly in a wicker basket with fresh fruit, crisps and chocolate bars. Anita sat in the passenger seat with the shotgun.

Compared to when they had left the farm the previous morning, Lisa felt confident and well prepared. Simply being clean, rested, and fed and watered, had restored her positivity, along with the fact that, this time, they knew what to expect. Well partly, at least. Everything seemed to be coming together for them at last. Meeting Richard and Charlie when they did, had been nothing short of miraculous.

Despite having known each other less than 24 hours, it was hard to say goodbye. Tears were shed, and grateful hugs exchanged, as well as contact details and promises to get in touch as soon as they could.

Richard walked down the drive to see them off. Charlie stood on the steps of the house waving. He opened the gates using a button on the back of one of the gate posts. They creaked slowly apart. When they were fully open, Lisa edged the Discovery forward and out into the lane.

The moment the nose of the car was far enough forward for her see past the conifer hedge; she saw them.

She screamed.

Anita saw them at the same time. "Jesus, what the ... Richard!" She twisted round in her seat to see where Richard was.

A group of four infected were only a few feet away to their left and already moving with intent towards the car, obviously attracted by the noise of the gates and the car engine.

In the rear-view mirror, Lisa could see Richard standing by the gate post, watching the gates as they closed. He wasn't looking towards the car.

"Richard!" Anita shouted and waved furiously at him. His gaze didn't shift from the gates.

Lisa scrabbled to find the button that opened her window. In the time it took to find the right one, ram her finger on it and open it enough for him to hear her, a man and a woman had reached the car and were banging and clawing on the passenger window. Anita shrieked and cowered away in horror.

The other two had slipped behind the car towards the slowly closing gates.

"Richard! Richard!" Lisa screamed through the open window. She banged on the horn. Richard looked up just as the infected reached him.

But Lisa was distracted by the sound of Anita opening her own window.

"Nita! What ...!" Things were spiralling out of control. She could feel her chest starting to tighten.

Anita stopped when her window was open a couple of inches.

108

The infected growled and snarled, their hideous faces pressed against the window, thick brown spit smearing the glass. Lisa could smell their fetid breath. Anita raised the shotgun and pointing the barrel through the crack at the top of the window, pressed it against the forehead of the male. She flicked the safety and fired.

The sound was thunderous in the confined space of the car. Anita was thrown backwards into Lisa's lap by the recoil. Lisa barely heard her own screams beneath the ringing in her ears.

The man was gone. In his place, a red mist hung in the air. The woman immediately took his place. Anita sat up and, with shaking hands, reloaded the gun and repositioned it against her forehead in the same way. She fired again. The woman disappeared.

"Richard ..." Lisa whispered. She turned around.

The gates were closed. There was no sign of the other two infected. She opened the door and got out, running to the gates. Anita shimmied over and followed her.

In the middle of the gravel driveway, halfway towards the house, the remaining two infected crouched over Richard's body. They were tearing at him with hands and teeth, pulling and ripping his flesh. His eyes bulged in terror and his mouth was open wide in a silent bloody scream. Lisa screamed and sobbed with rage. She shook the gates, kicking and punching them.

At the other end of the drive, Charlie stood and watched from the bottom of the steps. She pulled at her hair, her face a mask of grief and confusion. She began to walk falteringly towards her husband and his attackers.

"No, Charlie! Get back in the house. You can't help him. Quickly! Run!" Lisa shouted.

Charlie didn't seem to hear. She called out.

"Richard!"

One of the infected raised its head and looked up the drive towards her. She took another step forward.

"Richard!" she cried again, louder this time.

The infected, a man in his thirties, in jeans and an Aston Villa football shirt, got clumsily to his feet. He started moving towards Charlie, moaning, arms outstretched, hands and face covered in Richard's blood. She let him get too close before she turned to run. She almost made it to the top of the steps but seemed to catch her heel and stumble. She wobbled precariously for a moment, her arms flailing to try and pull herself forward.

Then she fell. She tumbled backwards down the steps and into the open arms of the Aston Villa fan. Lisa turned away. She closed her eyes and covered her ears to block out the sounds.

They didn't need to talk about what to do next. They waited in grim silence for Richard and Charlie to reanimate. Lisa shook her inhaler and sucked in a couple of puffs. Anita gently called out their names.

"Richard. Charlie. We're over here."

Richard was first. Lisa closed her eyes as he strained to reach them through the bars of the gate. Anita took aim and fired.

A few minutes later she did the same for Charlie.

They got back into the car and sat in silence. Anita reached for Lisa's hand and held it. Lisa squeezed back. They sat like that for a long time.

Anita broke the silence. "It's all our fault. We killed them. They'd be fine if they hadn't helped us."

"I know," was all Lisa could manage.

Anita looked at her. "But they *wanted* to help us. Richard came to find *us*."

"Even so, we should've been more careful. We should've checked."

"All of us should. Richard included. We were all too careless. Far too careless. We've got to do better if we want to survive."

"We owe it to them to stay alive, Nita, or they died for nothing."

Lisa put the car in gear and programmed the satnav with her home postcode. They planned to use it to keep them on track but use the map to find minor roads that avoided populated areas. As they turned up the lane, a few more infected appeared at the far end, heading quickly in their direction, obviously attracted by the gunfire and the sound of the car engine running. But they pushed on past them, easily getting through the small group, before turning right at a junction that led away from the village.

"Look, Lisa!" Anita pointed to their left where a significant number of reinforcements were shambling down the high street.

"We just got away in time," Lisa replied.

"Whatever happens next, we're not going to be able to hang around in one place for very long."

Their strategy of sticking to minor roads was working. For the first time since they had left the farm the previous day, they were actually making significant progress. Before they left, Lisa had shown Anita their destination on the map. It was on the other side of the M42, which was about ten miles ahead of them to the northwest. Their route was flanked by the M40 to the southwest, and the M6 to the northeast, placing them in the middle of a triangle of major motorways, which they had to avoid. But one other route, the A46, cut straight through middle of the triangle. This was going to be impossible to miss, but Lisa thought there was an underpass they could use between Stoneleigh and Kenilworth.

Compared to the previous day, when their route had been thick with infected and fleeing survivors, there seemed to be no-one around. They met no traffic, and any properties they passed either appeared deserted or were in the process of being fortified.

Gates, doors, blinds and curtains were all firmly closed. Some people had constructed makeshift barricades around their homes using cars, wheelie bins and bits and pieces of whatever they could find, like fencing and chicken wire. They passed one house where a man was fixing wooden boards across the ground floor windows of his home. He stopped what he was doing to turn and stare, hammer in hand, as they approached. He followed them with an expressionless gaze as they passed before turning back to his work.

There were a few infected around, but just ones or twos, on driveways or in front gardens ambling about, heads down. They also looked up as the car approached, raising their arms and opening their mouths wide, reaching forlornly towards them as they passed quickly by. Lisa watched every single one in the rear-view mirror until they were out of sight. Even though they had no chance of catching the car, they followed it doggedly, apparently through instinct or reflex rather than conscious thought or decision.

They skirted around Stoneleigh Park and Showground until they turned into a narrow lane that brought them to the concrete underpass that Lisa had remembered. It passed beneath a raised bridge section of the A46. They slowed to a stop as they approached and sat, with the engine idling, to assess the situation. The underpass was narrow and dark, but they could see that the road beyond curved round to the left and out of sight.

The road above was a tangled mess of abandoned vehicles. Two or three infected moved between the cars. Lisa felt anxious and indecisive, wary of what was above and what might be beyond. According to the map, the edge of the small town of Kenilworth was just ahead. They would have to go through a section of the town before they were back into open countryside.

Her mind was made up for her when one of the infected on the bridge turned towards them. It was a burly workman in blood spattered orange overalls and a battered safety helmet. He moved towards the edge of the bridge and reached over the railings, snarling and grasping for them, despite the fact that they were at least twenty feet beneath him.

Two more joined him and others emerged from different directions. The gruesome crowd gathered on the bridge, jostling for position, pressing against the barrier, leaning and stretching over the railing. The barrier seemed to be leaning too, crumpling beneath their weight.

"Lisa, move!" Anita called out at the same time as Lisa hit the accelerator.

But she was too slow.

The burly workman crashed onto the bonnet of the Discovery. Its head hit the windscreen in an explosion of flesh and matter.

Both women screamed in unison, as the glass shattered into tiny fragments. It stayed in place, but Lisa could see nothing through the mass of cracks and splattered body fluids. She braked sharply. She saw the workman roll off the bonnet on the driver's side, just as a second massive thud rocked the vehicle. This time it was on the roof and another body bounced onto the road behind them.

Pressing hard on the accelerator, and using only mirrors to gauge her position, Lisa drove blindly through the underpass. At the same time, she grappled for the torch in the door pocket and used it to punch a hole in the windscreen. She used the steering wheel to pull herself forward, peering through hole at the road ahead.

As they picked up speed, fragments of glass blew into the car as the windscreen crumbled. Both women flinched and ducked, trying to protect their faces. Anita pulled the cuffs of her jumper over her hands and covered her face with them.

"We have to stop and clear it." Lisa was pulling over as she spoke. "If it cuts us, we could get infected."

"Jesus! I never thought …! Stop! Hurry!" Anita glanced behind them at the silhouettes of the mangled infected dragging themselves in pursuit through the underpass.

Lisa used the torch and Anita the butt of the shotgun to knock out the rest of the loose glass. They got rid of the worst of it, just as their pursuers reached the car. She put her foot down again, leaving them open mouthed and empty handed.

But the wind that blew through the empty windscreen forced her to slow down almost immediately. Tears blurred her vision and the noise was deafening. Anita slouched in her seat and covered her face again. Lisa eased her foot off the pedal until it was bearable. They could barely move above 20 mph. The infected disappeared out of sight behind them,

They carried on down a long, straight, tree-lined lane. On the right, a neat laurel hedge marked the boundary of the Kenilworth Golf Club. There were a few cars in the car park, but otherwise the place looked deserted. A day or two before, Lisa might have thought about going in to see if they could get some help with their now badly-damaged vehicle, but she pressed on, and Anita didn't even raise an eyebrow.

They reached a junction on the outskirts of the town. Ahead of them, and on both sides, were large properties. The houses were opulent and well-maintained, and the gardens were neat and colourful.

It was bizarrely quiet for a Saturday morning. There was not a car, nor a person, in sight, living or dead. Straight ahead, a wide strip of grass dotted with mature trees sat between the main road and an access road to the properties. A sign read: "Knowle Hill".

The only indication of anything untoward, was a single, overturned, brown wheelie bin lying on the strip of grass, its contents spilling out across the road. A piece of pink, shiny cellophane was blowing silently down the street. They could hear the distant wail of a burglar alarm.

Lisa felt her anxiety levels rising again. So many houses, with so many doors and windows, so many walls and corners, so many trees and hedges. The sense of protection that the big Discovery provided, was diminished by the wide, empty space where the windscreen had been.

"Which way, Nita? I don't like it here."

Anita was poring over the map, muttering rapidly to herself.

"Erm … erm … left. No! Right! Right!"

"Are you sure?"

"Yes, yes! I'm sure. It should take us round the edge of the town until we join the A452 at the other side."

"Right it is then."

Lisa turned right and soon felt better as the land gradually dropped down on the right-hand side of the road. Most houses were now down at the bottom of a steep bank on their right, and the left side of the road was thickly wooded.

After a mile or so, they came to another junction, on another road lined with houses.

"Right again. Then next left," Anita almost whispered as she looked up and down at the map, all the time keeping her finger on their position.

Now, they were surrounded by houses.

"I really don't like this." Lisa clenched the steering wheel. Despite the breeze blowing in through the windscreen, she was sweating,

A flurry of movement ahead caught her eye.

Anita saw it too. "Just keep going, Lisa. Don't slow down, and don't even think about stopping." Anita's voice was low but firm.

The source of the activity was a small convenience store in the centre of a small row of shops. The storefront window was smashed and a small car, with blacked-out windows, was parked with its open boot facing into the building. A boy was hurriedly passing boxes from inside to another boy, who was loading them into the car. Two other loose-limbed youths were positioned at either end of the small parking area. One was armed with a baseball bat, and the other was wielding a machete.

"Oh, God! What now?" Lisa muttered as they approached the scene.

The boy with the baseball bat eyeballed them. He stepped into the road and raised his weapon as they passed. The other glanced in their direction but was preoccupied with an infected in a nearby garden. The Discovery sailed past. The whole interaction played out in total silence. Both women sighed in relief as baseball boy turned back towards the shop and the more pressing matter in hand.

They continued for ten or fifteen minutes, mostly driving slowly along deserted semi-residential streets. A few infected roamed around in the fenced-off car parks of commercial buildings, but other than them, they saw no-one. Lisa's knuckles were white as she gripped the steering wheel, focusing on the road ahead. The looting incident had really rattled her. She was suddenly aware that it was not just the infected that they should be afraid of.

Anita seemed tense too. Other than constantly checking the map and barking out one-word directions, she was silent.

"How far, Anita? Till we get out of here?"

"Not far. Nearly there. Another mile or so."

Their anxiety eased as the properties grew larger in size, fewer in number and were set further back from the road. Houses gradually gave way to open fields. They picked a spot with good visibility in all directions and pulled over.

"Jesus! That was horrible!" Anita leaned back in her seat and rubbed the back of her neck.

"Awful!" Lisa took out her inhaler and shook it but didn't take a puff.

"You ok?" Anita asked.

"It's nearly empty. I'm going to have to save it for when I really need it."

"Will that work? Will you be ok?"

"Don't know. Never had to ration it before."

"Jesus! I ..."

"I'm ok for now. Don't stress about it. Let's have a look at where we are."

Anita spread out the map. "I know we're heading to Solihull, but where exactly?"

"Here. Attwood Common." Lisa pointed to a spot on the map. "It's on the other side of Solihull. A village really. We'll have to get over the M42 at some stage. We'll have to deal with that when it comes, but for now, we can still stick to back roads. Loop south and round, through Warwickshire, like this." She drew a wide loop on the map with her finger.

She continued. "It'll take longer, but avoid any more built up areas, and keep us as far away from Birmingham as possible. At worst, we'll have to pass through a few little villages."

"So, we head towards this place." Anita pointed to the map. "Knowle? And then take a left?"

"You've got it! Let's go! It's still only 11 and we're halfway there." Lisa replied.

119

A couple of miles before they reached the junction for Knowle, they noticed a cloud of dark smoke in the distance, rising above the treeline. Swirling grey plumes dirtied the clear azure blue of the sky.

By the time they reached the junction, they could hear the roar of the fire and the cracking and splintering of burning wood. Smoke billowed across the road. Their intended route to the left, was thick with it. Dense, acrid fumes drifted in through the open windscreen making them cough, and their eyes sting and stream with water. The source was a large white house a hundred metres or so away. Flickering orange tongues of flame arose from its roof and upper windows.

"Well, that's our route." Anita said.

"D'you think we can get by?" Lisa thought she knew the answer already but asked the question anyway.

"Not without a windscreen."

"Maybe ... Jesus!" Anita gasped.

A smouldering figure staggered out of the smoke towards them. It was a featureless, black likeness of a human form. Neither age nor gender were distinguishable. It reached its withered arms out towards them. A dark cavity appeared from where its mouth would have been. Smoke drifted from the empty space.

Lisa froze. She couldn't seem to drag her eyes away. She couldn't make sense of what she was seeing. Was it an infected? Was it alive or dead? What the hell was she looking at?

Anita was staring at it, too. But, when a couple of other dark figures appeared through the smoke behind it, she turned to Lisa.

"Go right! Just go right! Now!"

Lisa swung the car to the right.

She didn't see what hit them. Her attention was focused on the burning figures in the rear-view mirror. She heard Anita scream, at the same time as the impact hit the passenger side and sent them rolling and tumbling in a violent blur of blue sky, greenery, and white airbags.

When the world stopped spinning, they were head down in a deep ditch on the side of the road. Dense shrubbery surrounded the car. Anita was slumped forward in her seat, not moving. With fumbling fingers, Lisa undid her own seatbelt and shook the girl. Hard!

"Anita! Wake up! We've got to move! We've got to get out!"

Anita lifted her head and stared at her blankly. She looked completely baffled. Lisa undid her seatbelt for her, then, pushing foliage out of her way, climbed out through the open windscreen onto the bonnet of the car.

She grabbed Anita's wrists, trying to pull her out of the car. "Come on! Please!"

Anita was mumbling and shaking her head. "Give me a minute. Just a minute."

Lisa glanced back up to the road. The large truck that had hit them was stationary. The driver was facing them, rubbing his chest, his face twisted with pain. Blood flowed down his forehead from his

121

scalp. He saw her. Their eyes met. He raised his hand and made a move to get out of the cab. She shook her head and furiously gestured at him to stay where he was. He didn't understand. He opened his door and got out, walking unsteadily towards them.

The first burning infected was on him before he even saw it coming.

Lisa tried to block out his screams as she refocused all her attention on getting Anita out of the car.

Another infected appeared at the edge of the road and tumbled into the ditch. Twigs and branches ripped and tore its charred and fragile flesh.

Anita was on her feet.

The screams continued.

The infected was between the car and the edge of the ditch.

Anita was clambering awkwardly onto the bonnet.

The infected stood up. Its blackened toothless mouth opened in a silent moan.

Yellowed eyes fixed them in its gaze.

In one final, superhuman effort, Lisa heaved Anita off the bonnet and up the other side of the ditch.

They scrambled into the field beyond. Anita fell to her knees. Lisa hauled her to her feet and dragged her, running, along the edge. The girl tripped and stumbled but kept moving.

They made for a bridge that passed over a canal, and scrambled down into the dark, wet tunnel. Anita sank to her knees, panting. Lisa hunkered down beside her. They huddled together and waited until long after the screaming had stopped.

Lisa checked her watch. It was after midday. They'd been crouched under the bridge for over an hour. She was miserable. Stiff and shivering. They were both freezing. But it was more than just the physical discomfort. She'd really felt as though they were going to make it this time. Now look at them! Things had been going so well.

Too well. She'd become complacent. Again! She replayed the accident in her head, over and over, cursing herself for being so stupid and not focusing on the road ahead. She tried to tell herself they'd been lucky. It could have been so much worse. Apart from a big bump on the side of Anita's head and a few scratches and bruises, they were remarkably uninjured. But it didn't help. She was furious with herself.

Quietly, she got to her feet. Her legs cramped and screamed in complaint. She listened. Anita eased herself into a standing position as well. She leaned against Lisa as she stretched out her legs, one at time.

Lisa took her by the shoulders and looked into her eyes. "Are you ok? Can you move?"

Anita responded with a nod and a weak grin.

They crept out from under the bridge onto the canal tow path, inching tentatively from their hiding place. When they reached what felt like a safe distance, they turned to look back at the road. The Discovery was only a glint of metal in the shrubbery, but they could see the truck, which effectively blocked the whole road. Nothing moved and all was quiet.

The towpath stretched out in front of them, following the gentle curve of the canal. A small hedge separated it from open fields beyond. On the other side, willow branches dipped gracefully into the water. Birds twittered. It felt so calm and tranquil, only the lingering smell of smoke in the air, a reminder of what they had left behind. They walked in silence, both women lost in their own thoughts, content just to put as much distance between themselves and the road as they could.

But, as soon as Lisa began to let go of some of her acute feelings of fear and anxiety, emotions of hopelessness and despair flooded in to take their place. She was only two or three miles away from home as the crow flies, but it might as well be on the other side of the world. She had no idea how they were going to get there and was seriously beginning to wonder if they ever would.

For the first time since the start of their journey, she began to truly question what she was doing. Was she being stupid, reckless and selfish, to even think there was a chance that she could get home? Would Neil even be there? If she couldn't even get to Solihull from Coventry, how would he have managed to get there from Lincolnshire? What was she thinking, dragging Anita on this wild goose chase at a time when they should be holed up somewhere safe just trying to survive?

They should have stayed at the farm and waited. They should have stayed with Richard and Charlie. She'd thrown that offer away and got a lovely couple killed into the bargain. That was her fault too. Of

124

course, it was. It all was. Now, they were out in the open for the second time, with no food or drink or warm clothes. They'd lost the only weapon they had and burned through two cars that had been generously lent to them. And now Anita was hurt because of her careless driving. It was hopeless. She was hopeless.

She tripped and realised she was crying. Tears were running down her cheeks blurring her vision. She wiped her eyes and tried to concentrate on the uneven ground beneath her feet. But, after a few more steps, she stopped and allowed herself to weep openly.

Anita put a hand on her back but didn't speak. Lisa cried harder, her whole body racked with deep shuddering sobs. She cried for the train driver, for the boy in the green hoodie, for John and Lynda, for Brian, and for Richard and Charlie. She cried for the burning infected and the truck driver. She cried for Anita and her family. She cried for her own friends and family, for the people on the train, the people of Wolston and the families in their cars fleeing to who knew where.

She cried for herself and for Neil. Where was he? Please let him be alive. Please let her just get home to him.

An image formed in her head of Neil sitting at their kitchen table. His back was straight and strong. He was concentrating and his shoulder muscles flexed as he worked with something in his hands. He suddenly became aware of her presence and turned around, calmly smiling at her, his eyes twinkling. It felt so real that she lifted her hand as if to reach out and touch him.

Her tears began to slow. She sighed deeply and sat down on the grassy bank at the side of the path. She wiped her eyes. Anita sat beside her, putting her arm around her shoulder.

"This is so shit," Anita mumbled.

"Damn right," Lisa responded.

"Better?"

"Actually … yes!"

She really did feel better and stronger again.

She knew Neil was waiting for her. She couldn't explain it, but she just knew it.

Her desire to get home returned in a rush, pushing all other thoughts and feelings aside.

She got to her feet, straightening her back and her resolve simultaneously.

"Sorry about that." She offered Anita a watery apology.

But Anita was staring at her intently, the corners of her mouth twitching as she fought to suppress a smile.

"What's wrong?" Lisa asked.

"Your face," Anita giggled. "You're a mess." She dissolved into peals of laughter.

Lisa grinned. "Come on. Let's keep moving. I need to find a mirror."

They carried on along the path. A few carefree ducks bobbed on the canal, enviably oblivious to the chaos going on beyond their own little world. The Indian summer sunshine of the past couple of days had started to give way to grey skies moving in from the west. A light breeze rippled the surface of the water. They walked slowly, Anita in front and Lisa close behind, eyes mostly on the ground below as they picked their way around deep holes and furrows.

"It looks like rain." Lisa pointed to the clouds.

"We're going to do this, Lisa."

"I know. We just need to find somewhere to rest for a bit and work out what we're going to do next."

Twenty minutes later, Anita stopped so suddenly that Lisa bumped into her.

"Look. Over there. That might work."

She was pointing ahead to a small cottage that marked the start of what looked like a series of locks. It stood on its own … isolated. It looked deserted … untouched.

They approached it cautiously. Nothing stirred.

They peered into the front window. A tidy, but cosy, sitting room looked undisturbed. Two sofas faced a small TV, and some magazines were strategically scattered on a low coffee table. More windows revealed a tiny kitchen and a bedroom containing a neatly made bed, complete with a hand-crocheted bedspread. Apart from an upturned coffee cup on the draining rack by the sink in the kitchen, nothing was out of place. They went back to the front door.

"Doesn't look like anyone's been here for a while," Anita observed.

"Can we get in?" Lisa asked.

Anita put her hand on the door handle and jiggled

127

it a few times. "Locked!"

"No kidding," said Lisa sarcastically. But she was looking at the wire brush door mat Anita was standing on. When Anita stepped back from the door, she picked it up.

"Yesss!"

Lisa picked up a single brass key. She tried it in the lock and the door swung open.

They stepped quickly into the room and closed the door behind them.

"That was way too easy," Anita muttered looking around nervously.

Lisa checked the small bedroom and bathroom, and then started going through the kitchen, banging cupboard doors and rummaging in drawers.

"What are you looking for?" Anita joined her in the small room.

"Weapons!" Lisa brandished a large carving knife.

"Good shout." Anita joined the search.

It was soon clear that Lisa had salvaged the best and only option from the contents of the kitchen, so Anita shifted her search to the living room. She opted for a cast iron poker that was resting in a stand near the fireplace.

Weapons chosen, Anita threw herself onto a sofa, and Lisa, who had discovered the store cupboard during her search of the kitchen, went to make them a coffee. She was pleased to discover the electricity was on and, while the kettle was coming to the boil, she opened a carton of long-life milk and liberated an unopened packet of Chocolate Hobnobs from the back of a shelf.

"I'm sure they won't mind in the circumstances." She spoke aloud but was largely reassuring herself.

"Jesus, Lisa! They're probably either dead or long gone. And even if they do come back one day, I don't think they'll be bothered about a couple of biscuits," Anita called into the kitchen.

Lisa was beaming when she came back into the sitting room carrying two steaming mugs of coffee, with the packet of biscuits tucked under her arm.

"I don't know about you, but I'm planning on having more than a couple." She handed Anita her coffee and eased onto the other sofa.

What followed was a long and honest discussion about what they should do next. By the time they had finished their coffee and most of the biscuits, they had a new plan.

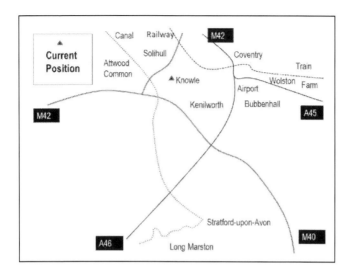

Chapter 6

Day 3 - Knowle

Anita leaned back on the sofa. She yawned and stretched her long arms above her head.

"So, that's it then. We're walking, but by a more direct route. Oh, and a more *dangerous* route."

Lisa nodded. "Yes, but I don't see what choice we have, now we don't have a car."

"Again!" Anita sniped.

"Ok, I'll take that. But it's doable, Nita. We're only four or five miles away. We could walk it in a few hours. Through Knowle, over the motorway and through Solihull. Simple."

"Why do I think it's not going to be *simple*?"

"Who knows, we might even find another car?"

"Yeah, sure."

"Come on, Nita. Besides, there's hardly anyone around. We've hardly seen anyone. They've all either left or barricaded themselves into their homes."

"Yeah, sure, but you forgot to mention the bunch of brain-dead, flesh-eating, infected folks, roaming around the streets looking for their next snack."

"Of course, I didn't, but we have the advantage. We can think and move fast. They can't do either. And we're learning all the time about what they can and can't do. About how to ... kill them ... if we have to."

"Head! It's gotta be the head," Anita muttered.

"You see! And besides, they seem to be kind of dormant when there's no-one about. If we're really quiet and careful, they might not even see us! We just need to be careful, Nita ... quiet and careful."

"Stealth and speed."

"Yeah, stealth and speed." Lisa leaned across the coffee table and put her hand on Anita's knee. "We can do it, Nita. I know we can."

Anita nodded. "But we're gonna need to be better prepared. We can't just walk out there ..." She pointed at the window. "like this!" She pointed back at Lisa's dress and leggings. "We need better gear, protective stuff, and better ... *weapons*. I'm not being funny, but a kitchen knife and a poker aren't gonna cut it!"

Lisa nodded. "Agreed. And I've thought of that,

too. We could do with backpacks to carry water and stuff."

"Food! We'll need food." Anita looked at the empty biscuit wrapper.

"Yeah! Look, over here." Lisa got up and went over to the window. She pointed at a long, low building, across a field on the other side of the canal. "It's a Garden Centre. I know it. It's on the edge of Knowle. We should be able to get a lot of what we need there."

Anita walked over to the window.

"Looks like that's our first port of call then." She hesitated and took a deep breath. "This is gonna be hard, Lisa. Really hard. We're gonna have to be strong. Dig deep."

"I once read something about how, if you choose who you want to be and choose to adopt the mindset of that person, it can help you become them. It's all about self-belief and self-fulfilling prophecies and all that. It's hard to explain."

"So, what are you saying, exactly?"

Lisa turned to face her. "I think I'm saying that, if we choose in our minds to be survivors, we can do it. We can make it happen. We can survive."

"Well, we've done it so far, so in a way we are already."

"Already what?"

"Survivors." Anita grinned at her. "We are survivors, Lisa."

Lisa nodded. "We are. We are survivors."

When they left the cottage just after 2pm, it was

raining. The clouds that had been building earlier, were now thick and heavy and the sky was a solid dark grey. The gloom felt more in keeping with the death and destruction all around them than the blue skies and bright sunshine of the past couple of days. Lisa was wearing the one waterproof jacket they'd managed to salvage from the cottage. Anita had fashioned herself a rustling, temporary cape from a black bin bag.

They crossed the canal via one of the locks and, keeping as low as possible, scurried quickly across the field. They approached the garden centre from the rear, heading quickly for the cover of a long poly-tunnel that lay between them and the main building. Breathing heavily, they sheltered behind the structure as they recovered and listened for signs that anyone else was around. The rain was heavier now, pattering on the plastic of the poly-tunnel and making it hard to hear anything else.

They nodded at each other and edged towards the entrance of the tunnel, slipping inside. At the far end, a hunched figure in a green overall lifted its head and looked towards them. Both women reacted instantly. Before it could make a sound, they charged. Anita went low and hit it in the chest with her shoulder. The speed and impact of the blow knocked it onto its back. Lisa threw herself on top of it and plunged her carving knife into its eye socket. It went limp.

She stood up and straddled the body, pulling the knife out and holding it ready to strike again if it moved. It didn't. She wiped the knife on its overalls.

Anita stared at her, open-mouthed. "Jesus, I'm loving our new survivor mindset thing!"

Lisa took her inhaler out of her pocket and shook it. She looked at it before putting it back without taking a puff. She took a long slow breath.

"You ok?" Anita asked.

"It's nearly finished. I need to save it."

"What happens if it runs out?"

I don't know. It's never happened. But I don't think it'll be great. Anyway, I'm ok for now. Let's keep moving."

The big yard was laid out in a network of wooden structures laden with displays of potted plants and garden ornaments. They moved gradually closer to the building, crouching low and moving from the cover of one structure to another until they could see a set of double doors. One of the doors was open but a few feet away a couple of infected lingered by a large wheelie bin. Another green overall clad male infected was accompanied by a small female in a green polo shirt and black utility trousers. The sorry pair were facing the bin, heads down, dripping wet and barely moving.

"They're too close. We'll never make it." Anita whispered.

Lisa was looking at a small greenhouse a few metres beyond the doorway. She pointed at the chunky gravel beneath their feet. "We need to distract them. Draw them away."

"Nice!" Anita nodded and began to pick out a selection of larger, heavier stones.

Her first throw fell short. However, the mere click of stone on stone stimulated a response. Both infected instantly raised their heads and turned towards the sound but didn't move.

The second throw was better and clattered against the glass but didn't break it.

The female started to move towards the greenhouse.

When the next stone smashed one of the panes, the male followed her.

When the next missile smashed another pane, they both began to moan and moved more quickly towards the sound.

The women dashed for the open door. Anita was fast and got there first, slipping inside and out of sight. Lisa was right behind her, but the infected were quick to react, too. They were moving fast. Surprisingly fast. The male was close. Too close. The moaning intensified. It made the hairs rise on the back of her neck. She wasn't going to make it. She looked straight ahead and pumped her arms and legs.

As she reached the door, she was sure she felt his outstretched fingers brush against her back, before Anita grabbed her arm and dragged her inside, pulling the door shut behind them.

The doors had push bar mechanisms on the inside, and the women clung to the bars as the infected outside roared and pounded in fury.

Lisa had to shout to be heard above the noise. "They can't get in. They're fire doors. There aren't any handles on the outside. We can let go."

She let go and stepped back. "Anita! It's ok. We can let go!"

Anita looked at her but held on for a few minutes more, before she too released her grip.

The banging and growling continued.

They turned their attention to the room. A single bulb on the ceiling provided enough light for them to see that it was a small storage space, crammed with bags of compost and irregular towers of brown cardboard boxes. The only other exit was a single, windowless door at the back.

Lisa went to this door and pressed her ear against its surface, but all she could hear was the infected outside. A line of white light shone through the thin gap where it met the floor.

"We've got to go in and get what we've come for." Anita shrugged.

"Yeah." Lisa tried the handle. "It's locked."

Anita examined a unit on the wall. "There's a slot for a key card here."

"Great!" Lisa kicked the door.

Anita looked at her. "They'll have one." She nodded in the direction of the barrage of noise.

"Don't even think about it, Nita."

"Come on, let's just open the door a crack and see what we can see. What choice have we got? If we can't get through, we'll have to go back out that way anyway."

"Shit!" Lisa turned and went back to the double doors.

Anita opted to open the door as she was taller and

stronger. Lisa's job was to look for the key card. She crouched low to stay out of the reach of nails and teeth.

Anita pushed the bar down and eased the door open a few inches. The noise increased in volume as the enraged group of infected became even more agitated. Multiple grey fingers with dirty, discoloured nails spidered through the space.

At first, all Lisa could see was a mass of moving legs as the small crowd clamoured around the door. They were actually pressing it shut, and Anita had to fight to keep it open wide enough for Lisa to get a good look. But, somewhere, in the blur of noise and movement, Lisa caught a glimpse of a key card hanging on the belt of what she thought was the female in the polo shirt.

"I see it," she hissed. "Hold it steady."

Anita strengthened her grip on the door, and Lisa slipped her arm through the opening to grab for the card. In one movement she snatched at it and threw herself backwards. Anita released the door and it slammed shut, accompanied by a new salvo of pounding and enraged snarling.

Lisa was on her back, clutching the card, which was still attached to its owner by an elastic cord. She secured the card by twisting the cord around her fingers and grappled with the knife in her other hand. Anita took the knife from her and cut the cord in one swift movement. Lisa grinned as she held the card up triumphantly.

They were even more pleased with themselves when they slid the key card down in the slot and heard the mechanical whir as the door unlocked. They pushed it open slowly, momentarily dazzled by the bright light that flooded in.

As their eyes refocused, they looked around. They were in the back corner of the main shop. Nothing looked out of place. The shelves were neatly stacked, and the aisles were clear, but they waited and listened. From the front of the shop, they could hear a dull, repetitive knocking, but otherwise all was quiet apart from the gentle purr of the strip lights and the hum of the ventilation system.

"We should check it's clear first," Lisa suggested.

Anita nodded and mumbled her agreement.

They systematically swept the shop, checking the aisles one by one, gradually working their way from back to front. It was a vast space. As they moved, Lisa mentally noted things that might be useful. They could still hear the knocking sound. It seemed to be coming from the checkout area.

As they approached the front of the shop, Lisa saw the source of the sound. A female worker was sitting in her seat still facing her till. She was trapped in the small booth and the knocking was the sound of her chair hitting the counter as she rocked back and forth. Her throat had been torn open and old, dried blood had turned the front of her green polo shirt a rusty brown.

One step closer and she saw them. Her vacant expression became a glare and she reached for them, rocking faster on her seat, turning the knocking into a loud banging. She opened her mouth to moan, but no sound came from her ragged throat.

Anita strode over and finished her with the poker in one swift movement.

"Poor cow. If that ever happens to me, promise you'll do me the favour."

"You don't have to ask, … and I know you'd do the same for me."

Confident that the shop was secure, they split up and set about gathering what they needed for the journey ahead. They brought their spoils back to the checkout area at the front of the shop and got ready to leave. Lisa was now wearing a pair of thick cargo pants, a warm fitted waterproof jacket and a solid pair of walking boots. Anita had swapped her trainers for a pair of boots but had opted to stay in her jeans and leather jacket. Lisa tied her hair back with a camouflage sports bandana.

Anita shot her a look. "Hey! Rambo?"

Lisa chucked her a bright pink version of the same and she pulled in on.

In return, Anita handed Lisa a pair of gardening gloves.

"They'll protect your hands."

They packed a couple of small backpacks with as much water and as many snacks as they could carry. Lisa had also picked out a torch, a roll of gaffer tape and a pack of wire garden twines. Anita raised her eyebrows.

"They might come in handy. Who knows?" Lisa stuffed them into her backpack before Anita could persuade her otherwise. "Anyway, what are the funky goggles for?"

Anita was trying on a set of protective, clear plastic goggles.

"If we're gonna get up close and personal with any more of our fierce friends, I don't want any blood and guts getting in my eyes." She positioned them on her forehead.

"Actually, that's not a bad shout. I might get some too."

"Thought you might!" Anita handed her a pair.

Both women had selected a more effective weapon. Lisa had gone for a curved, serrated pruning saw with a vicious point.

"Nice!" Anita admired it, turning the point back and forth and probing it with one gloved finger. She had gone for an axe that she positioned in a pale leather carrying sling over her shoulder and across her body. She also had a crowbar. She swung it at an invisible enemy a couple of times, testing its weight and manoeuvrability.

"Let's have another look at these cable ties and tape," Anita said.

Obediently, Lisa got the items out of her bag again, looking at Anita questioningly. The girl disappeared for a moment and returned with a wooden broom handle. Using the cable ties and tape, she fixed Lisa's saw firmly to the handle. She tested it by driving it into some bags of compost a few times before handing it back to her with a grin.

"You were right. They might come in handy after all."

Lisa tried the saw, now a lethal, hooked spear, on a few bags of compost herself.

"Nice!" She nodded with a tight-lipped smile.

"Ready, Survivor?" she asked Anita.

"As I'll ever be, Fellow Survivor!"

They looked at each other for a long moment, then turned and approached the main doors.

Anita levered the sliding doors open with the crowbar and they squeezed out. The doors sprang shut with a dull thud. A car park sat between the building and the road. It was clear apart from a couple of empty cars. The rain had eased into a light drizzle, but the sky overhead was still dark and threatening.

Lisa felt her heart begin to pound as they left the safety of the building. But she wasn't afraid. Well, of course, she was ... a bit. But the feeling that had really set her heart racing was one of anticipation, almost ... excitement. She felt different. Strong. Determined. Ready.

Ahead, Anita's leather-clad back was square and strong. Both of her hands were on the crowbar that she held out in front of her. She was lithe and fast as, glancing from side to side, she moved quickly into the road and paused ... looking both ways, before her gaze settled in the direction of the village of Knowle just ahead.

When Lisa joined her, they began to walk slowly up the middle of the road, constantly scanning around them for signs of movement. Like Kenilworth, it was unnervingly quiet. From the corner of her eye, Lisa thought she saw a curtain twitch in an upstairs window, but when she looked up nothing moved. A wind had picked up. Trees rustled and, from somewhere ahead, she heard an echoing clang of metal on metal.

They approached a junction. Straight ahead was the main high street and to the left another deserted, tree-lined, residential road stretched into the distance.

"Which way?" Anita whispered.

"The High Street is the direct route, but it goes straight to the motorway and into Solihull itself. It could get hairy. The other road is longer but more rural and possibly safer."

"Oh, Jesus! We said we were going direct. Let's just get there."

Anita walked straight on towards the High Street. Lisa looked longingly for a moment at the quiet, leafy road on their left before she followed her.

As soon as they hit the High Street, they heard the moaning. It rose and fell above the sound of the wind, but it was definitely moaning. They were familiar enough with the sound now to be sure. The clanging metal was louder, too. Both sounds were coming from up ahead, but they couldn't see anything. There were shops, cafés and restaurants on either side of the road. Most were boarded up.

On their immediate left was a large traditional pub: The Red Lion.

"Neil and I drink there sometimes," Lisa said, mostly to herself.

"You used to," Anita quipped.

She was right. Usually the place was buzzing, day and night, with people spilling out onto the pavement to smoke. You could never get a parking space. They'd often have a drink there before going to Loch Fyne for dinner. He'd have a pint of bitter, and she'd have a glass of white wine, or Prosecco if she couldn't face the bitter aftertaste of a "pub" wine.

Now, it was silent and still. The doors were shut, and the curtains were closed. Someone had attempted to board up the shattered front door. One of the windows was broken; a torn curtain was caught on the broken glass. It was dark inside. She shivered. This felt weird. Creepy.

All the places they'd passed through up to now had been largely unfamiliar. The whole thing had had the feel of a very long, very bad dream. She'd been able to stay detached. Now, though, in this familiar place so close to home, reality hit her like a slow blow to the stomach. She felt physically sick.

"You ok?" Anita asked.

"Yeah, it's just so … you know …"

She was interrupted by movement ahead. An infected stumbled out of an alleyway on the left. It came from the same direction as the moaning and the clanging noise. Lisa stiffened, tightening her grip on her spear. The infected was lurching itself towards them.

They pulled their goggles down. When it was close enough, Lisa stepped towards it. In one swift move, she raised the spear and brought it down in a firm strike on the top of its skull. It dropped like a stone. As it fell, she held the spear fast and the blade slid out from the wound. A dark, viscous liquid dripped from its tip.

Another infected appeared from the same direction. This time, Anita stepped ahead drawing her axe from its sling. She barely missed a stride as she stopped it in its tracks with a single, solid strike.

A slow but steady stream of infected trickled out from the alley. The two women dealt with them calmly and efficiently, taking turns until the trickle stopped, and all was quiet again except for the metal clanging.

They were sweating and panting, their clothes and faces splattered with gore.

"Great idea about the goggles." Lisa wiped hers clean with her sleeve.

"We're definitely getting the hang of this." Anita surveyed the corpses that littered the street with an expression of grim satisfaction.

Lisa realised that she, too, felt strangely satisfied. What was wrong with her? It was confusing. She didn't want to think about it. What was that damned clanging, anyway?

She went into the alley. At its end, a metal gate was blowing in the wind.

She strode towards it, intent on silencing it.

Anita called out to her.

"Wait, Lisa! The noise is attracting them. It's our friend."

Lisa stopped and turned back. She patted Anita on the shoulder.

"Let's get out of here."

They made steady progress through the village

and out towards the motorway. But they smelt and heard it before they saw it. The unmistakable odour of decaying flesh reached them first, followed a couple of hundred metres later by the sound of a multitude of moaning. They stopped and looked at the road ahead. It rose up towards a roundabout that sat above the motorway. The noise and smell was coming from below.

"Man!" Anita said.

"It's the M42. The Solihull Junction. The town centre is on the other side." Lisa gestured beyond the roundabout.

"Are you hearing this? There's got to be hundreds of them. The noise and the smell ..." Anita was frowning and chewing her thumbnail. "I don't know ... I really don't know."

Lisa tried to reassure her, "Let's just have a look first. Let's just see. We can come back"

"Oh, Jesus," Anita groaned. "What if ...?"

"We can move faster than them. You know we can. Think about it. We can't give up now. We knew this was coming. We knew it could be bad."

"Yeah but not as bad as this! Seriously, Lisa! Have you lost your mind?"

"Come on. We can do it. You know we can. We're survivors, aren't we?"

"Oh, Jesus! Please, Jesus. Just a look then."

Lisa took Anita's hand and coaxed her up towards the roundabout.

The noise and the stench intensified the closer

146

they got, and by the time they reached the top of the southbound entry slip-road, it was overwhelming. Both women had to cover their mouths and noses to stop themselves from retching and gagging.

They crouched behind some bushes to look down at the scene. It was utter carnage. A tangled mass of vehicles, a few still shiny and intact but most mangled or burnt out, stretched as far as they could see. Hundreds of infected wandered amongst the vehicles. Some writhed and twisted in their cars.

The end of the slip-road was blocked by a mini pile-up, effectively preventing any of the infected from leaving the main carriageway.

"See, they can't get up here," Lisa whispered.

"What about the other exits?"

"Wait here."

Lisa scuttled across the road towards the top of the exit slip-road on the other side. She dropped onto her belly and wriggled forward to get a better view.

She signalled a thumbs-down sign before belly-crawling back the way she'd come. She was breathless when she slipped back behind the cover of the bushes.

"That side's open," she panted. "They could come up there. Honestly, though, if we're quiet and careful, I think we can get over. They can't see us."

"Jesus! Let's do it then."

Keeping low, they inched their way forward on their hands and knees, pausing every few minutes, listening for any increase in noise or activity below.

It felt like more, but it took only ten minutes or so until they were safely past the slip-road and onto the main bridge. There, in a spot where they were completely out of sight, they took a break and stretched out their cramping limbs, before crouching again to crawl the remaining distance past the top of the exit slip-road.

Lisa was focused on the road ahead. It was empty. They were almost there. She could see the gardens of the first few properties just ahead. She felt a thrill of excitement. They were going to do it.

Then, above the low moan of the infected, she became aware of a distant, thumping sound. It was far away but getting quickly louder. As well as the thumping she could hear what sounded like the whirr of an engine.

She pushed on. Just a few more minutes and they'd be clear.

The sound got louder. Closer. The infected heard it too. Their moaning intensified.

She paused and glanced over at Anita.

The girl was staring at the sky to their left.

Lisa followed her gaze.

The distinctive dark outline of a helicopter was travelling towards them, fast, from the south, following the path of the motorway.

For an instant, Lisa couldn't decide whether to run or freeze.

She froze.

When it reached them, it swooped down low, hovering directly above their heads. The wind from its rotating blades pinned them to the ground. They could hardly lift their heads. The noise was deafening. Combined with the, now frenzied, cries of the infected, it created a wall of sound that obliterated everything else.

Then, sheets of paper began to flutter from the sky, swirling in the wind, blowing across the motorway, the roundabout and into the streets beyond.

Lisa managed to turn her head and look up. The side door of the helicopter was open and a man in army fatigues was gesturing at them furiously. Lisa just stared at him. Her head was empty. She felt distant … detached … like she was watching a movie scene that she wasn't part of.

"Lisa!" Anita's voice cut through the fog. "Get up! Run!"

Anita was standing. Her body was bent and braced against the blasting currents of air. Her long braids flew around her head like a medusa. She was pointing towards the slip-road.

A group of infected were coming over the top. They looked angry, hungry and dangerous.

The helicopter arced and soared, up and away over the motorway again, continuing north.

Anita was running. Lisa scrambled to her feet and followed her.

Another group of infected were coming up the other side of the motorway on their right.

They reached the road. Infected were appearing from all directions … both sides, in front and behind. The noise seemed to have served as a rallying cry …

drawing them out … summoning them.

"They're everywhere!" Anita cried out. "There's nowhere to go!"

"Just keep going. We can avoid them, outrun them!" Lisa yelled.

Fired by adrenaline, the women blasted through the group in front, weaving between them, twisting and dodging to avoid their grasping, clawing hands.

But, more and more appeared. The road ahead was a mass of seething rotting flesh, bearing down on them.

"There's too many!" Anita sounded desperate. "We're not going to make it!"

Lisa frantically glanced around her.

A large white shape on a driveway to their left caught her eye and she instinctively spun and ran towards it. It was a huge camper van, the type the Americans call an RV. One door was ajar. She was at the door and inside before she had time to think about it.

Anita was right behind her, but so was a large, beer-bellied, greasy-haired, male infected, in baggy shorts and a too-tight polo shirt. He got to the door a fraction of a second before her.

Again, without thinking, a primal survival instinct kicked in as Lisa braced herself in the door frame and, screaming, kicked out with both feet. She hit it square in the centre of the chest, and it toppled backwards. Anita scrambled over it, kicking and stamping on its flailing limbs. She tumbled into the van and Lisa slammed and locked the door behind her.

Gasping and shaking, they cowered by the door. Outside, a multitude of infected clawed and scratched at the van. The noise was deafening. The whole vehicle swayed and rocked.

Lisa closed her eyes. She covered her ears to try and block out the sound. Flashbacks of the train toilet flooded in. With it came the fear. The same paralysing terror and fuzzy, light-headed feeling. She felt herself losing control. She could hear herself breathing fast and loud, and her pulse was pounding inside her head, but she couldn't control it. She put her fingers in her ears and began to hum. Not a tune exactly, just a flow of monotonous random notes. Anything to drown out the noise. She was only vaguely aware of Anita by her side, who was also lost in her own ocean of terror.

It was a long time until the noise outside subsided. The deluge of scratching and clawing gradually gave way to just an occasional bumping and scraping. Somehow, the van had remained secure and upright. It was big and heavy. A smaller vehicle would almost certainly have succumbed. Lisa didn't want to think about what could have happened.

Warily, they moved into the interior of the van on stiff and cramped limbs. Most of the curtains inside were drawn already and, keeping out of view, they closed those that were not in a series of tiny movements, including the one that separated the cab from the rest of the space.

The van was packed with bags of clothes, boxes of food, camping equipment and packs of drinking water. Whoever had loaded it had been preparing

151

to get away. Lisa thought about how the door had been open and wondered who they were and what had happened to them. There were no signs of a struggle.

Anita was more concerned about finding the keys. Having checked the ignition, she was now rummaging around in drawers and compartments.

"I don't think they're here." She sat down heavily. "Shame. It could've been perfect. Our own little mobile fortress. Sweet."

"Well, we're not going anywhere tonight. We might be able to have a proper look in the morning. It's getting dark now."

"Yeah, totally. Sounds like there's only a few out there now. They might all be gone by the morning."

"But there were so many, Anita! They'll all still be out there … somewhere ... they're not just going to … go away."

"Hmm … yeah, I know that. They just won't be … right outside." Anita chewed at her thumbnail again. She stood up abruptly and started to open a can of baked beans. "Well, I'm hungry and I'm knackered. We should try and eat, then get some sleep. We can think about everything properly in the morning. Want some?"

She offered Lisa a can of beans and a spoon.

"I'm not really hungry." Lisa took them reluctantly.

"But you know you should eat … yeah?"

"I know," Lisa said and winced as she put a spoonful of cold beans in her mouth.

They made up a couple of beds, and Anita

snuggled down in one, as Lisa had agreed to take first watch. Her chest was tight. It hadn't really settled down since they'd got into the van. She wouldn't be able to sleep until it felt easier. It was always worse when she lay flat.

And she'd taken the last puff of her inhaler earlier. She hadn't said anything to Anita, and the girl didn't seem to have noticed. They had more than enough to deal with without worrying about her having a full-blown asthma attack. She would become just another part of the problem if she couldn't breathe. She dreaded what the coming day would bring, in more ways than one.

She wondered where Neil was and what he was doing, anxious again that yet another day had passed, and they'd still had no contact. If he'd made it home, maybe he'd given up waiting for her. By now, he might think she was dead, *or worse*. If only he knew that she was so close.

A muffled bang on the back of the van made her jump.

They were still out there.

It was going to be a long night.

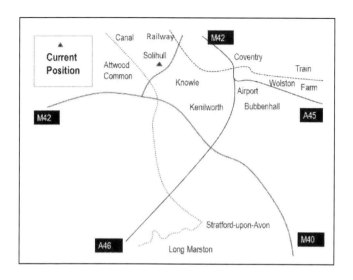

Chapter 7

Day 4 - Solihull

Lisa let Anita sleep through, but the girl woke just before dawn.

"What are you doing, Lisa? Why didn't you wake me? It's way past my turn."

"I couldn't sleep. Thought I might as well let you rest."

"Jesus! You look awful! Are you ok?"

"My asthma's playing up a bit. All the drama from yesterday set it off."

"What about your inhaler?"

"It's run out."

"Oh, what does that mean?"

"It means it's empty. Finished."

"I know that! You know what I mean. What does it mean for *you*? Are you gonna be ok?"

"Dunno. I've never run out before. I suppose I'm going to find out."

"Shit. Look, at least lie down and shut your eyes for a bit. *Try* to sleep. We've got a big day ahead. You'll be fit for nothing!"

"Yeah, you're right. I'll try."

She didn't think sleep would come, but it evidently had. After tossing and turning for a while, she awoke from a dreamless sleep to the sounds of Anita rustling around. Lisa sat up, yawning and rubbing her eyes. Her chest felt better, but it was still tight.

Anita turned to look at her. "You look better. How d'you feel?"

"Yeah, a bit better. How long have I been out?"

"About four hours. It's almost nine. I said you needed to sleep."

"Shit!" Lisa jumped up. "We need to get going. What's it like out there?"

Anita grabbed her arm. "It's fine. They've mostly gone."

Anita sat down and patted the bench opposite her.

"Sit down a minute. I wanna talk to you." She had a crumpled piece of paper in her hand. "I grabbed this yesterday, after the helicopter."

"Idiots!" Lisa grumbled. "What the hell were they doing? They nearly got us killed."

"I think they were trying to help. Look!" Anita held

156

out the piece of paper which was a crudely produced leaflet. It contained some large, bold text and a blurry image.

"What does it say?" She took it from Anita, trying to smooth it out, squinting at it through still sleepy eyes.

"It's about a safe zone. It's telling any survivors to make their way there." Anita looked at her, waiting for a response.

Lisa studied the leaflet. It gave the details of a military "safe zone" at an airfield near Stratford-upon-Avon. It simply advised any "survivors" of the "outbreak" to make their way there. It gave directions on how to get there from different locations and the blurry image was a map. Lisa looked at it for a long time.

Anita pressed her, "What d'you think?"

"We've come this far. We're so close now. Neil will be waiting. He promised."

"But everything's different now. It's been three days. How do you know he'll still be there? He might have gone to the safe zone himself. He might have gone to look for you there."

"I just *know,* Nita. You don't understand. We made a promise to each other. We talked about it several times. We promised. *He* promised."

"Oh, Jesus, Lisa! I just don't know. You say it's close, but who knows how long it'll take to get there? Look at what happened yesterday. The day before. We might *never* get there."

Lisa was silent. She studied the leaflet. Her eyes blurred with tears.

157

"Do you know where it is, this Long Marston Airfield? How far away is it?" Anita asked.

"It's got to be twenty miles. Just think about it, Nita. We are only a few miles from home now, maybe three or four. We could be there in an hour or two. *Then* we can go to the safe zone. *With* Neil."

"But you've said that *every day,* Lisa. 'We're close. We're only a few miles away.' You have to face reality. We're not getting any closer."

"That's just not true, Anita. We *are* getting closer … just very slowly ...." Lisa's voice trailed off.

Anita sighed deeply. She stood up and walked towards the back of the van, peering cautiously through a crack in the curtains.

Lisa watched her. Waiting. Hoping.

Her chest was tightening again. She needed to calm down. Stop getting herself so agitated.

After a few minutes, Anita sighed again and turned to face her. "Ok! Look! As we're so close, let's have one more try to get there today. If we don't make it, we give up and head for the safe zone. Deal?"

Lisa smiled. She got up and hugged her. "Thank you! We'll get there today. I promise."

Anita shook her head. "We'll see. One more day. Ok?"

She pulled the curtain of the back window aside a couple of inches and nodded her head towards the outside. "Anyway, changing the subject, d'you want the bad news, the good news, or the other good news?"

"I'll take *all* the good news, please." Lisa nodded enthusiastically.

"As I said, it's pretty much clear outside. They've mostly all gone."

"Great. And?"

"Well the bad news will put that into some context. There are definitely no keys. I've looked everywhere. But we do have bikes! There are two on the back of the van! Look!"

"Oh yes!" Lisa jumped up to peer out of the window. Suddenly, the world seemed to be a brighter place again.

They freshened up, ate a breakfast of cereal and cold rice pudding and got ready to leave. Despite her poor night's sleep, Lisa was full of hope. She felt energetic and excited. It was about time their luck changed. It was happening. She could feel it.

They packed as much extra food as they could carry. Lisa kept watch while Anita unfastened the bikes from the rack. They were hybrids. A large man's one and smaller woman's version of the same model. Anita took the bigger one. Her long legs still reached the ground even when she was sitting in the saddle. She helped Lisa to strap her spear over her shoulder with a strap from the bike rack. They filled a couple of water bottles and fitted them into the holders.

They were a bit wobbly at first, as they got used to the unfamiliar bikes and the weight of their backpacks and weapons. During the time it had taken them to get ready, a few infected had emerged from the surrounding properties and had gathered in a straggly group that was moving down the road towards them. But they safely negotiated around the small group and were soon gliding smoothly down empty streets towards Solihull town centre. Lisa was elated. They were moving so quickly. All being well, they should be there within the hour.

But the town centre was blocked off by a series of abandoned military checkpoints much like the one they'd seen on the edge of Coventry on Friday morning. To get through, they had to stop and lift their bikes over the barricade.

The main shopping area was devastated. A smoky, metallic smell hung in the air. It smelt like what Lisa imagined war would smell like. Broken glass and rubble littered the streets. They had to get off and walk again, carefully manoeuvring the bikes around the debris. Some buildings were boarded up, but most had their windows smashed and doors forced open, their contents spilling out onto the pavement. Overturned shopping trolleys loaded with food and water had been abandoned where they fell. Broken glass, empty plastic bottles, torn cardboard and crumpled plastic packaging was scattered everywhere. Lisa saw a large, flat-screen TV sitting in the middle of the road.

There was evidence of fierce fighting, blood smears on walls and vehicles, and fallen weapons on the ground. Military grade rifles and pistols lay alongside makeshift implements like kitchen knives with reinforced hand grips, and baseball bats studded with nails.

And there were bodies. Bodies everywhere. Slumped in doorways and draped over the wreckage of burnt-out cars. The full collection of repugnant injuries were on display. Shredded limbs, spilling guts, gouged throats and disfigured faces.

Lisa was fighting a renewed battle with her spasming airways. Her chest felt like it was in a vice. Her breath was coming in small grunts. She felt woozy and light-headed. She *really* needed her inhaler now. When Anita stopped once to retch, all she could do was watch.

But they pushed on through the town and out the other side. They had to. After they were over the last barricade, they got back on the bikes and pedalled fast and hard until they reached the top of a long wide road that lead to the suburb of Shirley, and then on to Attwood Common.

Lisa dropped her bike and stumbled to the side of the road. She leant on a low wall and tried to catch her breath. Her vision was blurred, and a high-pitched whine rang in her head.

Anita was behind her. Lisa felt the girl put a hand on her shoulder.

"What can I do. Lisa? How can I help?"

"Nothing … " Lisa gasped. "Need … inhaler."

"Oh, Jesus!"

"Wait … Just wait … Will pass."

It took a while, but it did pass … eventually. Her breathing slowed and her airways began to relax. She gulped fresh air into her lungs. Every breath flooded her body with oxygen. Her head began to clear. The whine began to fade.

Anita sighed with relief. "Jesus! Thank God! You

really scared me. Are you ok?"

"Yes ... sorry 'bout that. I'm going to be ... I am ... I'm ok."

She was, but it had been close. Too close! Much too close! She'd been lucky. Next time, she might not be. She had to get an inhaler.

"I'm going to have to get an inhaler, Nita. I thought I could manage without one, but I can't. Sorry!"

"Don't be sorry. And don't be stupid! You can't help it. We just need to find a chemist." She turned back towards the town centre they had just left. "We'll just have to go back. There must be one ..."

Lisa interrupted her. "There is, but there's also one ahead. In the retail park. A big one."

"How far?"

"A mile ... maybe two? Not far."

"Far enough. Can you make it?"

"I have to."

The road was clear, and they pedalled freely for a couple of miles. They passed the college where Lisa had taken night classes in photography, the leisure centre where she played squash, and her dentist's surgery. Her vision blurred again, but this time it was due to the tears that filled her eyes and trickled down her cheeks. Everything was so familiar but at the same time changed forever. The streets and buildings were scarred and deserted. Where were all the people she knew that lived and worked here? What had happened to them and their families?

They reached the retail park. It, too, had witnessed violence and destruction and was trashed and desolate. Lisa stopped at the entrance. Anita pulled alongside her.

"Where's the chemist?"

"Over there." Lisa pointed to the other side of the car park. "Boots."

"Got it. Let's go."

"Hang on!" Lisa was hesitant.

"What's wrong? D'you see something?"

"No ... I'm just thinking. We're only a couple of miles away from home now. It's a straight road. I've got plenty of inhalers back there. I ..."

"Lisa! No! Just look at what happened back there. You *need* an inhaler. Jesus knows what could happen between here and there. What if we don't get there before you have another attack. It's not up for discussion. Come on!"

Anita pushed off and cycled across the car park.

Lisa took one last, long and wistful, look down the road ahead, then followed her.

They saw movement inside the store from about 50 metres away. They stopped and watched for a while from the cover of a car. The front window of the shop was smashed. Several infected wandered around inside as if they were browsing the aisles in search of their favourite brand of shampoo.

"How many?" Anita whispered.

"Can't get a good view. At least six. Maybe more."

"What d'you think? Too risky?"

"Maybe. It's impossible to tell from here."

"Where's the pharmacy section?" Anita asked.

Lisa grinned. "You genius! At the back! There's a

delivery area behind the shop."

They gave the shopfronts a wide berth as they cycled round to the delivery area. Conveniently, a Boots delivery truck signposted them to the right building. It had evidently been interrupted halfway through a delivery. A few broken cartons of toothpaste and mouthwash lay on the ground, and the back doors to the shop were open. They left their bikes propped up against a railing and crept inside.

They entered a large storage area. Rows of shelving piled high with boxes lined the room. Ahead, another set of double doors that led into the shop was also open. Lisa could see the aisles at the back of the shop where the baby care section was. She knew the pharmacy was just beyond it. They crouched down and crawled through the doors into the shop.

The light inside was blinding. It took their eyes a few minutes to adjust to it after the semi-darkness of the storeroom. Lisa pointed to the Pharmacy sign over to the right. Anita nodded and cast her eyes towards the infected at the front of the shop. They seemed undisturbed. She pointed to them, then to herself, and then at the floor. Lisa interpreted her signing to mean that she would stay where she was, to keep watch on them. She nodded her agreement.

With Anita focused on the infected, she crept over to the pharmacy area. She crawled beneath a gap in the counter and, still crouching out of sight, started to search the shelves. The inhalers were all located towards the far end of the section, a few shelves up.

She could see the familiar blue colour of the row of Ventolin boxes about shoulder height. She was going to have to stand up to get them.

She could hear the shuffling of the infected. They sounded close. She looked up at the Ventolin. She might as well grab a few while she was here. Who knew how long it would be until she could get any more? Trembling, she slowly and silently got to her feet until she was standing at her full height. The Ventolin was right in front of her.

She could sense, more than see, movement on her left. She slowly turned her head. An infected was standing just a few feet away with its back to her. She reached over and began to ease the boxes of Ventolin off the shelf.

One. She stuffed it inside her jacket.

Two. She tucked it in beside the other one.

Three.

The infected snuffled.

Lisa jumped. The box fell from her fingers and clattered onto the floor.

The infected snapped its head round.

For a split second, Lisa met its glassy stare.

It opened its mouth to moan.

Lisa didn't wait. She straddled the counter and ran, weaving between the aisles towards the back door.

"Anita! Anita! Move! Move!" she shouted.

Behind her there was crashing and banging and a frenzy of moaning, but she kept running.

The door was wide open, and Anita was frantically gesturing her in.

She crashed through and it slammed behind her.

She turned to see Anita slide her crowbar between the door handles. On the other side, the infected slammed into it, but it stayed shut. They ran outside, jumped onto their bikes and pedalled without looking back.

When they reached the main Stratford Road, they stopped again so that she could unpack the inhalers. She opened one and took a puff, for comfort more than necessity. Her breathing actually felt better than it had all day.

They had started the last leg of their journey. She couldn't believe it. Another ten minutes and they'd be there.

A strange sense of detachment began to creep over her. For a moment she had a feeling that none of it was real and the whole thing was just a hideous nightmare. But, the whirr of the bicycle wheels, her aching legs, and Anita's heavy breathing alongside her, brought her back to reality. It was real. This *was* happening and she was finally about to get home, where Neil was waiting for her.

She was both energised and terrified at the same time. Energised by the fact that what had felt like an endless journey was almost at an end, and that she was going to be reunited with Neil at last. But, terrified about what she might find and that, after it all, he might not be there. She focused on the work of powering the bike faster and faster. She remembered someone, somewhere, once telling her that the quads were the strongest muscles in the legs, and that efficient cycling required them to do all the work. She concentrated on pushing the

166

pedals up and down with her thighs. She considered telling Anita to do the same, but then decided she probably already knew that. She was an athlete after all. Instead, she remained silent, intent on her goal.

The last stretch of road that led into the village was in open countryside. The village was built on old greenbelt land and gave the illusion of being in a rural setting. All five roads in and out were the same, a couple of miles of nothing but open fields or woodland. She'd once heard it described as an Urb-Rur development: it was a new urban style housing estate in a rural setting. Residents referred to it as "The Village", but it was less than 15 years old.

It contained a mix of different types and styles of homes, from small flats and tiny terraced houses, to large expensive dwellings and even blocks of luxury apartments. At its centre, was a village green and children's play area. The green purported to be a cricket pitch and the road beside it was ambitiously named "Boundary Lane". She had never seen anyone play cricket there, other than a few children in the school holidays using their jumpers as stumps.

The village had its own primary school and nursery, health centre, village hall, library and even a small gym. It had one main street offering all the amenities of a self-contained settlement. There was a pub, a wine bar and a couple of restaurants, as well as a chemist, opticians, dentists, hairdressers and dry cleaners. The main shop was a Tesco Express but there were other small independent retailers selling everything from designer clothes, handbags and jewellery, to birthday cards and Yankee Candles.

Non-residents had been known to scoff when residents referred to it as a "village", but it had a strong sense of community, like many true villages had. Lisa and Neil had lived there for almost all of their ten years together and were very happy. Neil drank in the pub and used the gym, and Lisa was a member of the local pop choir and book club. They had a small, but strong, circle of close friends and got on well with their neighbours. It was close enough to the motorway network, rail and air links to be able to get pretty much anywhere quickly and easily. If they needed bigger or better shops, Solihull was ten minutes away and Birmingham city centre was only a 30-minute drive, or a 20-minute train ride from the station just a mile away. It was perfect for them. Their lives had been perfect. Lisa doubted that they ever would be again.

As they turned the last bend, the edge of the village came into view. Lisa's heart began to pound. The image of Neil sitting at the kitchen table came into her mind again, him working then turning and smiling at her. This time, he got up and took her in his arms. She pressed her face into his chest taking in his smell …

Suddenly, something slammed into her side. Her bike jolted to a stop and she was propelled forward over the handlebars. Time seemed to slow down as she flew through the air. She heard Anita cry out and was vaguely aware of a dark figure wrestling with her friend. She hit the ground hard. There was a burst of pain and flashing lights, before everything went dark.

J.M.MCKENZIE

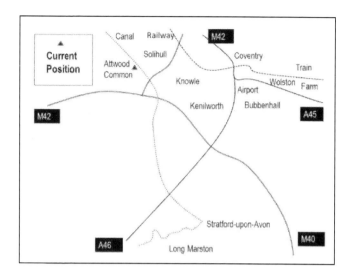

Chapter 8

Day 4 - Attwood Common

Lisa opened her eyes. The world was horizontal, and the tarmac felt rough against her cheek. Dazed, she pushed herself onto all fours, then back into a sitting position. She was in the middle of the road. It was empty in both directions. Anita and the bikes were gone, as were her backpack and spear.

She got unsteadily to her feet, testing her limbs for injuries. She was remarkably unscathed. The gardening gloves and thick cargo pants had done their job. The edge of the village was just ahead. She started walking.

She had no plan, nor any solid thoughts in her head as she walked. It just felt like the natural thing to do.

She walked over the humpback bridge that marked the entrance to the village, glancing down to the canal below. Everything was calm. Four or five ducks were bobbing on the murky water. Birds were singing. In the distance, she thought she heard children's laughter coming from the direction of the green. She felt peaceful and relaxed and utterly devoid of fear. A dog barked. She heard the buzz of a mower.

She turned onto the road that led to the centre of the village. The whole place looked completely untouched by the outbreak. There were no signs of looting or violence. None of the properties were damaged or boarded up.

There were some figures in the children's play area. A woman was slowly pushing a small child on one of the swings. The woman stopped pushing and turned to watch her as she passed. The swing slowed until it was barely moving, and the child also turned to stare at her. With a smile, the woman raised her hand and waved an acknowledgment. Lisa waved back. She felt good. Everything was ok.

She walked up the main street past the shops and restaurants. Again, all was well. Outside the wine bar, two elderly men on disabled scooters sat at a table. They were smoking and there were two pints of lager on the table beside them. Apart from them, the street was empty. The shops were closed but intact.

She reached the end of the road and turned onto her street. As she did, the neighbour's dog ran up to her, barking. She felt a tiny tremor of concern. That was unusual. He was an odd creature, prone to unexplained flare-ups of aggression. He'd bitten Neil on the leg once for absolutely no reason as he was getting out of the van. Since then, Peter and Jenny had kept him indoors, or muzzled and leashed when he was out.

She was almost there ... only a few more steps now.

She was at the front door when she realised she didn't have a key. Another pinprick of anxiety threatened to break through her state of tranquillity, before she noticed the door was ajar. But she was not surprised. Everything felt so right. She pushed open the door and walked into the kitchen.

Just as she'd imagined so many times, Neil was sitting at their kitchen table facing away from her. His back was straight and strong. He appeared to be concentrating, and his shoulder muscles flexed as he worked with something in his hands. She approached him slowly, her eyes filling with tears. All the fear and uncertainty of the past few days flooded over her. She knew he would be here. She knew he would be waiting for her. She reached out to touch him, her voice cracking as she spoke his name.

"Neil."

He turned around, suddenly aware of her presence. He stood up. His movements were awkward and jerky. A sound came from him that was not his voice, a sound that was now all too familiar. His eyes no longer twinkled with warmth but were clouded over and unseeing. His skin was grey. The thing he was working on was a human hand, ripped off at the wrist. He dropped the hand. It bounced on the kitchen floor spraying blood onto the light grey floor tiles.

She stepped back as he reached for her, a sneer deforming his features. He lurched towards her and gripped her around the shoulders, his bared teeth moving towards her neck. She put her hands against his chest trying to push him away, but he was too strong.

She cried out "Neil! It's me! Lisa." She felt his foul breath on her skin.

She grabbed the hair at the back of his head and tried to pull his head away, but it came away as a clump in her hand, bits of flesh clinging to the hairs. He bore down on her and she felt his teeth sink into her neck. There was pain and wet warmth, and she heard her own gurgling screams from somewhere outside her body before, for the second time that day, everything went black.

Lisa was struggling with someone who was calling her name.

"Lisa! Lisa! Jesus! It's me, Anita. You're ok."

Anita's face swam into view above her. She was frowning and looked concerned. Lisa was gripping Anita's wrists with both hands, pulling and twisting them. She let go. She tried to focus on where she

174

was. From the rocking movement and engine noise, she reasoned that they were in a vehicle. Her head throbbed and she felt dizzy and sick. She'd been dreaming. Still confused and disoriented, she was lucid enough to feel a massive sense of relief. She put her hands over her face.

"Oh my God! I had a terrible dream!"

"Clearly," Anita said wryly rubbing her reddened wrists. "But you're ok now. You're safe. Just chill."

"Where are we? Where are we going?"

"You were out cold after those little shits mugged us and stole our bikes. I half carried, half dragged, you back to the main road. It took forever. I was trying to find somewhere we could shelter before dark, when this truck came along. They've been out looking for survivors. So was the helicopter earlier, even though they nearly killed us. They're taking us to the safe zone."

Lisa sat up too quickly, reeling as a wave of dizziness hit her. "No! No! We were nearly there. I have to go back. *Please!*"

A rough male voice from the back of the truck addressed her.

"Lie down, Darling! You're not going anywhere but back to Long Marston, with us. It's almost dark, and you've got a bad case of concussion. You wouldn't last five minutes. Just settle down. We'll get you checked out by the medic, fed and watered, and after a good night's sleep you can take it from there."

"I'm sorry, Lisa. I didn't have a choice. I was really frightened. They rescued us. Rick's right. Just think

175

about it. You'd just get yourself killed, and what a waste that would be after all we've been through. Where would the lovely Neil be then? He might even be at the safe zone already. In fact, he probably is if he's got any sense."

The man spoke again.

"I can't believe you two have even got this far, fighting the undead with gardening gear," he snorted. "It's crazy out there, but you pair take the biscuit."

Lisa lay back and closed her eyes. Rick! Whether he'd saved them or not, already she'd taken a dislike to him and his sneering tone. Too woozy to argue, she drifted in and out of sleep for the rest of the journey.

The next time she woke was to the sound of heavy, metal gates creaking open. It was totally dark outside. Male voices barked at each other, and flashlights wavered as she was helped out of the van and into a brightly lit room. Her eyes hurt; her head pounded. She lay down gratefully on the low cot she was guided to, and allowed herself to be poked and prodded by, presumably, the medic. Someone asked her name, address and date of birth, and whether she knew what day it was. She mumbled her responses. Her pulse and blood pressure were measured, and her eyes were prized open one by one and an intense light was shone into them. Eventually, the lights were turned down and someone covered her with a fusty-smelling, rough blanket. She turned onto her side and slept deeply for the rest of the night, only occasionally aware of the hum of a generator outside and low voices in a corner of the room.

She slept most of the next day and night as well, stirring only when she was woken to have her pulse and blood pressure checked, or encouraged to sit up and drink some water. It was soothingly cool and quiet. During the day she was vaguely aware of a bustle of activity outside, vehicles coming and going, people moving back and forth and male and female voices. Part of her wanted to find out where she was and what was happening, but a bigger part just wanted to sleep. The sleepy part won until sometime just after dawn on the second day.

She awoke properly for the first time in almost 48 hours with what felt like the worst hangover she'd ever experienced. Her head throbbed, and she still felt sick and dizzy. The room she was in was actually a tent. There were four single cots in the space, but she was the only occupant. She was still happy just to lie there in the hope of sleeping it off.

A woman entered.

"Ah! You're awake at last. Good."

She was tall and slender, in army fatigues. Her long, dark hair was tied back untidily in a loose braid. She had dark circles under her eyes. She checked Lisa over again.

"You'll live," she said with a weary smile. "Take it easy for a couple of days and you'll soon be back to normal. You can go over to the main accommodation if you want. Your friend is waiting for you in the mess tent, I believe. I'll get Rick to take you over and show you around."

"What day is it?" Lisa asked.

"It's Tuesday. Six days after the attack. Feels like a hundred," the medic sighed.

Five minutes later, Rick appeared. Lisa recognised his voice from the previous night.

"Morning! Enjoy your nap? Sarah says you're ready to join the others now. Get your stuff together and I'll take you over."

Glancing around, Lisa realised she didn't have any "stuff". She didn't even have her gloves or goggles. He stood over her, watching in a way that made her feel uncomfortable for reasons she could not quite put her finger on, as, gingerly, she sat on the edge of the bed and put her boots on. Her head throbbed even more when she bent over, and after fiddling with them for a bit, she gave up on the laces. Rick turned and headed outside, and she shuffled after him.

She emerged from the tent, wincing in the bright sunshine. She was standing in a wide-open, grassy area surrounded by tents of various sizes. Some were small and dark green like the one she had been in, but others were much larger and made of a white, lighter fabric. A few soldiers were milling around near a line of trucks. Beyond the tents, she saw a helicopter taking off in the distance.

Rick led her over to one of the larger tents. Inside were long rows of tables and chairs. There were people everywhere. Civilian men, women and children were sitting at the tables. Some were eating, some were nursing hot drinks in tin cups and talking, a few were reading or playing cards, and some were just sitting quietly staring into their drinks. A few children were running about between the tables.

Since the beginning, Lisa had not seen so many healthy, living people all together in one place. It felt strange, surreal, and in complete contrast to the isolation of the past few days, when they had barely seen another living soul.

Someone called her name, and Anita jumped up from a group of people at a table in the far corner. She ran over, her face breaking into a broad grin, and hugged Lisa tightly.

"Are you feeling better? You look better. Isn't this great! We made it, Lisa. Jesus! We're safe. Come and meet some of the others."

She took her hand dragging her over to a table occupied by a teenage couple, three women in their early thirties, and two men, who looked like a father and son. The women stood up and welcomed her, making room at the table. The teenagers glanced at her in a disinterested way, and the two men looked up briefly, the younger one offering a distracted smile. She sat down. Bemused, and although she was not really hungry, she accepted a coffee in a tin mug and a mess tin full of porridge sprinkled with a generous spoonful of white sugar.

Anita was talking constantly, rejoicing that they had made it to the safe zone, telling her all about the camp and its residents and routines. Her chatter was punctuated by flashing smiles, pats and hugs. Her dark cheeks were pink with excitement. Suddenly thrust from the quiet stillness of the medical tent into this crowded noisy environment, Lisa was disoriented. It was so strange to suddenly be with other survivors.

But Anita seemed to have settled right in. She was more animated and talkative than Lisa had ever seen her. For the first time, she truly appreciated the magnitude of what the girl had done for her, and what she had given up in terms of her own needs and desires by accompanying her on her quest. At that moment, she realised she loved her for that. Whatever happened from now on, she would never forget it.

She listened as the group exchanged their survival stories, theories about what had caused the outbreak and about what the future held. But Lisa was struggling. As well as the nausea and banging headache, the realisation that she had got so close to home, and Neil, before she was snatched away, was beginning to sink in. She felt flat and down. She couldn't make herself care about these strangers and their stories and theories.

As the group talked, she looked up from her porridge from time to time, nodding, smiling or frowning in the right places. But she had only one thing on her mind, and that was to get out of there as soon as possible and find Neil. Admittedly, he might be here, as Anita suggested, but she seriously doubted it. If her instincts were right, she had to get out of here as soon as possible and head back to Attwood Common. She wasn't totally stupid though. She understood that she needed to rest and recover for a bit, or it would be a suicide mission. But, as soon as she felt better, she had to leave. This time, to avoid any more near disasters, she was going to need a better plan.

After breakfast, Anita took Lisa on a tour of the camp, partly to help her get her bearings, but also to see if they could find Neil, or at least rule out the possibility that he was there.

"I've asked around, but no-one has come across a Neil. But I don't really know what he looks like. And I don't know his last name! Your last name! Jesus! How crazy is that?"

"Crazy!" Lisa nodded, instantly regretting it as fresh new waves of pain crashed against her skull.

"Well?" Anita said.

"Huh?"

"What is it? Your last name."

"Oh, it's Saunders. What's yours?"

"Holder. Anita Naomi Holder. Come on Lisa Saunders. Let's go and find your husband."

The girl chattered away as she strode across the compound. Lisa hurried after her, as quickly as her headache would allow.

"As well as the army tents and the mess tents, there are 18 disaster relief tents. Each one takes about 40 survivors and they're still putting up more. There's got to be 700 people here already, and more are arriving every day. Jesus! Isn't that amazing?"

"Amazing," Lisa quietly agreed.

"It all seems pretty well-organised. They must have a register of some kind coz everyone has to give their name and address when they arrive."

They made their way to the main tent where most of the army comings and goings seemed to emanate from. After several initial futile attempts to attract someone's attention, they were eventually directed to another smaller tent towards the far edge of the camp.

Inside, a spotty boy soldier, who could have been no more than 18, worked his way through a ring binder containing the names of all the occupants of the camp in alphabetical order.

"No, sorry ladies, there's no record of a Neil Saunders arriving or leaving since the camp was first set up on Day 4."

"Have people left?" Lisa asked.

"Not many, but a few. Sometimes people have found out that their relatives have been in another camp, or holed up somewhere else and they've gone to try and find them."

"Other camps?" Anita and Lisa asked in unison.

"Yes." He looked up in surprise. "There are eleven in England, four in Scotland and two in Wales, so far."

"Do you have a record of the people in the other camps?" Anita asked.

"To an extent. I can't promise that they're up-to-date, but when we have been able to communicate with any of the others, we have taken names."

"Can you look for my parents?" Anita continued. "Please? Mr. and Mrs. Holder. From Epsom."

The boy flicked though a couple of other ring binders. After a few moments his fingers stopped on an entry and he looked up.

182

"Natasha and Peter? Northcroft Road? There's another person listed with them. A Tyler Holder."

"My brother. Jesus! That's them. They're all alright!" Anita sat down and closed her eyes. "Oh, thank God! I can't believe it." She was shaking.

"Oh, I'm so pleased for you, Nita." Lisa dropped to her knees in front of her and took her trembling hands in her hers. "That's fantastic news."

Anita looked at her. "I'm sorry, Lisa. Neil's not on the list. I feel bad."

"It's ok, Nita. Honestly, I know he's at home. I just know it. It's all going to be fine."

Thanking the boy, they turned to leave the tent.

"You might want to check the message boards, just in case," he called after them.

"Message boards?" Lisa asked Anita.

"I know where they are," Anita said, pointing to the other end of the row of tents. "I've already had a look but let's check them out again."

At the opposite edge of the camp, close to the perimeter, was a row of wire-mesh barriers that served as the camp message board. As they got closer, the women stopped and took in the scene before them. The barriers were covered with hundreds of messages.

Some were neatly typed, others were handwritten, and some were scribbled on scraps of paper with whatever had been to hand at the time. Some were on postcards, some were wrapped in plastic to protect them from the elements, and others were tattered and torn, or had partially disintegrated in the recent rain, their ink smudged and barely legible.

Some were factual, giving details and descriptions of missing people, while others were emotional and desperate pleas for help to find loved ones. Most were from survivors, who, having made it to safety themselves, were seeking information about friends and family, but some were more altruistic, providing information about people they'd met on their journeys.

There were prayers and poems, prophecies and postulations. There were ribbons and faded flowers and photographs. Hundreds of images captured in happier times, of missing men and women and children of all ages, gazing out from the crowd of lost souls.

Lisa's mind flashed back to all the infected they'd seen, and those that they'd killed, over the past few days. Were any of them these people? A tear rolled down her cheek. She brushed it away and concentrated on searching for anything that might mention Neil. Had he met anyone heading for the safe zone? Had he given them a message for her?

Together they scanned the sea of messages for something of any significance. For almost an hour they looked. It was a harrowing task. The tragic and desperate words and images haunted them for days afterwards. Eventually, emotionally exhausted, they agreed that there was nothing of relevance. They'd covered the entire length of the barriers twice. Lisa's head was thumping again. She was desperate to lie down.

Anita took her to the large tent that they were

sleeping in and showed her to her cot. They were arranged in four rows of ten, lined up nose to tail. The layout aimed to prevent strangers from having to sleep side by side, affording a scrap of privacy in the most public of circumstances.

Lisa slept for the rest of the afternoon and woke at six, her headache easier for the first time since she'd arrived. She got up and wandered over to the mess tent, thirsty and relieved to be finally feeling a bit better. Anita was sitting with the same group as before at the same table. Lisa joined them and, for the first time, started to listen to their stories.

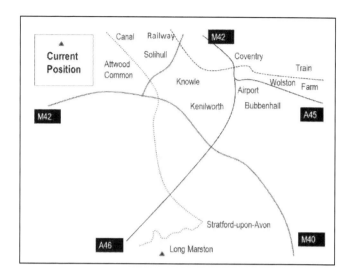

Chapter 9

Day 6 - Long Marston

The mood amongst the survivors was a strange mix of relief at having made it to a place of safety, and shock and distress about their experiences before they got there, heightened by an acute anxiety about the future. All had lost people to the infection. Some had been forced to commit unspeakable acts to survive. Most had no idea where their missing friends and family were. Husbands and wives had not returned from work that day; children had not come home from school. Many, like Lisa and Anita, had been away from home when it began and had not been able to return, nor contact their loved ones.

The teenage couple always sat away from the rest of the group at the far end of the table. Lee and Emma were from Solihull. They were studying in Stratford-on-Avon and had stayed on for a drink after lectures on the day of the outbreak. They had been in a bar down near the river when the first reports of the crisis began to filter through. They'd not taken much notice at first, but as the evening had gone on, and the bar slowly emptied around them, they had begun to realise how serious it was.

When the bar staff announced that they were closing early and advised them to go home, they decided to heed their advice. It was only then they discovered that none of the buses or trains were running, and that all the phone lines were jammed so they couldn't contact their parents. They were left with no choice but to wait it out until morning, and had spent the night huddled together on the bandstand in the middle of the riverside park opposite the town centre.

The next day, from their relatively safe vantage point, they watched the chaos that was ensuing across the river and were afraid to move. Terrified and confused, they had crouched on the bandstand for most of the morning. When a few infected eventually appeared on their side of the river, they chose to make a run for it, heading out of the town into the Warwickshire countryside. Unknowingly, they had headed straight towards Long Marston and were picked up by the military on Day 2 before the camp had even been properly established.

They had been there ever since. They hadn't found out anything about their friends or family from the army records, the message boards, nor any of the other survivors. (Lisa shuddered when she recalled the destruction they had seen in Solihull and was not surprised that the pair had heard nothing.) However, the young couple seemed oddly unconcerned, apparently content to simply be together, smooching and snuggling in their cosy corner of the mess tent. They had that enviable teenage ability to be completely absorbed in each other, and indifferent towards everything and everyone else around them.

The three women were friends from London, who had been in Oxford for an extended hen weekend. Two were married and had young families back at home with their partners. They had arrived in Oxford on the Thursday night and were due to leave on the Tuesday morning. Fortuitously for them all, the bride-to-be was marrying a senior civil servant, and he had contacted her as soon as he realised what was happening. He instructed them to lock themselves into their room at the Malmaison and stay there until he sent help. By the time they were successfully extracted by a bemused Special Forces team 24 hours later, they had consumed the entire contents of their mini-bars and in-room snacks, and used up all of the free toiletries.

The two married women had since discovered that

189

their families were safely ensconced in another camp in Sussex. They were fortunate, and they knew it. Lisa thought at times that they almost seemed to be enjoying themselves. They were calm and seemingly blissfully unaware of the real horror unfolding outside the perimeter of the camp. If they were disturbed by some of the stories they had heard, they were concealing it remarkably well.

Lisa and Anita's experience had been tougher than that of Lee, Emma and the trio of women. However, they had had it easy compared to the father and son. Their story was as hard to hear as it was for them to tell. The son, Peter, was profoundly traumatised and his father had an air of deep sadness about him. They were rarely apart and spent most of their time alternating between bouts of weeping and efforts to comfort and console each other. There was a faraway look in their eyes that told Lisa they had been damaged, possibly irreparably, by what they had experienced. She had never heard their story directly, but Anita had told her what had happened to them, sparing none of the shocking details.

On the night of the outbreak, the father, Geoff, and his wife, had both made it safely home from work to their home in the sleepy market town of Alcester. Peter, who worked with his father in the family business in Evesham, had also made it home, collecting his small son from the child-minder, before securing the house and waiting anxiously for his wife to get back. She worked in Birmingham city centre, which had been badly affected early on.

She did make it home later that evening but was injured and seemed unwell. She had been attacked in the street on her way to her car. She had got away and managed to drive herself home, despite having been badly bitten on the shoulder. Peter had cleaned and dressed her injuries as best he could and had given her some paracetamol for her fever. He assumed that she was experiencing a simple bacterial infection. However, when her condition deteriorated a few hours later, he had taken his whole family over to his parents' home. As well as seeking help and support in dealing with his sick wife and frightened child, he had also simply wanted them all to be together as the terrible events of that first night unfolded.

After settling his wife into bed with their son, Peter joined his parents downstairs to follow events on the TV and social media. Of course, the inevitable had occurred. His wife had died and reanimated, killing both her own son and her mother-in law when she had gone up to check on them. The first that the two men knew about it was when the infected trio had made their way downstairs. What happened next was a horror that required no explanation.

The listening to, and retelling of, hundreds of different stories of survival was the main activity in the camp, as people waited to find out what the future would hold. For Lisa and Anita, a clearer picture began to emerge of how the infection had spread so far, so quickly. As they already knew, there had been multiple attacks on trains and other forms of public transport. The timing of the attack to coincide with the rush hour had meant that millions of commuters were moving about, and the infection had spread rapidly. Many people, like Peter's wife, had been bitten but had made it home and subsequently infected their families. Towns and cities fell with startling speed, emergency services were overwhelmed, and panic and confusion took over. The military were mobilised within 24 hours, and urban areas were evacuated, unwittingly carrying the infection in ever-increasing numbers into rural areas. It was a perfectly planned and executed attack. Communication channels were choked, and the lack of accurate information and advice led people to behave in ways that enabled the infection to spread rapidly.

By Day 3, the whole country was in the grip of the infection. What was left of the government and the military agreed that their first priority was to create safe zones at various locations around the country and move all survivors into these secure areas as soon as possible. In the first instance, the aim was to try and halt the spread. After that, they could begin think about what to do next.

They sent units out daily in trucks and helicopters both to find and bring back survivors, but also to distribute leaflets telling people where the safe zones were and how to get there. Most people in the camp had been picked up by one of these patrols. Very few had got there independently. Lisa and Anita instantly gained the admiration and respect of everyone who heard their story. Two young women, surviving out there on their own for so long was almost unheard of.

The airfield was the perfect location for the safe zone. It was a large flat site surrounded by countryside, with clear views in all directions and a couple of readymade watchtowers. Its perimeter was already securely fenced, due to its historic function as a military base, and latterly as a venue for outdoor events such as drag racing, car boot sales and concerts. Lisa recalled spending a wild night there with Neil at a music festival, a few years ago.

But it was barely recognisable now. At the very heart of the site was a large, triangular grassy space delineated by interconnecting runways. A wire fence had been erected around this and it was here that the main camp had been set up. The army had reinforced the pre-existing perimeter fencing around the outer edge of the runways to form a second line of defence. Powerful floodlights, powered by the generators, lit up the space between the camp and the wooded boundary of the airfield. Troops patrolled the runways 24 hours a day, ensuring that any infected who made it onto the site never reached the camp itself. In addition to all of this, the remote rural setting meant that the numbers of infected in the area were low.

While there was clearly an ever-present risk of attack from outside, the biggest threat was the introduction of the infection into the camp, and its transmission between the survivors within. Everyone was checked head to toe for bites, scratches, flushing or fever before they were allowed in. Anita explained to Lisa that this had been done to her by Rick, while she was still unconscious on the truck. She pushed away the image of his rough hands exploring her body and touching her skin without her knowledge or permission.

A quarantine area had been set up in some buildings outside the main camp. Anyone with suspicious injuries or symptoms was held there in isolation for 48 hours. An occasional burst of gunfire from that direction signified the demise of some poor soul who had proved to be beyond help.

There were still many unanswered questions, mainly around who had carried out the attack and why. Various religious and far-right, extremist groups were the chief suspects, but no-one had actually claimed responsibility. Or, if they had, no-one had been left to hear their message. If someone had been trying to get the world to sit up and take notice, their plan had seriously misfired. What would be the point in destroying the whole country … maybe even the whole world?

Was it just the UK that was affected? No-one seemed to know the full story. Although initial reports had claimed the whole of Western Europe was involved, the word on the ground was that it was just the UK. But then, where was the help from our allies in Europe? Why were survivors not being airlifted out of the country to safety? Geoff raised the point that they might want to avoid the risk of spreading the infection to the continent. As an island, the UK was the perfect natural containment area. Lisa thought he was probably right. They were most likely to be on their own - for the moment anyway. Where *was* the government? Had they survived? What were they doing?

The only activity the military seemed to be engaged with, and interested in, was getting all survivors to the safe zones to halt the spread of infection. When survivors asked questions about what was going to happen next, they were met with silence and blank looks. If anyone had a plan or an inkling of an idea about what the future might look like, they were keeping it very close to their chests.

The military were constantly busy organising the survivor searches and maintaining the infrastructure and organisation of the camp. Some survivors with particular skills and abilities had been commissioned to help them with specific tasks, but for the majority it was all about existing ... and waiting.

Their day began early. Sleep did not come easily in a space occupied by 40 troubled souls. The nights were filled with whispers and quiet weeping, coughing, moaning, and restless tossing and turning on the flimsy cots. Occasionally, nightmares would evoke cries or screams of terror, followed by murmurs and more crying. Throughout the night, there was a steady procession of people tiptoeing barefoot in and out of the tent for a cigarette, to use the portable toilets or simply to get a bit of privacy or fresh air.

As soon as it was light, it was viewed acceptable to get up, and the whole camp was usually awake and up and about just after dawn. There were no showers, as water was largely restricted for drinking. Every survivor was given a plastic bottle containing a small daily allowance for washing and other essentials. People would use the last of the previous day's allowance to freshen up the best they could before heading to the mess tent for a refill and a cup of tea or coffee.

Meals were staggered, with different serving times for different tents. Lisa and Anita's breakfast slot was between seven and seven-fifteen. The queues were long and slow but no-one seemed to mind. It passed the time. Lunch was at a quarter to one and dinner at six-thirty. Food seemed to be plentiful, and drinking water was unrestricted. In between meals, people lingered in the mess tent, lay on their cots or wandered around the camp. After dinner at eight, people would slowly make their way back to the sleeping tents, many just relieved to have made it through another day, content to lie down and invite sleep to envelop and comfort them, ready to see what, if anything, the following day would bring.

This general air of passivity infuriated Lisa, and she could see that it was beginning to irritate Anita, as her initial euphoria was fading. Admittedly, it was early days, and people were shocked and exhausted, but it felt wrong to just be hanging around, waiting to be told what to do. Lisa was itching to leave, but Anita and the medic insisted she stay and recover for at least another couple of days. She knew herself that she was not fully fit. She still had a dull headache and bouts of terrible tiredness, when all she wanted to do was lie down and sleep. She recognised that she wasn't ready and accepted that she had a better chance of success if she was strong, fresh and clear-headed when she made her next move.

And so, she waited. She slept in her creaky cot, she queued for her meals, she sat in the mess tent with the others nursing cups of coffee, and she wandered round the camp and watched the comings and goings of the military.

In the centre of the camp was a small, wooded area known as The Copse. She'd found a quiet spot there, where she could sit, unnoticed, on a pile of discarded pallets under the shade of an ancient oak tree and watch what was going on.

As time passed, a subtle, but tangible, air of tension was building among the soldiers. At first, they had seemed tired but still friendly, exchanging banter with each other and the survivors. Now, when they returned to camp, they were quiet and subdued, shoulders slumped and heads down. Fewer and fewer survivors were arriving at the camp and those that did were in a bad way, either physically, when they were taken straight to the quarantine area, or mentally, when they were clearly exhausted, and deeply traumatised.

The number of infected that were getting onto the airfield was increasing, too. At first, only one or two a day had reached the camp perimeter. That had grown into a slow but steady trickle when, every hour or so, one would emerge from the treeline and weave across the open ground towards the runway. Initially, the patrols had dealt with them easily, but by Thursday, the trickle had become a steady flow and, outnumbered, the soldiers were forced to retreat back inside the camp. They still patrolled the fence, but now dealt with the clamouring groups of infected outside from behind the safety of the barriers.

By Friday, the bursts of gunfire that had previously been sporadic and alarming, had become part of the regular background noise in the camp. Occasionally, a particularly large group of infected would threaten to breach the perimeter simply through the pressure of bodies surging against the fence. It would sway and lean inwards precariously provoking screams of terror from nearby survivors. There would be running and shouting and gunfire for a while until order was restored.

There were piles of bodies accumulating around the outside of the fence. The stench permeated into the camp, especially when the wind blew in the wrong direction. At first, groups of soldiers had gone out in trucks to try and clear them but latterly they had given up what was proving to be a pointless task.

Lisa occasionally saw Rick coming and going in the midst of it all, but he either didn't recognise her or was ignoring her. He was unshaven and had a new gaunt, hollow-eyed look about him that she didn't like. It made her nervous.

She suspected that the military were gradually losing control. Everything pointed to it. The trucks rarely went out anymore. The helicopters only made a couple of trips a day now. How much fuel did they have? How much ammunition? How much food and water? She got the feeling that they were waiting now as well, keeping up appearances but waiting to be told what to do next, just like the survivors. The other survivors appeared oblivious, just content to be alive and to wait until someone else sorted it all out for them. They seemed paralysed by inertia. Lost in their own little worlds of shock, grief and denial.

The deception was easy to maintain because the military didn't mix with the survivors. There was a firm and deliberate *us and them* culture. They slept and ate in different areas. They were in charge and they made that very clear. They communicated formally with the survivors only when they had to, and that was not very often. If anyone asked what was going on and what the plan was, they always got the same answer. They were searching for survivors. Trying to get them all to safety and stop the spread of infection. There was no mention of what would happen after that. Lisa was sure they didn't know.

From her discreet observation point, she had tried to work out how many of them there were. There had always been three or four groups of two or three soldiers out in the trucks or helicopters, and a guard patrol of another two or three. Including the catering team, the medic and the register boy, there could only have been about 20 of them at the most. Not enough to protect hundreds of survivors from the thousands of walking dead that seemed to be headed their way.

By the Friday evening, Lisa was sure that all was not well in the camp, and that it was only a matter of time before the safe zone was no longer going to be safe. In fact, it was in danger of becoming a potential death trap. It was now over a week since she had awoken to the horror on the train, and the urge to get home was stronger than ever. She felt good now, too. Fully recovered and reenergised. Her headache was gone completely, and she felt fresh and alert. It was time to go.

After dinner, she asked Anita to go for a walk with her. They walked away from the survivor tents towards the edge of the camp. It was a clear moonlit night. There was no breeze, and the smell of death was strong. The groans of the undead seemed to come from all around them. Bursts of gunfire rattled in the background every few minutes. She stopped at the pile of pallets under the oak tree and sat down. She patted the space beside her, but Anita stayed standing.

"What's going on, Lisa?"

"I'm leaving in the morning. You don't have to come, but I'd really like you to. It's not safe here anymore."

The girl didn't speak.

"We were never going to stay here forever, Nite. Come on. You knew that. I know you think it's safe here but just look around you. Listen! We're surrounded. They're losing control, and the people here are all asleep! They're in total denial. When it all goes wrong - and it will, very soon, believe me - it's going to be *really* bad. All these people in one confined space! It doesn't bear thinking about. I honestly think we should take our chances outside again, before it all kicks off."

"Oh *Jesus*, Lisa! Just say it! Don't treat me like an idiot! You just want to try and get back to Neil. Again! Don't try and pretend that now you suddenly don't think it's safe here anymore."

"I'm not pretending! It's *not* safe! I've been watching what's going on. They're losing it! Of course, I want to try and get back to Neil. Nothing's changed as far as that's concerned. But, I'm serious. I've got a really bad feeling about this place."

"Oh, why can't you just face it, Lisa! You're never going to get back home to him. You can't do it. You'll never make it. *You're* the one who's asleep. You need to wake up!"

"I *am* awake! I'm the only one who is! They're losing the fight. Any day now, we'll be overwhelmed."

"You don't know that. They're getting ready to get us all out. To move into the next phase. In the meantime, we are with other people, we have somewhere to sleep, food and water, and the protection of armed soldiers. Have you forgotten what it was like out there?"

"Of course, I haven't, but we did ok! We survived. We almost made it!"

"Yeah, but we *didn't* make it, did we? Yes, we survived, for a time, but I don't know how to be honest. I think we were lucky. It was only a matter of time."

"Of course, we weren't *lucky*. We were strong. Smart. Determined. We could be again."

"Look, Lisa, even if Neil is alive, and that's a massive "if" - I'm sorry but that's the truth - the first thing he's going to do when he realises you're not coming home any time soon, is to come and look for you *here*!"

"No! He wouldn't! He ..."

"Oh *Jesus*! What is wrong with you?"

"I'm sorry, Nita. I'm going. I have to. You don't have to come with me. I want you to, but you don't have to."

"You *know* that's not going to happen! You know I can't let you go back out there on your own. You're so selfish! I hate you! What choice do I have? I *have* to come."

"You're making the right decision. Yes, you have to come. Not for me, but for *you*! Honestly."

"*Oh my God*!" Anita wailed at the sky.

She began to weep. Lisa got up and tried to put her arms around her, but she pushed her away. Lisa let her cry, waiting in silence until her sobs subsided.

Anita's voice was thick with emotion when she eventually spoke. "What's your plan, then? It'd better be a good one!"

Lisa hugged her. She felt a mixture of relief and exhilaration that they were leaving, and pure ice cold, gut-tightening fear of what lay ahead. A huge burden of guilt and responsibility bore down on her. She knew she had forced the younger woman into a corner. She *had* to make it home, now more than

202

ever. As well as finding Neil, she had to keep her friend safe, too. This time she couldn't fail. The stakes were way too high. They were running out of options. She started to describe her plan.

J.M.MCKENZIE

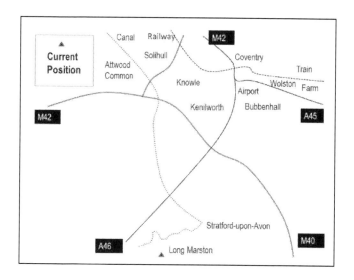

Chapter 10

Day 10 - Long Marston

The next day, they were up before dawn. They managed to track down Rick and explain their intentions. He looked exhausted: a shadow of the arrogant character who had brought them into the camp just a few days ago.

"Whatever! Your decision!" He seemed disinterested and ambivalent.

"Follow me."

He trudged over to a nearby supply tent, lifted the flap and gestured inside.

"Take whatever you need."

205

He turned as if to walk away then paused, turned back, and stared at them. Lisa saw something in his eyes. A flicker of emotion.

"You'll need these."

He unlocked a metal container and handed them a couple of pistols. He showed them how to turn the safety catches on and off, how to aim and fire and how to carry them securely. He watched as they stuffed as many as they could of the army issue pouches of dried food that they called MRE meals into a couple of rucksacks.

"There are thousands of these things around the site you know. You'll never make it to the main gates on foot."

"We'll take our chances. We know what we're doing," Lisa said.

"Seriously, I know everyone thinks you're a couple of superwomen who've seen and done it all, but even *you* don't know how bad it's got out there."

"Well, thanks for the advice and all that, but we've made up our minds and we're going. So, we'll just have to face whatever we face." Anita spoke this time.

"Between you and me, Ladies. You might just be doing the right thing. Hrmm …!" He hesitated. "Things aren't looking too good here. Not going to plan … if there ever was a plan."

"You don't have to be a genius to see that" Lisa said. "Come with us."

"I can't. Not an option. Like you say, I'll have to face whatever I have to face, but … I could give you a lift to the main road."

"Really? Why would you do that?" Lisa looked at him suspiciously.

"Wow! That would be amazing! Thank you!" Anita frowned at Lisa.

By nine, they were in the back of a speeding truck with Rick at the wheel, weaving expertly through throngs of clawing infected. The view of the camp behind them was gradually obscured by the horde as it closed back in after their passing. It suddenly seemed tiny and insignificant in their midst. Lisa was surer than ever that those left behind were doomed. They were already vastly outnumbered, and it was impossible to foresee anything but a negative outcome, unless something changed dramatically in the next few days. She tried not to think about it. She turned away and focused on the route ahead.

The crowds thinned out the closer they got to the edge of the airfield. Rick made a U-turn close to the main entrance and indicated to them to get out. There were a few infected around but not enough to give them any serious trouble. As soon as they had left the vehicle he headed back to the camp. He never said a word, but Lisa saw something in his face. Maybe, admiration. Maybe envy.

"Jesus! Weird guy." Anita muttered.

They sprinted up a small mound immediately on their left, towards the carcass of an old, World War Two fighter plane, its nose painted in a fearsome mask with glaring eyes and bared, pointed teeth. They slid underneath the body of the plane and lay on their bellies in the long cool grass.

They were near the main road that led back to Stratford-on-Avon. The previous night, Lisa had explained her plan to Anita. She'd had a look at some local maps that the soldiers were using and had worked out that, if they travelled due north, they would hit the River Avon in just a few miles. The river was part of the British Waterways network and linked to the Stratford Canal in Stratford-on-Avon. Then, it ran all the way into Birmingham, passing right along the southern edge of Attwood Common.

Ever since they had been on the canal side in Knowle, she had been thinking about what it was like down there. There were few, if any, infected or survivors along the towpaths. The canal boats were sturdy and high-sided. They were fuel-efficient and self-contained. If they could find one and get it going, they'd have a comfortable shelter, a place of safety and a vehicle, all rolled into one. In Lisa's mind, it was the perfect solution.

Anita hadn't been so sure, almost scathing. *Wouldn't they be locked up? Didn't they need a key to turn the engine on? Even if they did find one that they could get into and start the engine, could she even steer it? What about locks? Did she know what to do with these?*

Lisa had explained that she had been on a canal boat holiday with some friends when she was at university. The boys had steered the boat, but it hadn't looked all that difficult. You didn't even need a licence, for God's sake! People could turn up at the hire centre and be on the water after 15 minutes instruction. How difficult could it be?

"Be positive, Nita," she'd pleaded. "We can do it; I know we can!"

"We could just stay here," Anita had moaned.

From their vantage point, they scanned the area and identified their route. They decided to avoid the road itself but to keep close enough to it to be able to use it as a guide to their direction of travel. The night before, they had also discussed how to stay as safe as possible while they were on the move. The infected were not the only danger. It was a group of fellow survivors that had mugged them for their bicycles, and they had to try and avoid any similar encounters. They had agreed to try and move quickly from one place of cover to another and keep out of sight as much as possible.

They identified a clear route to a small cluster of bushes a few hundred metres away. On Anita's signal, they wriggled out from under the plane and ran over to it, concealing themselves again before identifying their next point of cover and then repeating the whole process. Although it may have been unnecessarily cautious, it gave them a sense of security. The moments spent in the hiding spots provided a temporary, but welcome, respite from the heart-pounding anxiety of running across exposed ground.

They travelled like this for several miles making good progress in small stages. There were infected around, but most seemed intent on travelling towards the camp and didn't notice the two women.

On a couple of occasions, they were forced to

crouch in silence barely breathing, staring at each other with wide eyes and fingers on lips, as an infected stumbled past their hiding place. Generally, they were easy to see or hear as they meandered across the fields or rustled through the bushes, but, increasingly, the smell was the first indication that one was nearby.

Ten days into the outbreak, most were in the advanced stages of decomposition. They were more disgusting than ever, their skin now more green than grey and beginning to sag from their bodies in drooping folds. They smelt putrid and rotten, like meat that had spoiled or a strong cheese that had been out of the fridge for too long. The smell was cloying and lingered in the air and in the women's nostrils long after the infected had passed. The only thing Lisa could recall that even began to get close was the odour of her grandfather's infected leg ulcers. On a couple of occasions, she'd been visiting when the District Nurse had changed his dressings. As the bandages were unravelled, the bottom layers had been soaked in a pinkish, yellow fluid. When the bottom layer of pus-soaked gauze was removed, the odour arising from the moist open sores was enough to send her gagging from the room.

It was around midday when they reached a large water treatment plant about a hundred metres from the river. Helping each other to slip under the fence, they made their way to the centre. Concealed between the wide basins and oblivious to the aroma of raw sewage, they celebrated the completion of the first stage of their plan with a bottle of water, fortified with a sachet of energy powder and a jam sandwich from one of the MRE ration packs that Rick had given them. They rested in the relative safety of their location for a while, feeling virtually jovial about how well things had gone so far.

Next, they needed to find a boat. They left the shelter of the sewage plant, crossed a small road and, following a line of trees, made their way down to the river. At the point where they reached it, they had a good view along its length in both directions. It was a warm and still afternoon, but it was cool and shady under the trees that lined the riverbank. The dark water silently coursed towards its destination. It moved with power and speed, only evidenced by the passage of small twigs and leaves on its surface. The foliage that adorned its banks was alive with wildlife. Small birds flitted across the surface of the water, feeding on unsuspecting insects. The two women savoured the tranquillity and normality of the moment. It was easy to imagine for a moment that nothing had changed, and all was still well with the world.

Apart from the nearby sewage works, the side of the river they were on was devoid of buildings for as far as they could see. However, the opposite bank was occupied by a row of large, luxurious homes, the gardens of which stretched down to the river, often marked by a deck, a boathouse or a jetty. There were boats moored at some of these, not canal boats, but small rowing boats and motorboats.

"What do you think, Lise? Can we get across?"

"Not sure, the river looks deep and fast moving. If we really have to, we could probably swim it, but I still think a canal boat would be way better if we could find one. They're bigger and stronger and more fuel efficient. Let's go a bit further up?"

"Your plan, your call," Anita nodded.

As they headed along the edge of the river, Lisa's thoughts drifted to the last time they'd walked along a riverbank together, after abandoning Brian and the X-Trail outside Coventry. There was pretty sure that this was the same river. She had a vague recollection that the Avon started somewhere in Northamptonshire and passed through Warwickshire and Stratford-on-Avon on its way to join the Severn at Tewkesbury.

It felt a bit like being reunited with an old friend after a long time apart. It had led them to safety then, and she was sure it would do so again now. So much had happened and so much had changed since then that it might as well have happened in another lifetime. Their world had changed forever. They had been changed forever by it. They were completely different people now from the two dishevelled and frightened girls who had picked their way along its muddy edge with no idea what was happening to them and what to do next. Now they were bold, resilient and clear-headed. They had a plan. They knew what they were doing. Slowly, but surely, they were adapting to their environment. And, like the river, Lisa felt that they were also bigger and stronger, with more power and more momentum.

She was jolted out of her reflections when Anita, who was a few steps ahead, stopped and turned back with a big smile, pointing at the river ahead. Lisa looked up to see a long, blue and white canal boat straddling the width of the river. It appeared to be caught at one end in some roots on the bank.

They approached. It looked deserted. Anita was fast. Scampering down the riverbank, she hopped nimbly across the exposed roots onto the small front deck of the boat. Lisa was slower, edging carefully down the steep bank and negotiating the slippery knot of twisted tubers. By the time she joined Anita on the boat, the younger woman had already opened the door and was peering inside. The smell was choking. Anita turned to Lisa her eyes wide and her hand raised in a warning gesture.

The infected rushed from the interior, knocking Anita off balance with a screech of rage. The decimated carcass of a small, grey-haired woman in a gore-splattered, yellow tee-shirt and blue jeans grabbed her by the throat and pushed her backwards, teeth gnashing inches away from her face.

For a split second, Lisa considered going for the gun that was firmly secured in the back waistband of her trousers, but instead seized a handful of hair, pulling the head back and away from Anita's face. Although some hair ripped away from the rotting scalp, she got enough of a hold to give Anita space to bring both her knees up and plant her feet in the centre of its torso. She pushed her legs out hard and

213

fast, propelling the creature back against the edge of the boat.

Its upper body swayed precariously over the water. For a moment it looked as though it might not go in, but Lisa provided a helping hand by lifting its ankles and deftly tipping it over. It entered the water and disappeared under the surface with a surprisingly small splash, more of a plop really. When it reappeared, it had already been carried a few metres downstream by the strong current. They watched its bobbing head drift into the distance.

"That was a close one." Anita rubbed her neck.

"You've got to slow down, Nita. Just slow down and think!"

They turned their attention back to the boat. Peering inside, they could see into the living and galley area of the boat. It was empty, but they couldn't see beyond into the sleeping area.

"Let's go over the top." Anita was already clambering up the side of the boat onto the roof.

"Take it easy. *Slow down!*" Lisa followed her.

They crept along the roof to the cockpit at the other end. The double doors were ajar, and some steep steps led down into the boat. The smell was strong again and they could hear movement inside.

"Another one," Anita whispered.

"I don't fancy tackling it in there. Too tight."

"Let's lure it to the bow end like the other one. We'll be ready this time."

"I don't know …"

"Got a better suggestion?" Anita raised her eyebrows expectantly.

214

"No."

"Come on then."

They made their way back to the other end of the boat and into the cabin. Inside the smell was even worse, but otherwise it was remarkably clean and tidy. The floral green curtains that matched the scatter cushions on the sofas, and the brightly coloured, hand-made pottery on display in the galley area gave it a warm and homely feel. There was a closed door between the sleeping and living areas. The infected banged and scratched on its other side.

They donned their protective gloves and Lisa took out her pistol releasing the safety. Anita shot her a warning glance.

"Just in case," she reassured her.

"Jesus! Be careful with that thing," Anita muttered as she prepared to open the door.

It worked like a dream. Lisa positioned herself outside in the corner of the deck beside the door. Anita poised and ready to move, flicked open the interior door and, without pausing for introductions, sprinted back outside. She stepped up onto the bow of the boat, turned and waited.

The infected lumbered and crashed after her, crockery clattered to the floor. This one had been a very tall, heavily tattooed, balding, middle-aged man. As it burst through the doors, it paused momentarily blinded by the bright sunlight. It was so tall it was eye-to-eye with Anita standing on the bow. Lisa didn't hesitate. She launched herself at it, pushing off from the edge of the boat and using her whole bodyweight to ram it with her shoulder. It went over instantly, tipping into the water, this time with more of a splosh than a plop. The women high-fived as they watched it bobbing away after its companion.

"Nice!" Anita nodded slowly with a satisfied smile. "Very!"

Lisa was euphoric. They had their boat. It stank, and they still had to work out how to get it going, but they were in.

The bow end was so tightly snarled up in the roots that it was holding stable, even in the strong current. They made their way through to the cockpit. Lisa's eyes immediately jumped to the ignition panel. The key was in the slot, a jaunty, day-glow-yellow tennis ball key-ring dangling from its end. She beamed at Anita, her euphoria notching up a degree or two.

However, when she looked at the gear lever, tiller and array of various other lights and switches, her confidence began to waver.

"How difficult could it be, eh?" Anita's eyes glinted with amusement.

"Pretty easy when you have this!" Lisa jubilantly held up a fat and tattered, ring-bound boat manual.

For the next hour or so, they floated on the river as Lisa devoured the manual, working out what all the levers and buttons were for, and how to work every aspect of the boat. From time to time, she got up and examined a particular item, occasionally pushing a button or flicking a switch and noting the effect. She was in her element. This was what she did best. Making sense of complex information. Thinking and working things out. Planning. Anita left her to it.

It was early afternoon when, after a couple of initial splutters, the engine started running. Anita sprinted over the roof to the cockpit, where Lisa was standing hands on hips.

"I can't believe how well this is going!" Lisa grinned up at her.

"I hate to say it, but you're right. It's perfect!" Anita jumped down beside her. "Let's get going then! Tell me what I need to do."

"Hang on. We can't just set off. Stratford is just around the next bend. There are locks and tight turns to navigate. It's nearly two now. It could take us a few hours or more until we get the hang of this and are able navigate them confidently. Call me overcautious, but I don't fancy getting stuck in the town after dark. I think we should moor up properly here overnight and wait till morning."

Anita looked deflated. "'How difficult can it be?' You said!"

"I know, but we have to think. We have to use our heads. It's the only way this is going to work. It's the *only* way we're going to do this. We've got to learn from our past mistakes. Stop rushing into things."

"Ok. Ok. You're right. Look! Come and see what I've been doing."

Lisa followed her inside. She had opened all the doors and windows and tossed out any soiled soft furnishings and bedding. She had wiped down all the surfaces with a bleach-based cleaning spray. The

217

place smelt better. Not good, but better. She had been through the lifeless fridge and all the cupboards, thrown away any mouldy or rotten items and sorted out what was still good to eat. And there was a lot of that: a huge selection of tinned and dried goods and long-life cartons, as well as chocolate and booze. Tattoo-man had a nicely stocked bar going on.

Lisa picked up an almost full bottle of Mount Gay Rum. "Wow! This is even better than I imagined."

Anita waved a six-pack of snack size Kit Kats at her. "And chocolate! We have chocolate!"

After greedily polishing off the entire pack of Kit Kats, washed down with a glorious cup of rum-laced coffee, they went outside to see exactly what was tethering the boat to the bank and try to free it. As Anita untangled the rope that was caught in the roots, Lisa scanned the riverbanks. Apart from a couple of infected roaming aimlessly in one of the gardens on the other side of the river, they were completely alone. It felt wonderful.

Having freed the boat and moored it up properly, they spent the rest of the afternoon just appreciating the tranquillity and solitude of the river, enjoying the brief respite from the horrors of the new real world. They set the sun on the roof with another rum, before moving inside to prepare a dinner of pasta and a ready-made tomato sauce.

As they ate, Lisa imagined the little, grey-haired woman preparing food in the galley, washing dishes at the sink and carrying endless cups of tea, and sometimes something stronger, out to her husband at the stern. She imagined him standing, bare-chested and tattooed, at the back of the boat, one hand on the tiller, cup of tea in the other, as he navigated the boat down endless, sleepy waterways. She thought of them now, bobbing down the Avon together towards the Severn and onwards to the sea. At least they'd given them a fitting end.

Later, they drank some wine and played Scrabble by candlelight. None of the electrics worked as the battery was flat. It was charged by the engine, but they didn't want to take the risk of making a noise until they were ready to leave, or waste fuel just to charge the battery. Compared to the camp, they were in relative luxury and could easily do without electricity for a little while.

Throughout the night, they took turns to keep watch. While one was awake, the other slept, for the first time in days, in a proper bed on fresh cotton sheets under a soft fluffy duvet.

Lisa took the second watch from three until seven. She sat on the roof of the boat on a plastic chair, wrapped in a blanket. It felt magnificent to be outside alone in the depth of night and not feel afraid. The water lapped gently against the side of the boat. The only other sounds she heard were the calls of night birds and the rustling of small creatures rooting in the undergrowth. This was the best she'd felt for a long time. She had slept well, and was relaxed and well fed.

As dawn broke, she snuggled into her chair smiling

to herself. It was going to be a good day. Her plan was working. Anita had cheered up. She was sure this time she was going to make it. She was sure Neil would be there, waiting. She wondered where he was right then. Was he awake? Was he thinking of her?

She whispered to him, "I'm coming. I'm coming home. Wait for me, my Darling. Wait for me."

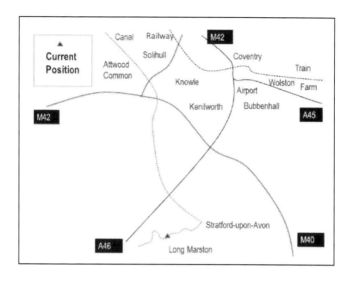

Chapter 11

Day 11 - Luddington

Anita's face was still puffy with sleep when, just after seven, she joined Lisa on the roof with a steaming cup of coffee. She pulled up another chair and they sat in silence for a while, sipping their drinks and relishing the normal sights and sounds of the Warwickshire countryside. For those few precious moments, they could almost forget that the world as they knew it was changed forever.

"We could just stay here," Anita murmured.

Lisa looked at her.

"It's a good idea. We could come back here, or find somewhere similar, once Neil is with us."

She got up, stretched, and folded her blanket.

"Breakfast?"

Anita muttered something unintelligible under her breath.

After eating their fill of porridge and canned peaches, they finally set off towards Stratford. Lisa stood in the cockpit at the stern, steering, and Anita perched on the bow, legs dangling over the edge, scanning the banks and the route ahead for infected, obstacles or any other signs of danger.

The noise of the chugging engine was reassuring. The boat felt solid and strong. They glided slowly up river. They were only a couple of miles from the town, but it meandered through open countryside. For the first half hour, the only sign of life, or otherwise, that they came across was an infected farmer fussing in its tractor on a road bridge over the river. Agitated, but unable to get down from the cab, it watched as they sailed beneath it.

Eventually, they heard the sound of rushing water from where the river ahead forked into two. Lisa slowed the boat to a halt and surveyed the route ahead. On the left was a fast-flowing weir, creating a mini-rapid as it tumbled into the river. Their first lock was on the right. She'd been mapping their progress in the Waterways Guide, so had anticipated this. She dropped anchor and they secured the boat to the tree-lined, left-hand bank, while they discussed their strategy for the lock.

Fortunately, it was surrounded by open fields, so they were going to be able to work out their technique, free from the added complication of having to fend off infected at the same time.

They left the boat and walked down the towpath to inspect the intimidating structure. The gates were closed, and the water was level with the river above the lock. They worked out how to open the sluice and the gates, letting the water drain into the river below the lock until the waterline was level. Anita waited by the gate while Lisa carefully guided the boat inside. They closed the sluice and the gates, waited for the water level to rise again, then opened the top gates and cruised through into the upper part of the river.

They were jubilant. But, although they had the technique right, and it seemed fairly straightforward, the implications of repeating the lengthy process in the presence of a threat from infected, or other, survivors were not lost on either woman. They would be extremely vulnerable.

Lisa found herself picturing a variety of frightening scenarios. Infected dropping from the sides of the lock onto the boat, or surrounding Anita as she wrestled with cranks and slow-moving gates and paddles. Annoyed with herself, she pushed the images away. They would be fine if they just took it steady and dealt with each situation as and when it arose. They just had to be patient and use their brains and their agility to their advantage.

But there was another image that she couldn't get

out of her head, one that frightened her even more than the locks.

The previous summer, she and Neil had spent an afternoon and evening in Stratford. They'd gone to see a production of Hamlet at the Royal Shakespeare Theatre. In the afternoon, before an early dinner in the theatre's restaurant, they'd taken a stroll around the riverside gardens.

They'd watched as a narrowboat was being manoeuvred around a tight corner under a bridge, where the canal entered the wide expanse of a basin in the centre of the town. They had tittered with sympathetic amusement, and cringed with embarrassment, as the, clearly novice, bargees tried in vain to negotiate the lengthy vessel around the tight corner.

The show went on for some time and drew a large audience of well-intentioned tourists and theatre goers, all offering advice. They scraped, bumped and wedged the boat against the unforgiving concrete walls, attacking it from different angles again and again until they finally chugged slowly away, red-faced but relieved, to a chorus of cheers and applause.

She estimated it had taken them at least 15 minutes to get out of the situation. The canal was narrow at this point, and the boat fitted snugly within it. She couldn't recall the specific details, but the crowds of onlookers on the bank had seemed very close to the boat.

The scenario playing in Lisa's head, was of Anita

and her, struggling to get their boat around that same corner watched by a crowd of onlookers. However, this time they were not encouraging tourists and friendly theatre-goers, they were a frenzied horde of rotting infected that were baying for their blood.

After they passed the weir, the river widened considerably. Continuing under a couple of bridges, which marked the start of the town, they held a steady course along its centre, keeping well away from the banks. They easily negotiated a second lock.

As they got further into the town, they began to attract the attention of a few infected hanging around some buildings on the left bank. However, the recreation grounds which ran along the right bank, opposite the town, were clear. They passed the bandstand where the teenage couple had taken shelter on the night of the outbreak.

When they reached the waterside area in front of the theatre, they both gasped. The whole area was seething with infected. It had always been a popular spot for locals and tourists to enjoy fish and chips or ice cream, a street performance, or a spot of people-watching. It seemed to be just as popular with the recently deceased. Every subset of society that could be found there before the outbreak, was represented now, but as a more ghoulish version of themselves.

Lisa put the boat in neutral and joined Anita on the bow, as they drifted in the centre of the river, taking in the spectacle. Colourful tourists with expensive cameras dangling from their necks, market traders wearing fat money belts, well-dressed elderly ladies, uniformed shop-workers, security guards, buskers, young parents, teenagers, children, and even some Shakespearean actors in full Elizabethan attire, all mingled aimlessly in a bizarre *danse macabre*.

For a while, the women just watched, captivated by the performance. This was the first time they'd been able to observe the infected in such detail from a safe distance. It was both tragic, and uncomfortably comic, at the same time. A few, that had noticed the boat, had made their way to the water's edge, moaning, and reaching towards it. Some of them toppled into the water and were immediately swept away by the strong current.

Up ahead was the exit where they had to leave the river to join the Stratford-upon-Avon canal. The route passed under a pedestrian bridge into a basin beyond. But, between them and the relative safety of the wide basin, was a lock. This time it was not going to be so easy. The lock was surrounded on both sides by hordes of infected.

The lock was full, and the bottom gates were closed. They were going to have to close the top gates and paddles to empty the lock before they could open the bottom gates. They would then have to wait inside the lock while it filled before they could enter the basin.

"Jesus! How are we going to do this? It's impossible," Anita said.

Lisa looked at the structure. It was a double lock, wide enough for two boats to fit in side by side. If she could keep the boat in the centre, they might be alright. Any infected that came over the edge would end up in the water and hopefully get sucked under by the powerful currents created by the surging water.

Lisa's mind was working overtime. She had the beginnings of an idea. She looked back at the crowds of infected. They had settled down and seemed to have lost interest in them while the boat had been floating quietly with the engine turned off. She ran to the back of the boat and turned on the engine again. Almost immediately, the noise levels on the bank increased and small groups of infected started moving towards them once more.

She pointed at them.

"Watch, Nita!"

After a few moments they started tumbling into the river and drifting downstream.

Anita watched, grumbling under her breath.

"There's hundreds of them. They're all over place. It'll take hours for them all to fall in."

"I'm not saying we wait for them *all* to fall in, but I have an idea. Just listen. You don't have to do it if you don't think it'll work. It's risky, but I think we could pull it off."

Five minutes later, Anita was hopping off the boat onto the other side of the river and sprinting for the cover of Lee and Emma's bandstand. Lisa had suggested she take one of the pistols, but the girl had opted for her old favourite, the axe from the garden centre. She'd swung it around a few times, as she had apprehensively limbered up on the roof of the boat.

When Lisa was sure the girl was safely ensconced in the bandstand, she steered the boat back towards the other side. She had to believe her plan would work, and she knew Anita was more than capable of executing her part in it, but she felt sick with anxiety as she left her friend alone on the other side. Although she didn't need to, she took a couple of comfort puffs from her inhaler.

She manoeuvred the boat as close to the river's edge as she could without risking any unwelcome guests inviting themselves on board, then she climbed onto the roof and started shouting.

"Hey! Over here! Over here! Come over here, you buggers!"

She picked up the metal ladle and saucepan that she had placed there in advance, and started banging them together.

The entire horde stirred as one. Heads raised and turned in her direction. They began to move, slowly at first, but quickly gathering momentum. Within a few minutes, a sea of bodies was surging towards the river. They were so close that she could smell them. The stench of hundreds of rotting bodies was overpowering. She coughed and retched and pulled her bandana over her nose and mouth to try and block it out.

But it was working. They started to fall in and more importantly to move away from the area around the lock and the bridge above it.

When the lock was clear, she glanced across the river to see Anita darting from one point of cover to another. She lost sight of the girl when she reached the main bridge that would bring her back over to the side Lisa was on.

It felt like a lifetime, waiting there, engine running, banging on the frying pan. The steady stream of infected had grown into a torrent. More and more of them appeared, coming out of buildings and emerging from side streets and corners.

Ten minutes passed. She had no idea how Anita was doing. She couldn't see the lock from her position. She could only just see the exit to the canal. She stared at the surface of the water in front of it, willing some turbulence to appear that would indicate that the lock was emptying.

Twenty minutes passed. She began to worry. What had she been thinking? She'd sent Anita out there on her own. She had no idea what to do next.

When thirty minutes had elapsed, she was on the verge of tears. Fear, guilt and sheer frustration threatened to overwhelm her. Then, a figure appeared on the footbridge waving frantically.

It was Anita. She'd done it!

As quickly as she had appeared, Anita disappeared again. In a fraction of a second, Lisa's emotions had lurched from despair to elation. Her adrenaline surging again, she steered the boat in a wide curve until she was facing the lock.

There was no sign of Anita, but the gates were open. As quickly as she could, she steered the boat under the bridge and into the lock, immediately cutting the engine again. Once the boat was in position, Anita bounded from behind a hedge and, working quickly and efficiently, closed the bottom gates.

The lock filled painfully slowly.

Anita was looking anxiously towards the theatre. Lisa couldn't see, but she knew they were coming. She could hear the wall of moaning getting louder and louder. She could smell them again.

She waited.

The lock continued to fill.

Anita was twitching, dancing impatiently from one foot to the other.

The horde reached the side of the lock. They flooded into the space, pushing and clamouring to reach the boat, tipping over the edge into the water in waves. The water was a frenzy of thrashing infected.

Then the lock was full.

Anita started to open the gates.

Because the lock was so wide, Lisa could see she only needed to open one.

She called to her. "One! Just one! I can get through. Get back on!"

She was focusing her attention on steering the boat through the narrow opening when she heard Anita cry out. A group of infected had reached the girl. She was battling to clear her path back to the boat, swinging her axe like a mad woman, screaming and yelling, hacking and slicing. The wet thump of the metal making contact with flesh was sickening.

Anita was grunting with effort. Gore sprayed and splinters of bone flew through the air.

The boat drifted into the basin.

"Nita! Nita! Now! Jump on! Jump on!" Lisa called in desperation.

Anita shook her head and pointed to the end of the basin.

"It's no good! Meet me at the other side!" she shouted. Then she sprinted down the footpath pursued by the infected.

Lisa steered in the same direction. The boat was slow. Anita was ahead of her. Now most of the horde had reached the basin and others were still appearing from all directions. There were hundreds of them. The entire basin was surrounded. There was nowhere for Anita to go. No way she could reach the boat.

The image that haunted Lisa for days to come was of Anita stopping and looking over at her, then shaking her head. She raised her hand and reached across the water for a moment, as if to try and touch the woman that had become her world over the past ten days, then she turned and faced the horde.

Lisa watched, helpless and open mouthed with dismay and horror, as the girl raised her axe and thrashed her way into the infected. Almost immediately, they completely engulfed her. She disappeared into their midst. Lisa strained to keep track of her amongst the throng … to pick out a flash of her bright pink headscarf, or the glint of metal from her axe. Nothing!

231

The next few hours were easily the most miserable of Lisa's life. She lost track of time as she stood on the roof of the boat, scanning the area for any sign of the girl.

Eventually, she was forced to attend to her own situation. The boat was drifting dangerously close to the edge of the basin and the clawing grasp of the multitude that surrounded her. She needed to secure it in the centre. She managed to do it with the aid of some ropes and boat hooks, but it took a while. When it was done, she climbed onto the roof again and sat, cross-legged, staring into the distance in the direction that Anita had taken.

She only stirred when it began to get dark. So much time had passed. She shuddered at the thought of Anita out there in the dark, alone, and afraid. But that was assuming she had even made it. She knew it was morbid, but she found herself searching the crowd of infected for anyone that looked like Anita.

The noise and stench emanating from the horde was stifling and relentless and she couldn't see much in the fading light, so, reluctantly, she made her way back down into the boat. She closed the doors and windows, pulled all the curtains, and then sat down at the small table, with her head in her hands, and a million thoughts spinning round in her head.

She swung between moments of positivity, when she was sure that Anita had made it to safety and that everything was going to be alright, to periods of utter despair and desolation, when she was convinced that she was gone.

They'd been so lucky to have got through everything they'd been through so far that she'd been sure they were both destined to survive. But maybe their luck had finally run out, maybe all they had done was to delay the inevitable.

As well as her misery about what might or might not have happened to Anita, she was also starting to have some nagging fears about her own situation. What was going to happen to *her*? How was she going to get out of this on her own? She chided herself for having such selfish thoughts when Anita was in such peril and might even be dead, but they kept pushing back through. Without Anita, she could never get the boat through all the locks that she knew lay ahead. But she couldn't give up the boat and travel alone on foot either. It was just too dangerous.

Her imagination ran away with her. A series of different terrible outcomes started to play out in her head. Starving to death on the boat, being torn to shreds by the horde on the waterfront or being overwhelmed as she tried to negotiate a lock on her own. Her head was pounding. She was dead-tired. She closed her eyes, then opened them again quickly. She couldn't sleep! She had to be awake in case Anita came back.

But now that night was here, that was unlikely. If she had made it to somewhere safe, she would stay there until morning. She wasn't stupid. By morning, the horde might have thinned out a bit, even drifted away like they had the night they were trapped in the camper van. If Anita was coming back, she would wait until then.

All Lisa could do now was wait.

She woke at dawn, slumped over the table with her cheek pressed uncomfortably against the hard surface. She sat up slowly, easing the stiffness from her aching limbs and back. She rubbed her cheek where the skin had been stuck to the table. She listened. It was quiet outside. The horde had settled.

Peering carefully through the curtains, she checked one side and then the other. They had definitely thinned out. There were still a few shuffling around the basin, but nothing like the numbers that had been there the day before. She considered her options, concluding that she just needed to wait and stay out of sight. If Anita was alive, she wouldn't be able to return until it was safe. Lisa couldn't risk being seen or heard and attracting them all again. She had to be patient.

She spent the day creeping around inside the boat. Waiting. She studied the Waterways Guide, memorising every section of the canal between Stratford and Attwood Common. She identified every lock and obstacle, and worked out which ones would be in potentially dangerous, populated areas, and where there were clusters of locks that would make for slow progress and be physically challenging. From time to time, she peeked outside to check on the infected, assessing their numbers and positions. Just in case.

She made herself some food around midday, hungry for the first time since their breakfast the previous morning. In the afternoon, she lay down on the bed and managed to sleep for a couple of hours. She awoke feeling positive. She had a sense of purpose. Anita was coming back, and she was waiting for her.

But when darkness fell again, the doubt started to creep back in. What was she *doing,* waiting here like this? She was wasting time. If Anita *had* survived, she might have decided to keep moving. To get away from the town completely. Not to try and return to the boat. To try and catch up with Lisa further up the canal. She might be long gone.

With every day that passed, Neil was more likely to think that she wasn't coming home. If he thought she wasn't coming, he wouldn't wait for her, and it would all have been for nothing.

She sat down at the table for the second night in a row. This time, she opened the rum and poured herself a generous measure. She'd hoped it would dull the edges and cheer her up a bit, but it had the opposite effect. She felt completely alone and wretched. Her plan was in tatters and she had no idea what she was going to do. She poured herself another. Anita was probably dead. She corrected herself. *Undead*. Anita was probably *undead*. Wandering around out there with the rest of them, with a vacant milky stare.

She poured herself another. Before she knew it, she'd emptied the bottle. Wallowing in self-pity, she indulged in a wanton bout of drunken weeping, before falling into bed, puffy-eyed and snotty-nosed, just after midnight.

She was awoken by banging against the side of the boat. Disorientated, she leapt out of bed. Her head reeled and she thought she was going to be sick. She was horribly dehydrated. She fumbled for the pistol on the bedside table and ran, barefoot, through to the main cabin and the source of the noise.

She stood, stock still, with the pistol gripped tightly in trembling hands and pointed it at the bow doors. The grey light of dawn was just creeping through the cracks in the curtains. More banging from the bow. Whispering.

People! More than one!

She tightened her grip on the pistol, her finger lightly resting on the trigger, ready to fire, the way Rick had shown her. Her chest tightened. She tried to steady her breathing. Where the hell was her inhaler?

Through the lace curtains, she saw a figure pull itself up over the side of the boat. With much grunting and panting, it heaved itself over, falling into the bow with a farcical clatter. A stifled snigger. Well, they definitely weren't infected. She had yet to hear an infected laugh, let alone climb over anything. Could it be …?

The figure got to its feet and she could see it was a tall male. *Shit!*

She kicked the bow doors open shouting, "Stop! I've got a gun! Don't move or I'll shoot!"

A tall, slim young man, with a mop of blonde curly hair, stood facing her. His mouth curved into a broad smile. He had perfect teeth.

236

"You must be Lisa. Anita said you were mad!"

Lisa registered the Australian drawl.

"Who the hell are you?"

"I'm James." The boy turned away to lean over the side of the boat.

"I said don't move! I mean it!" Lisa waved the gun at him. But she felt her heart rate slow and her breathing was easier.

James ignored her and continued to reach over the side, clearly helping someone else up.

"I said stop! Stop now!"

The boy winked at her as he hauled his companion up over the side. As soon as she saw the pink headscarf and black braids, the gun dropped to the floor and Lisa was on her in a flash, hugging and kissing her, crying and laughing at the same time.

"I knew you'd come back. I knew it! You little star! I bloody love you."

Anita was laughing and pushing her away. "You didn't think I'd let you go without me, did you? Not after all we've been through. You can't get rid of me *that* easily. Not until I've met the marvellous and mythical Neil, that is."

"Get up you idiot!" Lisa laughed. "Let's get inside before our 'friends' hear us and come back for another visit." Still chuckling, she helped Anita to her feet.

"Anyway, meet James! My hero!" Anita said, gesturing towards him. "I couldn't have survived the night, or got back here, without him. He's been brilliant."

She flashed James a smile.

237

"James, good to meet you. You're a star, too. I bloody love you, too. Thank you. Thank you so much!" Lisa shook him by the hand.

James smiled back. He had a great smile, big and warm and it went all the way to his sparkling blue eyes. Lisa instantly knew she could trust him. She looked at Anita. The girl was gazing at James in a way that suggested that she, too, had fallen for his smile.

Smiling to herself, Lisa turned and led them inside. She set about making a pot of fresh coffee and they settled down to tell her the story of the last 36 hours.

James was the manager of a pub on the other side of the river. On the night of the outbreak, after he'd sent all his customers and staff home, he'd barricaded himself inside the building and resigned himself to waiting it out. He'd been holed up in there ever since. He was Australian, and single, and, as he lived at the pub, had nowhere else to go, and no-one to go to. He was not easily fazed and was comfortable with his own company. He had enough food and water for weeks, maybe months, so was prepared for however long it took.

For the first 24 hours he'd laid low, cowering in his sitting room, listening to the carnage raging outside, watching TV and listening to the radio, until it all stopped. After that, he'd moved up to the attic, where he could see the expanse of the town along the river on the other side. And that was where he'd spent most of his waking hours ever since: up there, observing developments and working out what he was going to do next, trying to decide when to make his move … whatever that would be.

As the hours and days passed, the initial, frenzied activity gradually reduced to an occasional skirmish here and there, as other survivors emerged from their safe havens in search of food and water or loved ones. Few of them had made it and most had joined the throng of infected gathering on the waterfront.

His life had settled into a kind of unnatural, natural rhythm. He slept, ate and watched the daily goings-on from his viewpoint. He had ventured out a few times to get the lie of the land and do a little bit of scavenging. He hadn't seen any people, or at least living people, for days, until Lisa and Anita had cruised into town. He'd watched with interest that day as the barge floated in the middle of the river, the two women standing on the roof, seemingly assessing their options.

Until he saw them, he'd felt a sense of detachment from the other tragic and gruesome scenarios that he had witnessed. He had enough self-awareness to recognise that this was probably some sort of psychological protective mechanism that had kicked in, in response to the shock and trauma of it all. It was almost as though he'd been watching a TV show that he was not really part of.

But this time it was different. Maybe it was simply timing, or maybe it was something about them in particular? These women were interesting, they seemed to have a purpose, they looked strong and tough. He wanted to know more about them. He wanted to know where they were going - what they were doing and why.

What really did it for him was when Anita ran right past his door! He'd watched as Lisa had dropped her off and she'd sprinted for the cover of the bandstand. When she'd headed in his direction, he'd rushed downstairs to try and catch her attention but only caught a glimpse of her as she flashed, catlike, past the barricaded entrance to the pub. By the time he'd moved the furniture and loosened the planks that blocked the doorway, she was gone: a flicker of pink and dark hair bobbing across the bridge.

It had been enough though. Enough to get him engaged. Enough to make him want to help. To get involved. Enough to make him follow her.

He'd barely seen her, but what he had seen was the face of an intelligent and determined woman, and he wanted to be with her. It was that simple. He was sure that she and her friend were *true* survivors; they had what it took. They were not going to join the horde of mindless victims wandering forever on the waterfront. They were going to make it, and he was going with them. It was time for him to make his move. He grabbed the baseball bat that was constantly by his side and, without even a glance back into the safe interior of the pub, he was gone, jogging silently after her.

He had watched from the relative safety of the bridge for a few minutes, as she'd deftly hopped down to the lock, inserted the crank and started winding it to open the sluice gates. Then, not wanting to startle her, as much for his own safety as hers - the crank would make a pretty hefty weapon - he quietly made his way down to her position. But she was constantly looking around, and quickly spotted him. She fixed him in her gaze and watched him warily, as she continued to wind.

As he approached, he put the bat on the ground and raised his empty hands, as if to show he was no threat.

"Hi! I'm James".

"Hi, James! Why don't you make yourself useful instead of sneaking around like that?" she panted.

He made a move to help her with the crank.

"Not this! Them!" she snapped, pointing behind him.

He turned to see a small gathering of infected moving towards them.

"Can you distract them until I've got this?"

"Sure!"

He sprinted towards the group yelling and clapping his hands. They immediately turned their attention away from Anita and onto him, and he led them away from the lock back towards the town. He ducked out of sight when they were a safe distance away, reappearing at the lock a few moments later only to find another group closing in on her from another direction. This time he didn't wait to be asked, distracting the second group, then another and another, until the job was done, and Anita was waving at her friend from the footbridge, giving her the signal to bring the boat in.

But now, there were too many to distract. They were coming from all directions and the main horde was moving steadily closer. The pair crouched behind a hedge out of sight until the boat was in the lock and then Anita darted back down to open the gates into the basin. This time, James tried to protect her by dealing with any that got too close to her with his baseball bat. But there were just too many. They were separated and he lost sight of her. Eventually, he was overwhelmed and forced to retreat back to the bridge.

He was devastated, convinced that she was gone, one way or another. The basin was now surrounded on all sides. Either she'd made it onto the boat or she hadn't, but either way, he'd missed his chance. He was hit by an unexpected wave of sorrow and lonely desperation. His brief encounter with her had been intense, but it had been real and had felt good. He had felt hope for the first time in days and now it was gone - dashed away in an instant. He sighed deeply and sank to his knees.

Then he heard her! Screaming with rage, roaring with fury and physical effort. He heard the thud of solid metal on bone as she thrashed and struck out with her axe, followed by the gurgles of the dying dead.

Who was this woman! She was superhuman! He jumped to his feet and rushed to her aid, swinging his bat with renewed vigour, launching himself at her assailants.

When they were clear, they'd sprinted back across the bridge to the pub, and she'd helped him board the door up again before they both dropped to the floor, rolling onto their backs, gasping for breath, sucking air deep into their lungs.

When she could talk, Anita pushed herself up on one elbow and looked across at him.

"Nice to meet you, James!"

They spent the night, all of the next day and the following night waiting and watching for the horde of infected around the basin to thin out enough for them to try and return to the boat. They sat upstairs by the window when it was light, and downstairs in the pub when it was dark.

They ate and drank and talked. They talked for hours. Talked about the outbreak and shared their stories of survival, talked about their lives before, and the people that mattered most to them, wondering where they were now and whether they had survived. They cried a little and laughed a lot. They talked about the future and wondered what that might hold for them now. They felt as if they had known each other all their lives.

On the second night, they slept in each other's arms until dawn when they looked outside. It was as clear as it was ever going to be.

James knew there was a small rowing boat moored at the edge of the basin near the bridge. He'd seen it when he was out scavenging and had considered using it to explore further afield.

And so, they had returned to the barge and Lisa.

J.M.MCKENZIE

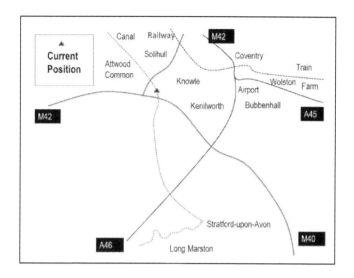

Chapter 12

Day 15 - Hockley Heath

Over the next couple of days, Lisa and Anita covered more distance than they had at any other stage of their long journey together. They made steady progress as they left Stratford and passed through a succession of small villages, encountering virtually no trouble. Wilmcote, Wootton Wawen, Preston Bagot, Lowsonford all appeared and disappeared, empty and hushed without exception.

They slipped silently under, and over, roads and railways, floated past train stations, caravan parks and pubs. The locks were way easier to manage with three: Lisa steering the boat, Anita opening and closing the locks, and James distracting, or disposing of, any infected that threatened to halt their progress. The further away they got from the town, the easier it became, until they reached a point where they were simply chugging along leafy waterways as if they didn't have a care in the world.

Some of these places were familiar to Lisa. Country pubs, where they had whiled away warm summer Sundays, sipping cider, people-watching and chatting. Villages they had strolled through hand in hand, admiring quaint cottages and picturesque gardens, while Lisa fantasised about living in a place like that, raising a family and growing old together.

It all felt so different now. Travelling on the waterways presented the locations to her from a new perspective: familiar landmarks became unfamiliar; recognisable features became unrecognisable. Add in the empty abandoned houses, deserted streets and beer gardens, and the effect was startling, that of tiny ghost towns existing in a parallel universe.

After the physical and emotional intensity of the previous 48 hours, it felt good to permit themselves to relax a little. There was time to rest, time to talk, and time to think. Lisa felt a sense of calm begin to envelop her. She was definitely getting close now. This time she was going to get there. And Neil would be waiting. She felt it as strongly as if it had already happened.

During the day, as she stood at the stern gently

guiding the boat closer and closer towards its destination, she listened to Anita and James talking in soft voices at the front of the boat. Their low murmurings were interspersed with occasional chuckles, peals of laughter and then long periods of silence. She wasn't sure, but she thought they were kissing in these long quiet moments.

She pictured them, eyes closed, wrapped around each other, lost in pleasure, shutting everything else out except each other. The relationship had developed fast. But why not? The phrase "life is short" had taken on a whole new meaning since the outbreak. Basic human needs, instincts and emotions were raw and exposed - all closer to the surface somehow, now that death was walking amongst them.

Inevitably though, as she watched their new relationship blossom, her head was filled with bitter-sweet memories of her own. Everything reminded her of him. Water washing over pebbles at the side of the canal in the boat's wake, took her back to a shingled beach in Cornwall where they'd spent a long weekend earlier that summer. She'd been sitting on the beach, knees against her chest, arms wrapped around them, watching Neil skimming stones at the water's edge. It was late afternoon, and the day was cooling down. She had a blanket around her shoulders. The remains of their picnic lay around her. She was a little woozy with wine ... sleepy, cosy and content. He would pick up a stone and examine it for its suitability for the task, turning it over in his hands, rubbing its curves with his fingers, brushing off dust and debris, smoothing it and polishing it. Then he would crouch, tilting his head and leaning his body to the side, one arm raised for balance, and throw. He would watch it skip across the surface. Rising and falling, once, twice, three times in long graceful arcs. When it finally sank beneath the waves, he would stand, disappointed, and then start the whole process all over again.

She could watch him like this forever, both envying him and loving him for the amount of pleasure he could get from such a simple thing. He'd always been like that. For him, life was all about the simple things. He had effortlessly perfected the art of living in the moment. Whatever he was doing, whether it was eating, reading, working with his hands, or lovemaking, he always gave it his full attention. Savouring every moment, insensible to time, making sure it was perfect, never rushing to finish.

She, on the other hand, was always thinking, always looking forward to the next thing, impatient, hurried. For her, the clock was always ticking, counting down the day, long lists of things to do, and how much time they would need forming and reforming in her head. She hated that about herself. Wished she could just stop and *be* sometimes, like he could.

And, that was why she was so sure he'd be there. She knew he could wait for her until the end of time, if that was what it was going to take.

In the evenings, they moored up and cooked dinner. James was a good cook, better than either of the women. They deferred to his superior skills in the kitchen, sitting together at the table planning their route for the next day and rejoicing on how far they'd travelled.

Anita cut her fingernails short and removed her nail polish with some remover she'd found in the main cabin. She re-braided her hair and plucked her eyebrows. They flicked through magazines, played yet more scrabble, talked about music they liked and books they'd read, films they'd watched and their favourite TV programmes. They told stories of before, stories of family, friends and lovers. Good stories, warm stories, memorials for people and times past - people who now felt hundreds of miles away, times that felt like lost history. The fear of the horror beyond faded a little, concealed for a time in both mind and eye by a thin veil of normality.

But at night, it would reappear. Up on the roof alone, when it was Lisa's turn to watch, reality furtively crept back in, stealing away the bewitching ordinariness of the evening. Watching and listening, alert and ready, searching the darkness for hostile shapes in the bushes, unexplained ripples in the water or unnatural sounds, the cold fingers of unease and dread would slowly return. But looking up at the night sky, where the moon and stars traversed the heavens like they had every night before, and would continue to do every night after, it was still possible to pretend, if only for a moment.

Anita and James were sharing the main cabin. Lisa

imagined them snuggled up together, arms wrapped around each other, legs entwined, faces close, lips touching. She longed for that intimacy again. Before, it had been the part of each day that she looked forward to the most. When the day's tasks were complete, all jobs done and lists duly ticked off, she liked to treat herself with moments of closeness.

During the evenings, when they were watching TV or reading on the sofa together, she would rest her legs across Neil's thighs as he absent-mindedly massaged her feet, and she'd puppy nudge him for more every time he stopped. She never grew tired of slipping under the bed covers and moving her body as close to his as she could get.

She was always first to suggest that they went to bed, hurrying upstairs, brushing her teeth and jumping under the sheets as quickly as she could, then waiting impatiently for him to join her. Invariably, he would dawdle for a bit, flicking through the TV channels, fixing them a drink or deciding to take a last-minute shower.

She would lie awake frustratedly waiting for him, willing him to hurry up, then reproaching herself for getting irritated. She knew he had no idea that she was waiting for him. He'd have been mortified if he'd known.

Now, when it was her time to rest and she had climbed into her cold, empty bed like a lonely, single woman, it struck her that something subtle had changed in the dynamics between her and Anita since James had come along. She couldn't quite decipher it ... couldn't explain it, or even give it words. It was something to do with the sense of self, and how it changed when you became part of a couple. Before James, that aspect of self-identity had been stronger in Lisa. Now, it seemed stronger in Anita. Lisa felt as though her perception of herself as one half of a couple was becoming weaker, fragmented.

But she was overthinking things again! This is when Neil would have told her to stop and get a grip. Of course, she was part of a couple. They were still a couple. Always had been! Always would be!

She turned over, shut her eyes and waited for sleep to come.

It was on Thursday, exactly 14 days since Lisa had been heading home from London, when they approached Attwood Common for the second time. They'd successfully negotiated the Lapworth locks, and had made it just past Hockley Heath, when Anita and James suggested it was time to stop for the night.

"But it's not far now! Just a few more miles!" Lisa was agitated.

"It's going to be dark soon, Lisa," Anita said.

"I know but we're so close."

"But you're the one who said we shouldn't travel after dark. We all agreed right from the start that it was too risky."

"But I know the way from here. I know it really

251

well! Neil and I used to walk this part of the canal. We could use the tunnel light."

"You said the tunnel light might attract the infected. What are you saying now?"

Anita sighed in frustration.

"Oh God! I don't know! We could get there *tonight*. I can't wait till morning. I just can't!"

"Look! Think about it! Tomorrow is going to be a big day. The biggest! We need to rest and be ready for … whatever. After all we've been through, why would you take the risk of losing everything now?"

"She's right, Lisa!" James added his support. "You know she is. What difference will one more day make when you've been travelling for so long? We don't want to arrive at night. Who knows what sort of situation we'll be going into? We need to be able to see where we're going, who we're facing and what we're doing."

"I know. I know. It's just that we're so close. It's killing me!"

She knew they were right.

But that night she barely slept. The excitement and anticipation of finally being reunited with Neil was almost more than she could bear. Even worse than that was the cold fear that kept nagging from deep inside that he might not be there, that he might have given up waiting after so much time had passed, or that he might be injured or dead, or worse. Whatever had happened to him over the last couple of weeks, tomorrow, she was going to find out.

She was up at dawn, pale and exhausted with dark circles under bloodshot eyes. She made some coffee and took a cup up to James, who was on last watch on the roof. She sat down beside him, and they sipped their drinks in silence as they gazed down the misty waterway ahead.

A bleary-eyed Anita stuck her tousled head out of the bow doors below them.

"Come on, guys! This is it! Let's get going!"

They decided to forego their usual leisurely breakfast, instead wolfing down some instant porridge, sweetened with Nutella and cooled with evaporated milk.

They were on the move within half an hour of waking.

The final stretch of the canal was dark and shady, its steep banks rising almost vertically on either side. This morning, the silence felt more ominous than comforting. Every rustling leaf or cracking branch took on a sinister tone. They were all tense and jumpy. Lisa was taut and silent, her knuckles white as she gripped the tiller. Even James understood the significance of the day which was, for his two companions, the culmination of two weeks of intense struggle and gritty determination. Everything hinged on what happened in the next few hours.

Anita was almost as anxious as Lisa. She knew the implications of Neil not being there alive and well. It was this belief that had given Lisa all her strength and drive throughout their journey. She dreaded to think how she would deal with it if he wasn't there.

They'd been travelling for almost an hour when they approached the moorings that Lisa knew as Lady Lane Wharf, the last settlement before Attwood Common. There was a little boating club there, that served a decent Sunday lunch and held occasional social events like beer and skittles or karaoke nights. There were always at least 20 or 30 boats moored there, along the side of the towpath. Most were permanent fixtures, ranging from the pristine, with neat little garden areas, sheds and washing lines on the bank, to the completely derelict, with rusting bicycles on their roofs, windows obscured by years of dirt and hulls dark with slime.

As they approached the last bridge before the wharf, Lisa noticed something hanging from the top. As they got closer, she could see that a large flag was draped across the side of the bridge. In the distance, she could hear the rhythmic, heavy thump of a bass guitar. Suddenly alarmed, but not entirely sure why, she cut the engine and allowed the boat to drift silently forward.

At the bow, James and Anita stood up, instantly tense and alert. As they stared straight ahead, James slipped his hand protectively on the small of Anita's back, and for a moment Lisa was overwhelmed with a longing to feel Neil's hand on her in the same way

She remembered the first time he had done that. They'd been on their first official date, in a noisy, crowded bar in Birmingham. It had been hard to talk, and after one drink, they'd decided to leave for somewhere quieter. As they were leaving, moving through the crowd, he had put his hand on the small of her back, gently guiding her towards the door. It had been completely natural; she was not even sure he was aware he was doing it. For her, it was all she knew in that moment. All her senses focused on that spot where she could feel his hand on her body. The room seemed to quieten, and her eyes lost their focus. She wanted that moment to last forever, and when he removed his hand as they emerged from the pub into the busy street, she could still feel a warm pressure where it had been. She had known in that instant that she would love him.

As they got closer, she could see that the flag was black, with the profile of a skull wearing a gold-crested helmet. It was vaguely familiar, but she didn't know what it meant. James suddenly hopped onto the roof and sprinted back to the stern. Anita glanced back towards them but kept her focus on the route ahead.

"It's the Hells Angels' flag," James panted. "I've seen it before."

"And ...?" Lisa raised her eyebrows.

She'd come across a few members of the Hells Angels and other biking fraternities in the past, and they'd always been perfectly charming despite their intimidating reputation. She opened her mouth to say more, but before they had time to debate the demonisation of the Hells Angels, two men in dark leathers appeared on the bridge above. Although the sun behind them made it difficult to see more than just their silhouettes, it was evident right away that they were armed and that they were pointing their weapons directly at them.

Things happened quickly from there. More leather-clad gunmen appeared from the trees on either side of the canal. Lisa fumbled with the key to turn the engine back on, unsure whether to go backwards or forwards.

She looked to James for guidance, but he was running back over the roof to Anita, who had the pistol raised and was aiming it at the group of men on their left. Lisa saw one of the men on the right raise his weapon and point it at the girl.

"No! Put it down Anita!" James shouted.

A single shot rang out. Anita cried out in pain.

Lisa dropped to the floor. Later, she couldn't remember if she had screamed herself or not. She made herself small, crouched in the cockpit, hands over her ears, her eyes squeezed shut. There was shouting and more gunfire, then a heavy thump as the boat collided with the bank. She curled herself into a ball. No! This couldn't be happening! Not now! *No! No! No!*

Seconds later, she was being roughly dragged to her feet, strong arms tugging her hands behind her back and fastening her wrists with something stiff that cut into her flesh. Her attacker stank of sweat and stale tobacco. He pushed her to the side of the boat, where another man dragged her onto the towpath pushing her onto her knees. She couldn't see Anita or James. A heavy foot on her back pushed her lower, face down in the dirt.

More shouting and sounds of a struggle. Someone fell heavily beside her, panting. Her nose and mouth were pressing into the earth, she was breathing in soil and leaves. She was choking. She was suffocating. She twisted her head to the side gasping for air.

James was lying beside her, also on his front. His head was turned away from her. He was still struggling and shouting, but several men were holding him down.

Lisa tried to steady her breathing, tried to think. She let her body go limp. The pressure on her back eased a little. James continued to fight.

"James," she croaked. "Don't fight them. Calm down."

"They shot her! Bastards!" His voice was thick. A boot kicked him in the side. Another caught the side of his head. He groaned and stopped struggling.

"That's it, James. Don't struggle. You're making it worse for yourself."

He was motionless, but she could still hear him panting. Either he had taken her advice, or he was unconscious, but either way he was calmer.

She could hear more movement coming from the direction of the boat, crashing and banging and more angry male voices. The sounds moved onto the towpath ahead of them. She strained to lift her head to see but it was impossible. She concentrated on trying to keep her breathing steady. Her inhaler was in her pocket. She could feel it pressing against

257

her hip.

Suddenly, she was yanked her to her feet by her hair. She spat the dirt from her mouth and blinked it out of her eyes. Ahead of her, Anita was standing on the towpath. Her head was bowed. One man was tying her hands behind her back with a thick plastic cable-tie. Another was in front of her holding her by the shoulders. Her hands were red with blood. It was dripping from her fingertips. She was injured but at least she was still standing.

The men started walking Anita along the path under the bridge. She seemed unsteady, stumbling and swaying. They took her by the elbows, one on either side. They disappeared under the bridge.

Beside her, they pulled James to his feet. A bruise was forming on his cheek, and his upper lip was puffed and swollen. He looked across at her. His eyes burned with a mixture of anger and distress.

"They shot Anita!"

He had difficulty forming his words through his damaged mouth.

"I know, but she's ok. She's walking."

The man behind Lisa pushed her forward. They were marched along the path in the same direction that Anita had gone, Lisa and James in front, with the men behind them. Lisa kept her head down, partly to watch her step, but also to avoid any eye contact that might provoke more violence. As she passed the spot where Anita had been standing, she had to step over the pool of blood that had congealed there. A trail of droplets marked the path her friend had taken.

As they emerged from the other side of the bridge, the pounding music got louder. She recognised the song. It was *Neon Knights* from the Black Sabbath album, 'Heaven and Hell'. It was the first music she had heard since the outbreak and, even in her current predicament, she almost laughed at its appropriateness as a soundtrack for the past couple of weeks.

They approached the buildings around the wharf. It was clear that any resistance would be futile. There were at least 20 or 30 men, and a few women, sitting or standing around in the garden outside the club house. They all turned to stare as they passed.

Most were armed, with their weapons casually slung over their shoulders. More weapons were scattered around. Shotguns rested casually against chairs, and large jagged knives were nonchalantly displayed on tables. Half-drunk bottles littered the ground, and a haze of cigarette and barbeque smoke gave the whole scene a nightmarish quality. She recognised the unmistakable scent of marijuana.

Lisa slowed as she tried to take in as much as she could. Numbers. Locations. Potential escape routes. Anything that might be useful if they were going to get out of there. Her escort jabbed her in the back with his rifle, but not before she caught a glimpse of a cage-like structure on a grassy area by the water. There were two or three figures inside. She couldn't be sure, but it looked like they were infected.

People jeered at their small procession.

"Keep moving, Darling. Nothing to see here," a

heavily tattooed woman in a vest top, with an assortment of piercings, growled at her.

"Not until later, that is! There'll be plenty to see, then," one of the men shouted, and they all erupted into laughter.

They moved beyond the buildings and back up the towpath beside a row of old boats. Each one had an armed man sitting in its bow. The men smirked and followed them with their eyes as they passed. Their expressions seemed to be a mixture of cynical amusement and curiosity. On one of the boats, a man was standing and yelling at someone inside. Lisa thought she heard sobbing coming from another.

They stopped when they reached a particularly dilapidated barge at the end of the wharf. A skinny, bearded man of undefinable age in a grubby, checked shirt was stretched out in a mouldy deckchair in the bow. He stood up slowly and raised his gun.

"Get in!" He gestured towards the door with his weapon.

They were bundled inside, and the doors slammed behind them.

The cabin was dark, and it took a few minutes for their eyes to adjust to the gloom. James saw Anita before Lisa did, and he rushed over to her. She was sitting on the floor at the other side of the cabin.

Lisa knelt down in front of her. Even in the dark she could see that she was deathly pale and small beads of sweat were glistening on her forehead.

"Oh my God, Anita!"

"I'm ok, I think. Don't worry," Anita said.

"You don't look ok. Where are you hurt?" James said. He was nuzzling at her body, trying to find the wound with his hands still fastened behind his back.

"Really, I'm ok. It's just my hand."

"Turn round," Lisa instructed. "Let me see."

Anita awkwardly shuffled round until her back was towards them.

Her hands were both dark and wet. There was an oily black puddle on the floor behind her.

"Which hand? I can't see." Lisa asked.

"My left. My wrist."

"Here! I've got it! There's a lot of blood. We have to stop it. Give me your bandana!" James's tone was urgent.

Anita bent her head towards him as he pulled the bandana from her head with his teeth.

"Help me Lisa!"

Somehow, using only their teeth, they managed to wind the bandana around her injured hand, twisting it as tightly as they could until she cried out in pain.

"That should work for now, but we have to get out of here!" James said.

"I know, but how?" said Lisa.

They didn't talk much over the next few hours. They sat on the floor, with their backs against the wall, all three of them dazed by the shocking rapidity of how events had unfolded. One minute they had been almost at the end of their journey, and the next, they were tied up in an old boat, having been captured by a group of Hells Angels, and Anita had

261

been shot!

Anita and James sat close together. The worst of her bleeding seemed to have stopped. He whispered words of comfort to her and she dozed, on and off, on his shoulder. Lisa, on the other hand, was in computing mode. Her mind was whirring … processing what little information they had … trying to work out what their options were, and indeed, if they even had any.

They were in the main cabin of the boat. Behind them, the door to the sleeping area was bolted shut and padlocked. All the windows were obscured, either by dirt or filthy curtains. Through the grime on the doors, she could just make out their guard in his deck chair. He was taking regular swigs from a rectangular bottle. It had to be booze and he was almost certainly drunk by now. If any of them did make a sound, he banged on the door yelling at them to, "shut up or he would kill them", and similar clichéd threats.

Outside, was large group of armed men and women in various stages of inebriation. Their boat was the last in a row of about five or six and there appeared to be others, like them, being held in them.

And infected! They had infected in cages! What were they doing? What did they want? What was going on? She couldn't make sense of it. Her head was spinning.

But, instead of trying to understand, she focused her attention on something she *could* do. She had to get her hands free … get all of their hands free.

Whatever came next, they'd have a better chance of dealing with it if their hands weren't tied up behind their backs.

Quietly, with one eye on the man outside the door, she shuffled herself over until her back was facing the corner of a cabinet. She began to move her arms up and down, slowly and steadily, rubbing the plastic tie against the sharp edge in a sawing motion. Anita was asleep on his shoulder, but James nodded his encouragement.

As she worked, she started to feel anger about the fact that a day, which had held so much promise, had ended in such disaster. The anger fired her energy and she moved her arms faster and harder. She allowed herself to go over and over the details of their capture in her mind. She was furious: furious with her captors, and furious with herself. How had they become so complacent? Over the past couple of days, they had drifted up the canal as if they were on a bloody holiday! They were in the middle of an apocalypse, for God's sake! What had they been thinking? Her arms moved faster and faster. This was not how it was going to end. Not after everything. She wasn't going to let it!

It was dark by the time the plastic fastening on Lisa's wrists finally began to loosen. James and Anita both had their eyes closed. They seemed to be asleep. Her back and shoulders were screaming in pain. Not long now. She could tell it was about to give. She could feel it.

But something was happening outside. Soon after it had got dark, the noise had increased. The music had got louder. Deafening. More frenzied. The thump of the bass vibrated the whole boat. She could feel it pulsating in her stomach. The raucous voices and laughter were loud and feverish. Bursts of gunfire crackled and popped. It all seemed to be building up to something. Lisa knew in her gut that it wasn't going to be anything good.

But now, there were other sounds, too. Activity on the boat next door. Raised voices barking commands. Banging and crashing. A woman crying … pleading.

Lisa stopped moving. She tried to listen.

James and Anita opened their eyes and sat up.

The new sounds faded into the distance.

The voices and laughter died down to a murmur.

The music continued.

The three of them looked at each other in silence. Eyes wide in fear and confusion.

Then, a single woman's scream rose over the music. It was a scream of absolute terror. It chilled Lisa to the bone! Her skin prickled and the hair on the back of her neck bristled. Anita let out a gasp.

The crowd roared.

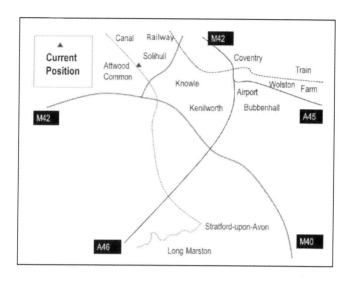

Chapter 13

Day 16 - Earlswood

The doors opened and their guard peered in.

"Time for the fun to begin, guys!"

"What's happening? Where are you taking us?" Anita asked.

"You'll find out soon enough," the man said. "Come on! You first!" He pointed at James.

"No!" Anita cried.

"It's ok. It's ok." James tried to reassure her, as he was roughly shepherded out of the door.

Two other men entered the room to escort the two women outside. Anita struggled and pleaded with them.

"Please, no! Don't do this!"

Lisa forced herself to stay calm. She kept her hands behind her back, confident that one good jerk on the tie would free them. She tried to catch Anita's eye - to give her a signal of some kind - but the girl was distraught.

Outside, the mood was ugly. All eyes were on them as they were led into the heart of the crowd. People parted like a wave to create a path for them. Low voices murmured jeers and insults. The air sizzled with anticipation. A gob of spittle hit Lisa on the cheek and dripped down her face. She resisted the urge to wrench her hands free and wipe it away.

The music thumped. Torches burned around the edge of the space. The air smelt of smoke and paraffin. But there were other smells. Smells that she knew well. Those of decaying infected and the metallic odour of freshly spilled blood.

Suddenly, they were in an open space. The crowd closed around them. Lisa stifled a scream. Anita dropped to her knees, sobbing, and James began to struggle against his captors.

A steel mesh fence had been erected around a wooden platform in the centre of the area. The space between the platform and the crowd was littered with bodies. Some were infected, with knives buried deep in their skulls. But, from the bright red blood that still oozed from their wounds, others appeared to be uninfected.

A man was dragging the body of a young woman to the edge of the platform. Her head lolled to one side, revealing where the side of her neck had been torn away. Two straining infected were chained to the inside of the fence at one end. Money was changing hands all through the crowd.

It suddenly dawned on Lisa what it was.

It was a fighting ring.

A tall, bald man in leather boots and trousers, stepped into the centre of the ring. His bare chest glistened with sweat. Reptilian tattoos crawled over his head and body. His back and shoulders were huge. In his hand, he held a long, curved sword. He raised it skywards. The crowd hushed.

He pointed the sword at James.

"You!" he shouted.

James was wrestled up the steps into the ring.

Anita sobbed harder.

The man walked over to the infected and prodded them with the sword. They writhed and snarled. The crowd cheered.

One of them had been a young man with a long beard and curly brown hair that reached his shoulders. The other was a middle-aged woman in a tattered nightdress. A curler dangled loosely from a single lock of hair on her otherwise balding scalp.

Someone in the crowd shouted.

"Je-sus!"

Others took up the chant.

"Je-sus! Je-sus! JE-SUS! JE-SUS!"

The man pointed his sword at the young male infected. He turned to the crowd with a quizzical expression.

"YES! YES! YES!" they shouted. "JE-SUS! JE-SUS! JE-SUS!"

"Place your bets!" the man shouted, and the crowd erupted in a frenzy.

Lisa could hear Anita's screaming above the wall of noise.

The big man unfastened James' wrists and pushed him into the centre of the ring. Someone began to undo Jesus' chains from outside the fence. The man exited the ring leaving James alone with the infected. He looked around, searching the faces in the crowd until his eyes found what they wanted. Anita! He mouthed something to her, and her screaming stopped.

Jesus was free from his chains. He staggered towards James, arms outstretched, teeth bared, brown saliva frothing from his mouth.

Lisa closed her eyes.

Although she didn't watch, James evidently put up a fight. The cries and shouts of the mob went on for a long time. Their "oohs" and "aahs" revealing every twist and turn of the battle. But eventually, a communal sigh of disappointment, and a long wail of anguish from Anita, indicated that it was over.

Lisa felt detached. Cold. She knew what had happened. She knew Anita must be devastated. She knew James must have been terrified and would have suffered unimaginably. But she knew that the ordeal wasn't over. That, for them, it was just beginning. For them, the worst was still to come. But she didn't seem to be able to feel anything. There didn't seem to be an emotion in her that she could draw on to adequately feel the horror of the moment. All she could think about was the fact that her wrists were almost free, and that they might still have a chance.

Then, the bodies had been cleared, the big man was back on stage and she was being dragged up onto the platform with Anita.

They stood on either side of him, facing the crowd. Anita was quiet. Her head was down - shoulders slumped. Lisa couldn't get eye contact with her. The man raised the girl's head by the hair. But instead of cheering, the crowd booed. He presented Lisa to them instead, and they booed again. He dragged them over to face the female infected and they booed louder still. The mood had changed. The jeers and insults took on a lewd tone. They didn't want more bloodshed. Now they wanted something else entirely. Lisa's blood ran cold.

The man pushed them away from him. Anita fell to her knees and stayed down. Lisa dropped down beside her. She couldn't see her face, but she whispered to her and hoped that she could hear.

"It's ok. We're going to be ok. I'm here. I'm with you ... I'm *sorry*."

The noise was building again. Cheers of approval and encouragement. Lisa looked up, just in time to

269

see the man swing his sword in a wide circle and decapitate the infected woman in one stroke. Its head hit the platform with a dull thud and rolled off the edge. Its body slumped at the knees and dangled loosely from the chains. More cheers of approval.

He moved back to the women and yanked their heads up by the hair, so that they were facing the crowd.

"Highest bidder! Two for the price of one! Let's go!"

Lisa looked defiantly at the faces leering up at her. Anita kept her eyes closed.

After more frenetic money waving and shouting a winner emerged. A small wiry man in dirty jeans and a Led Zeppelin tee-shirt came up onto the stage. His wide grin revealed a mouthful of crooked and discoloured teeth. He stank of sweat, smoke and stale whiskey. He put a hand on each of their shoulders in a gesture of triumph. Lisa shook him off. He slapped her on the side of the head. Her ears rang and stars appeared around the edges of her vision.

Then they were being led down from the ring and away from the crowd into the nearby building.

The air in the room was stale and sour. The torchlight from outside flickered through the slats of the window blind, sporadically lighting up sections of the room in an orange glow. There was a desk in the middle of the floor, a couple of filing cabinets against one wall and a, lumpy, leather sofa against the other. With a grunt, the man threw Anita onto the sofa.

"You can watch this time," he sneered at Lisa. "No offence, but I like 'em a bit younger."

He took a large, serrated knife from his belt. Its vicious blade was at least eight inches long. He pointed it at Lisa, ushering her to the end of the sofa by Anita's feet. He prodded her into position, until she was facing down its length, where Anita lay on her back with her eyes closed.

"Stand there! Don't move!"

"Nita! Nita! Look at me," Lisa said.

"No talking!" the man said and waved the blade in her face.

But Anita opened her eyes.

Lisa stared at her. Hard. She tried to say everything the girl needed to know with just her eyes. *I've got this! Hold on! Don't give up!* They held each other's gaze for just a fraction of a second. But it was enough. Anita nodded imperceptibly.

The man started to undress. He unbuckled his jeans and stepped out of them. He bent over Anita and started tugging at the waistband of her trousers with one hand while he held the knife to her throat with the other. She pushed him away.

"No! Stop!" she screamed.

He climbed onto the sofa and straddled her. Unable to control her one-handed, he stabbed the knife into the arm of the sofa above her head, and using both hands, yanked her trousers and panties down in one violent movement that pulled her body half-way down the seat.

Lisa's eyes rested on the knife. It was upright, still shuddering from the impact of the blow, its tip embedded in the leather. She took a step towards it, at the same time as she snapped her wrists free.

Anita screamed, kicked and fought, arching and bucking her hips to try and throw him off.

"A feisty one, eh?" he laughed.

He put his hands on her shoulders and pressed her down.

Lisa took another step.

The man lowered his body onto Anita's, fumbling with his crotch. All of his attention was focused on subduing her enough to achieve his aim.

Still, she screamed and struggled.

Another step and Lisa lunged for the knife. The noise of her movement was masked by Anita's screams, and the sounds of the wild party that was still going on outside.

The man was focused on his struggle with Anita.

With both hands, Lisa raised the knife over his writhing back.

She struck him between the shoulder blades. The blade went in more easily than she'd imagined. Slicing deeply up to its hilt, through skin, muscle and gristle. He yelped in pain. He let go of Anita. His hands clutched at his back. Lisa pulled the knife out. Blood gushed from the wound. She backed away.

Anita pushed him off her and jumped up. She backed away, too. They watched in silence as he struggled to his feet. Blood was pooling on the floor beneath him. His face was a mask of astonishment. He took a step towards Lisa. His lips parted and she thought he was going to speak, but instead frothy, bright red blood bubbled from his mouth and dribbled down his chin. Then it began to gurgle and pour down the front of his tee-shirt. He took another step towards her, then his legs buckled, and he fell onto his knees. A vacant look spread across his face and he toppled, face down, onto the floor.

The two women looked at his motionless body. Anita went over to him. She kicked him. Once. Still, he didn't move. She kicked him again, then again and again. She was sobbing.

Lisa stood up and freed Anita's wrists with the knife, then she threw it to the ground and wrapped her arms around her.

"He's dead! He's dead! Oh God, I killed him!"

It felt as though hours had passed while they waited for the sounds from outside to die down. Lisa went over to the window and peered out through the blind. Everyone was asleep where they had fallen in drunken stupors. It was quiet. Even the music had stopped. Most of the torches had burned out. A couple still flickered weakly.

Lisa whispered. "If we're going, we need to do it now. We don't want to be here when it gets light."

Anita nodded.

Lisa pointed in the direction of the canal and the boat they had been held captive in.

"That way. Along the canal."

Anita nodded again.

They eased the door open, and keeping low, crept around the side of the building to the row of boats.

Someone coughed and moaned in their sleep. They froze. But no-one stirred.

They carried on along the row of boats, away from the buildings and the fighting ring. No-one was around. They passed the boat they had been in. The tow path ended up ahead. Lisa knew the main path was on the other side.

"We need to cross!" she hissed and pointed across the canal.

A snarl broke the silence. Something moved ahead of them. Anita scuttled to the edge of the water. Lisa peered into the darkness.

"Lisa! Lisa!" Anita whispered.

"Wait!"

"Lisa! Are you crazy? It's an infected!"

"Just a minute!"

Lisa took a few paces toward the sound. The infected snarled again. She saw a glint of metal. Two milky eyes stared at her out of the darkness. More snarling, but the eyes didn't come any closer.

It was another cage.

She got as close to it as she could. She could make out at least two more infected inside. Maybe three. The door was secured with a nylon rope. She looked at the cage. She looked back at the sleeping forms in the flickering light around the fighting ring.

"Go! Get into the water! Head for the other bank." Lisa mouthed.

"What are you ...?"

"Just do it! Now! I'll be there in a minute."

Anita gawped at her.

"Go!" Lisa said again.

She gently nudged the girl towards the canal.

"And keep your hand dry," she added.

She watched as Anita eased herself over the edge, keeping her injured hand above her head. She let out a soft gasp as she lowered herself into the water. Only when Lisa was confident that the girl was moving towards the other side did she begin to untie the rope that secured the cage.

The cage door swung open. Lisa was in the water before the infected emerged. She watched from the edge of the canal as they staggered down the path towards the sleeping revellers. Then she turned and followed Anita.

The water was ice-cold. It came up to her chest. She kept her chin high to stop any water from getting into her mouth. She knew how dirty it was. She'd heard stories about the disease-carrying parasites and bacteria that lurked in canal water. Neil had once told her that you were more likely to die later from an infection than you were to die from drowning if you fell into a canal. She hoped Anita had managed to keep her injured hand dry.

She waded across as quickly as she could. The canal bed was soft and slimy underfoot. A couple of times, she stumbled on obstacles in her path, desperately steadying herself. Once, she felt something living brush across her legs. She shuddered, and stifled the urge to cry out, but kept moving.

Anita was waiting for her at the other bank, unable to haul herself out with one hand. She was shivering. Lisa hoisted her out, then dragged herself up beside her. From the other side, a scream pierced the silence. It was rapidly followed by another, then another until the night air was consumed in an uproar of screams and shouts.

"What did you do?" Anita asked.

"Nothing that they didn't deserve." Lisa's tone was grim. "Come on. We need to keep moving."

"But, it's so dark. What if ...?"

"Let's just go slowly and quietly. It's about a 20-minute walk to the village."

Lisa tried to sound convincing. But she'd never felt so vulnerable and exposed: on foot, in the dark, unarmed and dripping wet. She felt for her inhaler in her pocket. *Shit!* It was gone. She took a deep breath. Her lungs felt loose and clear. She couldn't remember when she'd last used it. It had been hours ago and yet she felt fine. Even with everything they had been through, her asthma had stayed away. She was drained and fatigued, but her breathing was easy. She shook her head, not sure what to make of it.

"Anyway," she said, shifting her attention back to Anita. "There won't be many down here. Think about how many we've seen over the past few days.

"I suppose ..." Anita said.

"The village will be different, but when we get near, we can lay low. Wait till morning to see what's going on."

She took Anita's good hand and, slowly, they began to move down the path.

They cautiously picked their way along. Their

clothes were sodden - their boots waterlogged and squelching. Although it was late autumn, it was cold. They were both shivering uncontrollably. Every rustle or crack in the undergrowth stopped them in their tracks, peering blindly into the dark for the source of the sound. It felt more like an hour than 20 minutes until they made out the silhouettes of a group of tall buildings ahead of them on the opposite side of the canal.

"That's the edge of the village," Lisa whispered. "We're here."

"What now? "Anita asked. "Where should we go? You said we should lie low till morning."

"Dawn can't be that far away. I know a place. It should be safe. Just follow me."

Lisa moved along the hedgerow feeling for something in the darkness until she found what she was seeking: a small kissing gate nestling in the hedge.

They moved into a small open area and Lisa led them along a rough path. They climbed some steps and reached another larger open space. The path narrowed the further they went then stopped abruptly in a small circular clearing. At the centre of the clearing was a bench.

"What's this?" Anita breathed.

"I know it sounds silly, but it's my special place." Lisa's voice faltered. "I like to come down here to think. No-one else ever seems to come here. It's on the edge of the village nature reserve. I can't believe I'm back here." Her voice broke and she stifled a sob.

Anita put her good arm around her shoulder.

"You did it. We've almost made it. If only ..." Her voice broke, too

"I'm so sorry about James," Lisa said.

The girl began to weep.

They huddled together on the bench. Anita cried and Lisa held her. There was nothing to say. No words to comfort her. They waited for dawn and whatever the coming day would bring. The home she shared with Neil was just a few hundred metres away. She could sprint the distance in minutes. If only it was going to be that easy. Somehow, she doubted it.

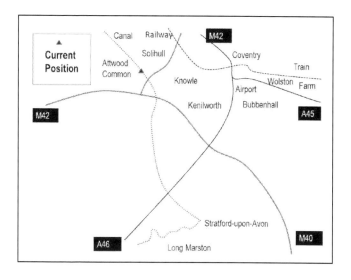

Chapter 14

Day 16 - Attwood Common

As the light began to change and the dawn chorus welcomed the new day, Lisa gently eased Anita's head from her shoulder. She uncoiled her stiff limbs and stood up.

Anita opened her eyes. She straightened up, groaning in discomfort. She looked puzzled for a moment, as if she didn't know where she was. Then a look of anguish washed over her face as she remembered.

"Oh, Jesus!" She covered her face with her hands.

"Oh, Nita! I'm so sorry!" Lisa put a hand on her shoulder.

The girl looked awful. Pale with dark circles around her puffy, bloodshot eyes.

"Let's have a look at your wrist."

Lisa gently lifted her hand and began to undo the makeshift bandage. "How does it feel?"

"Not great." Anita winced.

The wound was surprisingly small and clean. It looked as though the bullet had gone straight through. The bleeding had stopped, but her entire hand was hot and swollen. Lisa reapplied the bandana.

"We'll be able to get it cleaned and fixed up properly when we get home," she said.

Anita smiled weakly and nodded. A tear rolled down her cheek.

"If you can, we should get going. Are you up for this?" Lisa asked.

Anita looked down the path back towards the village.

"Yeah, of course I am. Come on."

They walked back down the path. On the way Lisa pulled a couple of sturdy branches from a tree and fashioned them into rough points, by stripping away the twigs at one end.

"They're not great, but they're better than nothing," she said, as she handed one to Anita.

There was a footbridge on their right. Facing them, on the other side of the canal, was a horseshoe-shaped apartment complex, about four storeys high. On the ground floor, various small shops and offices faced out over a central courtyard. A long, shallow water feature ran down the middle of the courtyard. Usually, the water flowed towards the canal and cascaded down some steps at the end, but today it wasn't moving. The steps were dry. The whole complex looked deserted.

At the centre of the water feature, a small arched bridge provided a walkway to the other side. There were four entrances to the horseshoe, an alley at each end of the small bridge and two more at the far end on either side of a large, designer furniture shop. Lisa and Neil would occasionally browse the shop on a Saturday afternoon, snorting at the extortionate prices. They'd once bought a duvet set there as a special treat. It was made from soft, white, Egyptian cotton, adorned with delicate coral pink embroidery. It was the most expensive bed linen they possessed, and they saved it for special occasions, like their monthly "duvet days" when, in between bouts of lovemaking, they drank wine, ate finger food and binged on box-sets.

"We need to take the exit to the right of the furniture shop."

Lisa pointed to it.

Anita nodded. She was scanning the buildings.

"Then, its straight ahead, across a road and up a narrow, little street."

"Ok. How far?"

"A couple of hundred metres, maybe?"

"And, then?"

"We'll come to a bar, The Tempest. Then, we go left, and the house is just across the road."

"Let's do it," Anita said.

They paused on the footbridge over the canal. A hundred or more windows looked down at them, but they saw no movement behind any of them. The pool was stagnant, full of leaves and litter. Plastic carrier bags, brown cardboard coffee cups and general waste were scattered on the ground. A few windows on the ground floor were broken and one or two were boarded up.

Here and there, brown blood stains smeared the silver-grey paving stones. Anita tapped Lisa on the shoulder and pointed up to where a dormant infected stood on a balcony high above them. Draped from the balcony railing, was a sheet with the words 'Survivors Inside' painted on it in red.

They had entered the complex when Lisa saw another two infected at the entrance to the alley on the far left. She turned to Anita to draw her attention to them, but the girl was looking at another group of three in a doorway on the other side of the walkway. They were all dormant. She held up five fingers and raised her eyebrows.

"We can outrun them," Lisa whispered. "You good?"

"I'm good."

"You sure?"

"I'm sure!"

Keeping close to the buildings on their right, they set off in a light jog towards the exit. Almost immediately, the infected in the alleyway lifted their heads and started to moan and move towards them.

The group in the doorway began to move as well.

As they passed the walkway, they saw two more at the end of the alley on the right. They lifted their heads and joined the pursuit. She glanced at Anita as she picked up speed, but the girl was already running.

They entered the alley at full speed and burst out onto the road. There were more infected on either side of them. Many more! She tried to count. 20, 30, maybe 40. *Shit!*

The street ahead was clear. Anita sprinted past her, heading for it.

"Run, Lisa! Run!" she shouted.

Lisa sprinted after her. She could see the bar ... see her street.

She flashed past the entrance to the gated community, Park Mews, that faced their house. Nearly there! A few more steps! Her lungs were bursting.

Anita was slowing ahead of her. She stopped. She looked back at Lisa.

"Keep going! Keep going! Left! Left!" Lisa shouted.

But Anita didn't move. She actually took a couple of steps back.

Lisa reached the end of the street. She could see her house. But she stopped running, too. She stood beside Anita.

In the street, right in front of her house, was another large group of infected. The entrance to the parking area beside their house was rammed with a barricade of cars and furniture.

The horde saw them and began to move.

There were infected closing in on them from all sides. They were coming from the other side of the bar now, too.

All she could hear was their moans. The air was filled with the cries of a thousand anguished voices. She wondered if this was what hell would sound like.

"NEIL!" she screamed. "NEIL! IT'S ME! LET ME IN, NEIL! NEIL ...!"

Anita grabbed her by the shoulder and tugged at her to move.

"What are you doing, Lisa? We can't go that way. It's suicide!"

Distraught, she shook her off.

"I have to. I have to," she wept.

"We've got to GO! There are too many!"

Anita started back down the street they had just come from.

Gasping and sobbing, Lisa followed her. Through her tears, the girl was just a blur in front of her.

Then Anita stopped again. She leant against the wall of one of the buildings, leaning on her stick for support. Panting, she pointed down the street.

"It's no good! Were trapped. I can't ... I'm done ... We're done."

Lisa felt a wave of rage rush through her. No! This couldn't be how it was going to end! Not here, like this. A stone's throw from her front door! Adrenaline surged through her. The pedestrian entrance to Park Mews was just ahead. It was a short alley with a wrought-iron gate at its end. Maybe, just maybe, the gate would be open.

284

She grabbed Anita's good arm and dragged her into the alley. They ran to the end. Lisa grabbed the gate and pushed at it. It didn't budge. She shook it and rattled it, screaming in fury.

Anita sank to the ground. She was spent.

The first infected turned the corner into the alley. Lisa stepped in front of Anita and raised the pointed stick out in front of her.

The infected advanced towards her. There were more behind it.

She thought she heard voices behind her.

Lisa thrust the point of the stick into the face of the infected. She grunted with effort as she speared it through the eye. It crumpled to the ground.

She heard Anita's voice. "Help us! Please! Let us in!"

A woman's voice called back, "I'm sorry! I can't."

She tried to wrestle the stick free, pushing against the head of the corpse with her foot.

The others were closing in.

"Please!" Anita wailed. "We're going to die!"

The point of the stick broke off. Lisa lashed out at the next infected with the blunt end. It staggered backwards with the force of the blow, only to move forward again.

She heard more voices. Arguing. Anita pleading.

The infected, a woman in a tattered blue business suit, was reaching for her. Its tights were shredded, and it was only wearing one shoe. Once stylish blonde hair was now matted and falling out in clumps. It gripped her shoulders pulling its face towards her, mouth open, teeth bared, snarling. The

285

smell of death and decay engulfed her. She pushed her hands against its chest, her fingers sinking into the putrefying flesh. Anita was screaming.

Suddenly, something exploded beside her head. She felt pressure and everything slowed down. The voices and screaming became low and distorted. Another explosion, and another. A wave of dizziness forced her to close her eyes. Her ears were ringing. She was sinking. Hands were grabbing her. Pulling at her. Dragging her. Far away, she could still hear Anita screaming. She let herself slip into darkness.

She regained her senses to the sound of the same arguing voices, but this time they were closer.

"Just hang on. Hang on!"

"But we *agreed* not to let anyone else in."

"For God's sake, they were going to be killed in front of our eyes. Where's your humanity?"

"The girl's been bitten. Look at her hand!"

Lisa sat up quickly, in spite of the spinning in her head.

"She's not been bitten! She was shot," she cried.

A crowd of fearful faces looked down at her from a few feet away. Men and women, young and old. Bleary-eyed children peered from behind them and between their legs. Some of the men were armed. Most people were still in their nightwear.

A pile of dead infected lay on the other side of the gate. Behind them, the rest of the horde continued to push against it, reaching and snarling. Anita was sitting on the ground a few feet away from her. Her head kept flopping forward onto her chest, as though it was too heavy for her neck. Her hand was bleeding again.

"Nita, are you ok?"

Anita raised her head with difficulty and looked at Lisa.

"Just … wiped … out," she gasped.

Her eyes stared out of her filthy face. Her hair was matted, and her clothes were smeared with a mixture of mud and blood. Lisa realised she must look the same. No wonder these people were afraid of them. She got to her feet. The crowd stepped back a couple of paces. She raised her hands, palms facing out.

"Thank you for helping us. I understand what that means … the risk you've taken."

"Don't come any closer," one of the men commanded. Lisa thought she recognised him.

"We're not infected. We've not been bitten. We're no threat to you. I live here. I'm just trying to get home."

A silver-haired woman stepped forward from the crowd.

"Lisa …! Is that you?"

"Oh, my God! Sylvia!"

Lisa gasped, stepping towards the woman, arms outstretched.

The crowd murmured and two of the men immediately stepped forward, aiming their weapons at her.

"I didn't recognise you! Oh, Lisa! I can't believe it!"

Sylvia threw her arms around her, and held her in a tight embrace, ignoring the protests of the crowd.

Lisa let her head rest on her friend's shoulder. She breathed her in. It felt so good. In that single moment it felt as though the end of her journey had begun. Just being with someone familiar, someone she knew and loved, was like waking up from a long, terrible dream. She closed her eyes and sighed.

From that instant, Sylvia took charge. Reasoning and negotiating with her, understandably anxious, fellow survivors, she carefully examined the two women one at a time, from head to toe, and reassured the group that they were uninjured apart from superficial scrapes and bruises … and a gunshot wound to the hand.

The men, albeit a little reluctantly, were persuaded to lower their weapons. A couple of other women approached the newcomers, offering soft words of support and concern.

Gradually, the crowd began to relax, breaking off in twos and threes, talking in low voices, returning to whatever they had been doing before the early morning drama. The two women helped Anita away towards one of the houses. Sylvia explained that they were taking her to the doctor's house.

She took Lisa gently by the elbow, leading her through a small gate towards some open patio doors, where long, white net curtains were billowing in the breeze. She guided her inside and onto on a voluminous soft, beige sofa, then sat down opposite her on a matching footstool. She silently took Lisa's hands in hers, her eyes full of questions.

Lisa's thoughts were racing. There was only one thing on her mind. Only one question she needed to ask. But she was afraid. Paralysed by fear. Afraid that the answer was going to be the one she dreaded. The one she didn't want to hear. She opened her mouth, but she couldn't release the words. She closed it again.

Sylvia spoke softly.

"It's alright, Lisa. Neil is alive. He's been waiting for you!"

Lisa crumpled. A huge animalistic howl swelled in her chest and rose up into her throat. It erupted from her lips, bringing with it every fragment of fear and effort, and doubt and belief, that she had carried inside her for the past few weeks. Her throat ached from the pressure of it as it burst through, and from the others that rose up to follow it. She gripped Sylvia's hands unable to speak, unable to breathe, battling to get some intelligible words out in between the howls that were now coming in waves.

"Where … is … he?" she managed.

"He's at home, across the street. He's been waiting for you since the first night. We tried to persuade him to wait over here with us, but he wouldn't. Said he had to wait for you at home, that he had to be there when you got back."

"I have to see him." Lisa stood up. "I have to go to him."

"I don't think you can do that right now. There are too many infected out there. But I have an interim solution. Come with me."

Sylvia got up to go outside again, beckoning her to follow.

Lisa followed her to the far end of the gardens, towards a tall town house where a child was playing with a small dog on some decking. As they approached, a young woman came outside and protectively took the child's hand.

"It's alright, Michelle. This is Lisa, Neil's wife. She's come home."

"Oh my God!" the young woman spoke. "Come in. Come in. Come upstairs."

Lisa followed her inside and up the stairs to the first floor sitting room. The room was dark, and she pulled the blind up half way. "We mostly keep the blinds down so as not to be seen by them."

She gestured Lisa over.

Barely breathing, Lisa stood at the window. Tears rolled down her cheeks. Her house was directly in front of her. The blinds were down. The horde was still milling about in the street below.

She could hardly believe it was real. She remembered the dream she'd had when they'd been mugged for their bicycles. Maybe she was dreaming now? Maybe she was actually lying unconscious or dying outside the wrought-iron gate, and her oxygen-starved brain was creating these images and sensations as it faded into oblivion?

"Just wait there. He'll appear soon enough. He checks in every day, just to let us know he's ok – oh, and for a bit of human contact, I suppose," Sylvia surmised.

"I'll get you a cup of tea and something to eat. You must be starving. How does a tuna sandwich sound? We have bread and mayonnaise but no butter, I'm afraid."

"That sounds fine," Lisa murmured, unable to drag her gaze away from her bedroom window.

The two women left the room and she stood, motionless, in front of the window. The house looked relatively intact. The front door appeared undamaged and the ground floor windows were boarded up with what looked like bits of their office furniture.

She was able to get a proper look at the barricade that blocked the arched entrance to the garage and parking area they shared with the other three townhouses in their row. Her red BMW and Neil's van formed the main structure of the barricade, parked nose-to-nose across the entrance. The space above and around the cars was crammed with mattresses, their garden furniture and the contents of their garage. She recognised some of the large black containers Neil used to store his camera equipment in.

Sylvia reappeared with a cup of tea and a sandwich. She put them on the coffee table and pulled an armchair closer to the window. "You might as well sit down. You could be there some time."

Lisa sat down.

Although she didn't think she was hungry, she wolfed down the sandwich. The tea was strong and made with powdered milk, but it was hot and sweet, and soothing.

When she'd finished, she allowed herself to sit back in the chair and relax a little. She made herself comfortable in between the cushions … and she waited.

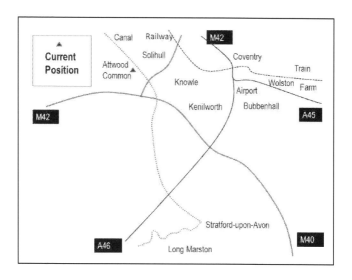

Chapter 15

Day 1 - Lincolnshire

Neil and his crew had just finished filming the final day's play of the National Bowls Championships in Lincolnshire. They were in the process of packing up as much as they could that night, but would return to dismantle the rigging fully the next morning. They were almost ready to get into the vans and head to the nearest pub for a well-deserved pint, when the familiar staccato BBC breaking news alert rang out from Neil's phone.

"Who's dead now?" Rob, the runner, quipped,

throwing a coil of black cable into the back of the van.

Neil chuckled as he packed away his camera. Rob had a point. Every time that alert rang out these days, it seemed that yet another celebrity had died. Was that really breaking news? He'd begun to ignore it unless he had nothing better to do than check his phone, which didn't happen often. He jumped into the driver's seat to wait until the others had finished up. Despite himself, he opened the BBC News app. His brow furrowed as he read the post.

"Erm ... seriously, Guys, it actually looks as if something major is happening this time," he called to the crew.

He got out of the van, phone in hand. The others stopped what they were doing and wandered over.

For the next ten minutes, they stood around reading news articles from different sources. The reports were sketchy and confused, accounts of riots and extreme acts of violence breaking out all over the country. They seemed to have started on trains leaving London but were spreading rapidly. There was video footage on Facebook and Twitter of panic and bloodshed, people running and screaming, and attacking each other.

Neil's thoughts immediately turned to Lisa. She was in London for a meeting and was due to travel home that afternoon on the train from Euston. He punched in her number. It rang out until the answer phone kicked in.

"Hi! It's Lisa. Sorry, I can't get to the phone right now. Leave me a *short* message and I'll get back to you as soon as I can."

"It's me, Lis. Just heard the news. Checking you're ok. Hope you get home safe. Give me a call when you get this.

"Love you," Neil said, before he hung up.

He spoke to the crew. "This doesn't look good, Guys. What do you say to packing up completely now and getting home tonight?"

"Good shout, Mate!" Craig, one of the other cameramen nodded. The rest of the crew agreed. Some of them were still on their phones trying to reach their families. Their normally jovial faces were pale and serious.

Packing up fully was usually a three-hour job. They did it in two. They worked silently. From time to time, one or other of them tried phoning home again, or checked the news and updated the others. Things were escalating dramatically. Neil tried Lisa a couple more times, with no success. He was beginning to worry.

By the time they'd finished, the phone lines were completely jammed, but the picture was a little clearer. What seemed to have occurred was some kind of coordinated bioterrorism attack. Those who were infected were committing frenzied attacks on those who were not, and this was how the infection was spreading. There were accounts of cannibalism. The army had been mobilised to try and regain control of the streets, and an emergency meeting of COBRA was already in session. It was around eight and beginning to get dark when the three-van convoy eventually set off. They had a three-hour journey ahead of them.

The first part of their route was on minor roads, and they made painfully slow progress. The traffic was unusually heavy, and some roads were closed, but they encountered no direct trouble until they joined the main road into Lincoln. Only then did they begin to witness signs of the developing crisis for themselves.

Sirens blared, alarms wailed, plumes of smoke spiralled into the air, and helicopters circled overhead. Police cars and ambulances sped in and out of the city, recklessly overtaking their convoy several times on the numerous, treacherous bends.

It was an easy, and unanimous, decision to avoid the city centre and go the long way round, heading east for a few miles to join the A46 bypass. But even that route was already choked with traffic, as a multitude of vehicles tried to flee the chaos.

They had their first direct encounter with the infection, where the main route out of the west side of the city joined the bypass. By then, they were virtually stationary, inching their way towards the well-lit roundabout about 100 metres ahead. A car had mounted the island and was stranded in its centre. All its doors were open. A woman stood by the passenger door with a toddler in her arms. The toddler was screaming.

A man was standing on the driver's side. There was something off about him. His movements were jerky, and his head was held at an odd angle. He was reaching over the car towards the woman and child. The woman seemed to be talking to him.

The man started moved awkwardly around the side of the car towards the woman and child. She backed away a few steps. For a moment, Neil thought she was going to run, but then she hesitated, seemingly pleading with him again.

He got closer.

The child's screaming intensified.

He was touching distance away from them.

The woman was screaming now too.

Run! Neil thought. *Run!*

Then, the man launched at them, knocking the woman to the ground. The toddler fell from her arms.

Neil opened his door and got out of the van.

"Neil! No! Get back in!" Rob shouted.

But Neil was already running,

An elderly man from a car ahead reached them first. He tried to pull the younger man off the woman, punching and kicking him. But the woman's body was already limp. The man was tearing at her throat with his teeth, shaking her like a rag doll. Dark blood glistened on the ground in the orange glow of the streetlamps.

The infected man released the woman and turned on the elderly man. The toddler was still screaming. Neil headed straight for the child. He was almost there when the woman began to move again. She rolled inelegantly onto her front and pushed herself onto all fours. Neil froze. It wasn't possible. Her neck was in tatters. She was drenched in her own blood.

She began to crawl towards the child.

"NEIL! GET BACK IN THE VAN! YOU CAN'T SAVE THEM! THEY'RE INFECTED!"

He turned to see the van beside him. Rob was driving. He had mounted the grass verge. The side door was open and Craig was shouting at him from within. Ian, the fourth occupant of the van, was staring past Neil to his right. The expression of abject horror on his face made Neil turn to follow his gaze.

Another group of people were walking towards him. They were all moving in the same jerky way as the man on the island. Many were sporting hideous injuries, their clothes soaked in blood. They were reaching towards him, snarling and moaning.

He didn't hesitate. He leapt towards the open door of the van. Craig pulled him in and slammed it shut. Rob put his foot down.

For the rest of the journey, Neil couldn't get his last image of the toddler out of his head. Standing there, screaming, as his savaged, infected mother crawled towards him. It was an image that would stay with him for a very long time. Wracked with guilt, he felt sick to his stomach when he thought about what happened next.

He was quiet for the next few hours, as Rob drove on. They were all quiet.

They didn't stop again, no matter what they saw. They just tried to focus on getting home - getting back to their partners, their parents and their children. They passed many more tragic and horrific scenarios playing out all around them, and many more burning vehicles and buildings, and roaming groups of infected. They negotiated road closures, traffic jams and diversions until it all became an endless blur.

Neil tried to stay positive. He hadn't been able to reach Lisa but that didn't necessarily mean anything. If she had been on the train, she might not have had a signal. She might have been asleep. He knew she'd had a late night the night before.

Now that the lines were jammed, there was nothing he could do. He just had to get home. If she was ok, she'd be heading there too. That's what they'd always agreed. What she'd made him agree to, after they were separated on September 11th.

At the time, she'd been obsessed by the fact that they'd been apart that day and that they didn't have a plan. She'd gone on and on about what they would have done if things had developed and they'd been unable to contact each other.

What would they have done? How would they have found each other? Where would they have gone? If he was honest, he'd thought she was overreacting, but because he loved her, he'd humoured her and had agreed to 'The Plan'.

The truth was, he just loved listening to her when she was like that. He loved watching her brain work as she analysed all their options and worked out their best strategy.

At some point during the night, the news reports

ceased and were replaced with standard emergency broadcast messages, advising everyone to stay in their homes and make them secure, or get to a place of safety and stay there. To a man, they agreed to ignore the advice and keep moving.

They eventually stopped on a quiet country lane on the outskirts of Tamworth, where they parted company with the other two vans. The guys in these vans lived in or around the Coventry area and planned to head south via Nuneaton.

Neil took over the driving again as they pressed on towards Birmingham. Craig and Ian both lived close to each other in different suburbs of the city near the airport, and Rob was based in Solihull, not far from Neil and Lisa in Attwood Common.

But they couldn't get anywhere near the city. Multiple roadblocks and other obstructions forced them to follow a tortuous route through the network of country lanes that criss-crossed the area to the south east of the conurbation.

It was getting light when Craig and Ian decided they wanted to try and make their way home on foot. Neil tried to persuade them to stick together, and try to get home when things had settled down a bit, but they were adamant. They were both desperate for news about their families. They dropped them off reluctantly in the little village of Hampton-in-Arden, exchanging emotional bear hugs and handshakes as they wished each other well.

It was around eight in the morning when they finally drove into Attwood Common. The village was quiet compared to some of the places they'd passed through. They passed a couple of infected on the canal bridge at the entrance to the village and a few more loitered outside the Tesco Express, as if they were waiting for it to open so that they could get their milk and daily papers. They presumed everyone was staying inside as advised, trying to stay safe until it was over.

They were mentally and physically drained when they finally pulled into the shared parking area at the back of Neil and Lisa's house. The other houses in the row were silent. Nothing stirred. Windows and doors were closed. Either their neighbours were hiding inside, or they weren't home.

Neil turned off the engine and rested his head on the steering wheel for a moment, suddenly afraid of what he might, or might not, find when he went into the house. He got out of the van and walked into the narrow passage that led to their back gate.

The gate was ajar. That wasn't necessarily significant. Sometimes the bolt was stiff, especially if the wood had swollen in damp weather, and Lisa sometimes chose to leave it open rather than struggle to close it. The house was still. It looked exactly as it had when he'd left it a few days ago. He had been the last to leave that morning. Lisa had left to catch her train while he was still drying himself after his shower.

He opened the back door and walked inside. At the far end of the room, the red light on the answerphone was flashing. He strode over to it and pushed the button. There were two messages. He pushed the play button and Lisa's voice spoke to him.

"Neil, it's me. I'm in trouble. I'm so scared. I don't really know where I am. I don't know what's happening. I'm so scared, Neil. I don't know what to do. I need you. I really need you."

She called out to someone else in the room. "What number is this? What's your number?"

There were muffled voices in the background.

"If you get this message, ring me here on 024 2356 2134 as soon as you can. I love you." Her voice cracked. "I love you so much. I'll try you again later."

He scribbled the number down on the pad by the phone.

He pressed the button again.

"It's me again, Darling. I'm ok. Sorry about before. I'm in a farm near a village called Wolston, near Coventry. I'm not far away. I'm safe at the moment. I'm with a few other people. I was on one of the trains. It was awful, but I'm ok. I don't know how, but I am ok. I'm going to stay here until the morning, then try to get home. If you get there before me, wait for me. I love you. Remember! Wait for me! I'm coming home."

The first message had been left at eight-thirty the previous evening, the second at three in the morning. He looked at his watch. It was eight-thirty. All the time he had been travelling, she'd been trying to reach him.

Fingers fumbling in haste, he dialled the number. Dismay washed over him as an automated message told him that all lines were busy and suggested he try again later. His next gut instinct was to jump straight back in the van and head for Wolston. He knew where it was, he could find the farm, and he could be there in half an hour. He took a breath. Or maybe not, if their twelve-hour journey from Lincolnshire was anything to go by.

What if she'd left already? What if she was on her way home?

"DAMN IT!" He kicked the wall. Why had he agreed to her stupid plan? He should have taken her more seriously, taken more interest, suggested that a better plan would have been to tell her she should stay where she was, wherever that was, and that he would come and get her.

"DAMN! DAMN! DAMN!"

"Neil?"

He turned. Rob was standing at the back door.

"Neil, I think we need to secure this place. We seem to have attracted a bit of attention."

He pointed to the front window.

Neil looked outside. Sure enough, there was a small crowd of infected gathering across the road and he could see a few others moving towards the house from the streets nearby.

"Ok. Sorry, Mate. You're right. I'm coming."

Neil fished Lisa's spare car keys out of the drawer full of batteries, keys and small tools that she referred to as his 'man drawer'. Keys in hand, he followed Rob back out to the van. Lisa's BMW was parked in the space in front of their garage. There were only two other cars in the parking area. They both belonged to Peter and Jenny at Number 7.

Where was everyone else?

Slightly concerned about what would happen if anyone else needed to get in - but convinced that it was more important to make the area safe - they blocked the archway with the van and Lisa's car, ensuring that there was no space big enough for anyone, or rather anything, to get through. Then they went back into the house, checking locks room by room, and closing blinds and curtains. Neil checked his emails but there was nothing from her there either.

It was around nine when they stood in the kitchen again. Neil flicked on the TV. An Emergency Broadcast image appeared on the screen. After a few moments silence, a woman's voice spoke.

"This is not a test. Repeat! This is not a test. A state of emergency has been declared in the entire United Kingdom. If you can, stay in your home or find a place of safety. Repeat! Stay in your home or find a place of safety. Ensure that all doors and windows are secure. Await further advice."

Neil turned away and put the put the kettle on.

"I don't know about you, Mate, but I'm parched," he said. "Let's have a cup of tea and think about what we're going to do next."

"Can I try the missus on the land-line?" Rob asked.

"Of course! Mate, I'm so sorry. I never thought. I was just thinking about Lisa. Totally selfish."

"That's ok. I get it, Mate. She's alright then?"

"Yes, she's in Wolston. She's on her way home."

"That's brilliant, Mate." Rob's tone didn't match his words. Neil turned back to making the tea as Rob went over to use the phone.

A few moments later he came back and sat down at the table.

"Can't get through."

Neil put a steaming mug of tea in front of him, carefully pushing a coaster beneath it. Lisa would kill him if he marked the table, national emergency or not.

"Sorry, Mate." He didn't know what else to say.

After they had drunk their tea, they took turns to sleep and keep watch. Rob had a couple of hours first, and Neil took his turn after him. But even though he was exhausted, he couldn't sleep, dozing for ten minutes or so at a time, then waking up again. He kept imagining Lisa out there by herself, kept getting up to peek out behind the blinds, certain that he had heard a car approaching, or the phone ringing.

By early afternoon, he was miserable. It felt wrong just sitting there waiting for her to turn up, but what else could he do? She could be anywhere? The feeling of complete powerlessness was gnawing at his insides. He checked his phone and his emails again. This time, there were a few messages from her sister, Gina, saying that they were safe, and asking them to get in touch, but there was still nothing from her.

By the time it got dark again, he had reluctantly accepted that she wasn't going to get home. Not that day anyway.

Around midnight, he knew he needed to sleep. He felt sick and could barely think straight. Rob had been dozing on and off all day, and offered to stay up to keep watch. As he climbed the stairs to the bedroom, Neil passed the office and decided to check his email one final time. Immediately, his notification pinged and her email address jumped out at him. The message had come in about eleven. She was still safe. *Good girl!* He opened the message.

Hi Darling, it's me again. I'm still safe. No longer at the farm but in a house in Bubbenhall. Been an awful day, but some great people have helped us. I'm still coming home. It's not going to be easy, but I'm getting closer. We're going to stay here tonight and set out again in the morning. If you get there first, just wait for me. Please just wait there, and I'll come. I promise. If I get there before you, I'll wait for you. Like we promised. I love you so much. Please be ok, my darling. Lisa Xxx

He messaged back immediately.

I'm here. I'm waiting. Tell me exactly where you are, and I'll come for you in the morning. Don't try and make it on your own. Stay where you are! Please! I love you too.

Relief, hope and excitement surged through him. He had a sudden burst of energy. He sat at the computer for an hour, praying for a response. Nothing came back. Disappointment washed over him. His adrenaline trickled away. His eyelids felt like they had dead weights on them.

He went to bed. This time he slept.

J.M.MCKENZIE

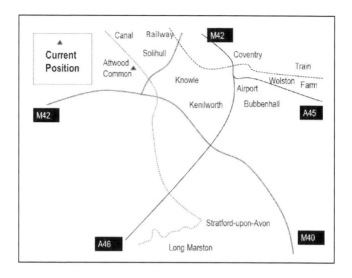

Chapter 16

Day 2 - Attwood Common

He awoke the next day feeling rested and more positive. The voice in his head was telling him that she was going to make it. He had underestimated her. She was smart, resilient and strong. If anyone could pull off something like this, it was her. She was meticulous. He was the stupid one. He would have gone charging through the countryside looking for her, with no idea where she was, and how he was going to find her.

He sat on the edge of the bed for a while as the memories of the previous day came flooding back. The image of the child kept flashing into his head. It was so vivid he felt as though he was living it all over again. The blood was black and shiny, and the little boy's eyes were wide with terror. His screams rang in his ears against the background of moaning, snarling infected. He wondered if the others had made it home, and what had happened to Craig and Ian.

He got up and looked out of the window into the street below. Overnight, the numbers of infected milling around had increased, but the village was still quiet.

He heard movements downstairs in the kitchen and went down to join Rob.

Rob was understandably keen to head home himself. Nothing had changed overnight. It was clear that the crisis was not going to blow over in a day or two, as they had first hoped. Although it would involve moving one of the other cars, Neil offered him the use of the van.

But Rob had already decided he might have a better chance on foot. During the night, he'd thought it all through. They knew all the roads into the city were blocked, and he doubted he'd get very far in a vehicle. If he encountered any infected, he was pretty sure he could outrun them as they didn't seem able to move very fast. His plan was to go down to the canal and follow the towpath for a few miles. It passed only a short distance away from his house. He was a runner and knew the route well. It was part of one of his regular weekend circuits.

He crammed as much of his stuff as he could carry

into his backpack without it slowing him down or hampering his movement, and armed himself with a sturdy metal rod from the rigging. They wished each other well, and he hopped over the barricade and set off jogging down the street that led to the canal.

Neil had mixed feelings as he watched him go. There was a bit of concern for his safety, and some guilt that he hadn't tried harder to persuade him to stay, but he understood that Rob had to do it. He had a wife of his own to get back to, and, unlike Neil, he still had no idea whether she was dead or alive. He'd have done the same if it was him. He felt a pang of envy. Envy that Rob was actually doing something. Something purposeful. Then the envy gave way to a wave of self-indulgent loneliness that, for a few moments, threatened to engulf him.

He shook it off. He had made his decision to wait, and that was what he had to do. He couldn't give in to self-pity. He had to keep himself busy. Make sure he was ready for when she got back.

He started by reinforcing the barricade in the archway. An infected teenage boy had managed to wedge itself between the van and the wall, and was writhing around trying to get through. He couldn't allow the parking area to get overrun. He needed to keep the access to the garage clear, as it was full of extra supplies. Three or four times a year, they went to Costco and stocked up on canned goods, bottled water and household cleaning materials. Everything they couldn't keep in the house, they stored in the garage. God only knew how long this was going to go on for. They might need those extra supplies.

311

He spent the next couple of hours dragging the heaviest things he could find from the garage and piling them onto and between the cars and the walls.

Around mid-morning, Peter emerged from the back garden of Number 7. He was clearly embarrassed that he'd not thought of doing it himself, nor come out sooner to help. He cited Jenny as the reason. According to Peter, she was terrified. Terrified to be left alone and terrified about what might happen to him if he set foot outside.

Neil said he "understood" and that Lisa would have been the same if she'd been there - although he knew that she wouldn't. He just wanted to make the man feel a bit better. Good God, there was no shame in being afraid. You'd be stupid not to be! They were in the middle of a nightmare. No-one else was out and about, and for good reason.

Only, Lisa *was* out there! Out there alone. But she was coming back to him, and the only thing he could do for her was wait … and believe.

That day was the first day of 'The Waiting'. If he'd known how long he was going to have to wait, it might have been harder. But he kept himself busy. Minutes became hours, and hours became days.

A couple of days passed.

But he trusted that she was coming home, and that no matter how long it took she *would* get there. He ate, slept and got up in the morning. He found things to do. He boarded up windows and fortified the front door. He dragged the mattress from the spare bed to help stabilise the barricade outside. Peter gave him the one from their spare bed, too. He checked for more emails several times every day, until the power went off and the internet went down.

On the third day, people in the village let their guard down. When it was evident that the emergency services were not coming to save them, they took matters into their own hands. They took to the streets, looting the shops and empty houses and killing the infected. It wasn't long before someone was bitten, and the infection spread like wildfire. The numbers of infected multiplied exponentially. Some people packed up and left.

A couple of days later, when the army dropped leaflets about a safe zone, more people left, this time including Peter and Jenny. He had to partially dismantle, then rebuild, the barricade to let them out, watching wistfully as they disappeared out of sight.

The residents across the road in Park Mews had secured their complex. There were a few of them in there, including Lisa's friend Sylvia. They seemed to be doing ok. From time to time in the first week, after everyone else had left, he'd go over there just for bit of company and to find out what they knew, if anything.

He'd let them know he was coming by shouting across the street to anyone who could hear to let him in. He had it down to a fine art, slipping into the passenger side of Lisa's car and out of the driver's side, sprinting across the road and hoisting himself up onto the balcony of the ground floor flat on the other side.

After some bad experiences, they had decided on a strict policy of not letting anyone else inside, but they made an exception for him. Nevertheless, two armed men always greeted him on the balcony, checking him over before letting him into the building. Sylvia tried to persuade him to move in with them - that there was plenty of space - but he just couldn't bring himself to do it. He had to wait at home. He had to be there when she finally made it.

By the second week, the increased numbers of infected began to curtail his visits to his neighbours. Shouting to be let in was too dangerous. It attracted them, and there were more of them than ever out there. He had tried counting them but had given up at a hundred. They seemed to have been drawn to the village from the surrounding countryside. No-one really knew why. The speculation was that the residents represented a food source, but they didn't want to think too long or hard about that.

Eventually, it became too dangerous to even try. Instead, he developed a daily routine of chatting to anyone who was willing to listen, using the white board from the office to write messages on. He checked in every morning and again in the evening. It was as much for their sakes as it was for his. They liked to know that he was ok … whether he needed anything.

Everyone in Park Mews knew he was waiting for Lisa. Some thought him insane, others stupid, but they all supported him. No-one, not even Sylvia, believed that she would come … that it was just a matter of time before he gave up and joined them. Until then, they respected what he felt he had to do.

On the morning of Day 17, a few days into the third week since the outbreak, he was woken at dawn by the cries of the infected outside. They were agitated. Extremely agitated. Their moaning filled the air in a wall of sound that made the whole house vibrate.

Somewhere in the distance, underneath it all, he thought he heard screaming. He went to the window. The street below was heaving with infected. They were flowing like a river towards The Tempest, where they merged with another stream coming from the other direction. The river then flowed down the road that ran along the side of Park Mews.

Then he heard gunfire. Something was definitely going on. He scanned the building opposite for someone who could tell him what was happening. No-one was there. Frustrated, he went downstairs to make a coffee.

He couldn't go outside into that hellhole. He'd just have to wait. He hoped everyone was ok. It sounded like someone was in trouble. The possibility that it was Lisa briefly entered his head, but he let it slip away. No-one could survive out there. That wasn't how it was going to be. That wasn't how she was going to come back to him.

He drank his coffee and waited for half an hour or

so, until the noise outside subsided.

No more gunfire either. That was good. Whatever had happened was over.

He went back upstairs and looked across the street again. There was a woman sitting in a chair by the window. He didn't recognise her as Michelle or Sylvia. She seemed to be asleep, her face partly hidden in the shadows. Her hair was thick and wavy and tied back in a ponytail. He couldn't make out the colour. His skin tingled as the hairs on his forearms stood on end. He blinked a couple of times trying to focus.

His breath caught in his throat.

The shape of her face was familiar, but he was probably just imagining it.

Then she opened her eyes with a start and stared right at him.

She looked like Lisa.

She jumped to her feet and placed her hands flat against the glass.

It was Lisa! It was her!

She was home.

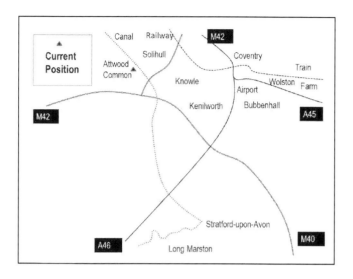

Chapter 17

Day 17 - Attwood Common

Lisa woke with a start, disgusted with herself for falling asleep. Her eyes immediately scanned the house across the road.

The blind in the bedroom was open. A figure was standing at the window looking straight at her. The body shape and broad shoulders were instantly familiar. She jumped up, placing her hands flat against the cool glass. His features were unmistakeable. His hair was longer and there was a heavy stubble on his jaw, but it was definitely him.

He saw her at the same time. Mimicking her

movement, he pressed his hands against the glass. He stayed like that for a moment, just staring at her, then he opened the window. His mouth moved. He was calling to her. She fumbled with the catch and pushed the window open.

Fresh air rushed in, carrying with it the sound of his voice.

"LISA!"

She reached out of the window towards him. He did the same. She couldn't speak. She was crying. They stood like that for a while, reaching across to each other, until he turned away and disappeared out of sight. She took a breath and swallowed, uncertain that her voice would work.

"Neil!"

He returned a few minutes later. She could see him bent over. He appeared to be writing. He raised a large board to the window. It was the whiteboard from the wall in their office. There were words written on it in red marker pen.

"I'M COMING OVER. TELL THEM TO LET ME IN."

She looked down at the street below. The horde had thinned out, but there were still large groups of infected in the street between the buildings. The sound of their shouting had agitated them. They were moving, active, heads raised, twisting left and right, seeking the source of the noise. She shook her head vigorously, raising one hand, palm out in a 'wait' gesture, and pointing to the street below with the other. He looked down, then nodded, pinching his thumb and forefinger together to form the 'OK' sign.

She didn't leave her seat at the window for the next few hours. Sylvia gave her the board and pens they'd been using to communicate with Neil, and they began the process of exchanging messages. She reassured him that she was ok and he her. He asked where she'd been, and she simply wrote 'LONG STORY'. He told her to 'EAT' and 'SLEEP'. She replied 'LATER'.

They exchanged news on what they knew about family and friends, which wasn't much. Neil had been in email contact with her sister, Gina, in Yorkshire for a few days at the start, but since the power had failed and the internet had gone down, that communication had stopped. He'd not heard from either of their parents, his brother, nor her other sister, Judith.

Sylvia came in at one point to report on how Anita was doing. Lisa felt guilty for forgetting about her friend, but Sylvia reassured her that she was sleeping, and that she was going to be fine. The doctor had cleaned her wound and had started her on a course of antibiotics.

Eventually, Sylvia and Michelle persuaded her to rest, and when she messaged him to explain, he replied 'GOOD'. She washed and changed into some fresh clothes that Michelle had found for her, before lying down on a comfy bed in an upstairs room. She slept soundly, blissful in the knowledge that Neil was alive and well, and just a few metres away.

Sylvia woke her just before it got dark. Neil was holding the board up which read 'TOMORROW'. She nodded and blew him a kiss before the light went completely and she could no longer see him clearly. She closed the blind and left the room.

She made her way to the doctor's house to see Anita. The girl was pale, but looked a hundred times better than when she'd last seen her, weak from blood loss and exhaustion, head rolling on her shoulders, clothes covered in dirt and dried blood. She was sitting up in bed. Her hand was wrapped in clean, white bandages and elevated on a couple of pillows. The two women embraced. Lisa felt the girl's body tremble in her arms.

Lisa drew back. Anita was crying.

"I'm sorry," she sobbed. "I should be happy for you but I …" She broke off.

"I know. I know. I'm so sorry."

"But you were right," Anita said, wiping her eyes and smiling through her tears. "You were right all this time. He was waiting for you. You never doubted it, and you were right."

"I did doubt it … sometimes," Lisa said.

The doctor came in to check on Anita.

"She still needs to rest," he said to Lisa. "You can see her again tomorrow."

Lisa took Anita's hand.

"Try and sleep," she said. "I'll come back in the morning.

"And, Nita, thank you! Thank you for everything. I could never have done it without you."

Anita nodded, lay back against the pillows and closed her eyes.

The doctor ushered Lisa from the room.

Anita was right, though. She *had* been right. He *had* been waiting for her.

It suddenly hit her properly for the first time. All the anguish and self-doubt about whether she was doing the right thing had been worth it. But there had been a cost, and it had been Anita's to bear. She owed her everything. While she was now on the mend from her physical wounds, her emotional ones were going to take much longer to heal, if indeed they ever would.

She spent the rest of the evening catching up with Sylvia on what had happened in the village since the attack had begun. The outbreak had been fairly slow to take hold at the start, largely because of the rural location. Then, people had become overconfident and thought they could get things under control by themselves. On Day 3, they had begun to venture out.

They started to try and get supplies from the village shops, to board up their homes and dispense with the small number of infected that were roaming the streets. But someone had been bitten and the infection had spread through the village like a tidal wave. Many families had got in their cars and left. Others had barricaded themselves into their homes.

The surviving Park Mews residents had secured the complex. At first, they'd waited to be rescued, but when it was clear that that wasn't going to happen, they'd shifted their focus to long term survival, and it appeared that they'd done pretty well so far.

If there was any such thing as the perfect set-up in an apocalypse, Park Mews seemed to be it. The basic structure of the complex could have been designed with exactly this scenario in mind. The terraced houses and apartment blocks were arranged in a square. All the fronts of the houses faced outwards, their front doors opening directly onto the street. The backs all faced into a secure communal garden, within which each individual home had its own private space, demarcated by decorative iron railings.

The only way to access the gardens on foot was through one of four wrought-iron, lockable gates at each corner of the square, or via the underground car park. The single entrance to the car park was on the main road, where a ramp led down to an electrically-operated shutter.

The ramp was directly opposite the entrance to Lisa and Neil's own parking area, and the noise of the electric shutter rising was the first thing Lisa heard every morning, marking the start of each new working day as the early-bird commuters set off on their daily journeys.

The survivors of Park Mews had made the most of their location and seemed to have a good thing going. The underground car park was stocked with enough food and water to last for several weeks. They had weapons and a medic in the form of a resident who was a local GP.

The shutter at the bottom of the ramp was firmly closed and barricaded, and since the power had died, it could no longer be opened electronically. But it could be opened manually, when it was deemed safe to do so, to enable foraging excursions using one of the many vehicles parked inside. They even had extra fuel stored in rows of jerry cans in a cool corner of the underground space. They had already started growing additional fruit and vegetables and were in the process of constructing a water collection system.

But more than all this, more than everything else put together, the survivors of Park Mews had something else that was going to give them the best chance of surviving in the long term. The residents of Park Mews were organised, united, and committed to one another.

The two women talked into the night. They shared their personal stories of survival, and those of others they had met. They laughed and they wept. They talked about what had, or might have, happened to family and friends. Sylvia had lost her husband on Day 3, when the infection ravaged the village. They talked about the past, and they talked about the future. When there was nothing left to say, they went to bed, Lisa returning to the room in Michelle's house, where she was as physically close to Neil as she could be.

She slept right through and woke the next morning with a thrill of excitement. Sunlight streamed in the window around the edges of the blind. It felt late. She leapt out of bed and rushed downstairs. Michelle and Sylvia were already at the window. They turned to look at her. Sylvia was smiling.

"He's coming."

She beckoned her over.

The street below was empty apart from a few infected. A rhythmic, metallic clanging was coming from the far end of the street to their left. The infected were shuffling towards it. She looked at Sylvia quizzically.

"The others are distracting them," Sylvia explained. She pointed toward the cars blocking the archway.

"Watch!"

Lisa looked towards the barricade. There was movement inside her car. The driver's door was closest to the street.

It opened.

Neil clambered out, standing up to his full height. He was holding a crowbar in one hand and, bizarrely, what looked like the domed lid of their barbeque in the other. Her heart skipped a beat or two, and she gasped out loud. Barbeque lid or not, he looked magnificent. He glanced up at the window for a split second before darting across the road to his left, disappearing out of sight beneath the building.

"Come with me!"

Sylvia hurried from the room.

Lisa followed her downstairs and outside, her eyes squinting in the sunlight. Sylvia slipped into a building a couple of doors down. Lisa followed.

She was sure they were in the stairwell of the flats diagonally opposite their house. She knew the flats. They had balconies that opened onto the street. The occupants of the ground floor flat were notorious for their loud parties that regularly went on all night. She and Neil had often been kept awake by the drunken chatter and music well into the early hours, half irritated and half amused … and, if they were honest, a tiny bit jealous.

Then, she was inside the flat. There were two men on the balcony outside. They were hauling someone over the wall. There was loud laughter. Sylvia stepped back from the door, a huge grin on her face.

Neil walked into the room.

They looked at each other for a second, almost unable to believe what they were seeing. He opened his arms, and she entered them. They closed around her. She had no words. No tangible thoughts. Her senses were flooded by the feel of him, the smell of him. She pressed herself into his body.

That night as she slipped into bed, she cuddled up against his broad, smooth back and lightly kissed the tattoo of a sun between his shoulders. He reached for her hand, pulling it across his body and holding it tightly to his chest as they fell asleep.

She was home.

J.M.MCKENZIE

ABOUT THE AUTHOR

J.M. McKenzie is from the UK Midlands. *Wait for Me* is her first full-length novel.

In 2019, she published a short story called *Puschkinia*, a gentle tale about a lost wedding ring and the role of an innocent child in breaking down prejudice and misunderstanding.

In 2020, she got through to Round 2 of the NYC Midnight Short Story Challenge with her entry in the spy genre called, *Option 3*. Later that year, she was proud to co-author *My Rachel* with S.J. Gibbs. This is a personal memoir of the lives of S.J. and her daughter, Rachel, who was born with severe cerebral palsy. Rachel is now in her early thirties and the book recounts the relationship between mother and daughter and their fight for life, truth and justice.

Along with her colleagues from JAMS Publishing (jamspublishing.com), J.M. has also contributed to a series of anthologies called, *Words Don't Come Easy, Words Don't Come Two Easy* and *Words Don't Come Threely*.

She is currently working on a new novel, *The Ice Factory*, which is about a traumatic loss of innocence. However, she hasn't ruled out the possibility of a sequel to *Wait for Me*.

Printed in Great Britain
by Amazon

64504123R00199